Turbo

Dick Parsons

Printed in the United States of America

ISBN: Softcover   979-8-88622-748-2
          eBook   979-8-88622-749-9

Republished by: PageTurner Press and Media LLC
Publication Date: 08/31/2022

To order copies of this book, contact:
PageTurner Press and Media
Phone: 1-888-447-9651
info@pageturner.us
www.pageturner.us

Turbans

DICK PARSONS

To
Anne and Mary

By the same Author

New Zealand - A Personal Discovery

A Fisher of Slaves

To be a NAAZI Family

Acknowledgment

My grateful thanks to Gillian Hancock
for her excellent proof reading.

Chapter 1

"Welcome aboard the *Ranpura* Miss Leafe. Please follow your steward to your cabin."

Miss Leafe was returning to India, where she had been born the youngest of three siblings. Her mother Lady Cynthia was married to Sir Henry Leafe, a High Court Judge in Allahabad in the Central Provinces of India. Christened Gertrude Henrietta, she had a sister named Alberta Louise and a brother, Stewart Norman. Alberta had been sent to school in England before Gertrude had been born and two years later, Stewart went to a preparatory school in Hampshire. When Gertrude was four Lady Cynthia took her to England to stay with her grandparents, until she too went to boarding school.

Since arriving in Instow, the little town on the confluence of the rivers Taw and Torridge in Devonshire, where Colonel and Mrs Hamish Leafe had chosen to retire, Gertrude had seen little of her parents, her only contact being their monthly letter which took some five weeks to arrive. Sent to school as a border at the age of five, her eagerness to learn had quickly made her a prized pupil. But though her teachers thought highly of her, her quickness of mind did not endear her to her peers, who delighted in teasing her because of her ugly name. This burden would be with her for most of her young life and though she made many acquaintances, she found it difficult to forge real and lasting friendships. Nor did she have a close attachment to her grandmother, a leading light in the local bridge club, who led a life of her own. And her husband, Colonel Hamish was either engrossed in his vegetable garden or lost in his model boat-making. So, Gertrude's path and those of her grandparents rarely crossed. Indeed, she saw more of Mrs Sharpe, the cook/housekeeper and her husband Bill, the handyman/chauffeur. Bill had been the Colonel's long-serving batman and as he spoke in his rounded Devonshire brogue, of his time with the regiment in India and taught Gertrude the names of the birds, plants and insects they found in the garden, a bond of friendship grew between this old soldier and the bright enquiring child. And it was he who softened her name to Trudi, which in time her grandparents and others adopted. Of her two siblings with whom she shared her school holidays, Alberta, nine years older than she, was always a remote authoritarian figure who she avoided whenever she could. She was closer to Stewart, but he, with his mechanical inclination spent much of his time with his grandfather as he shared his love for model making. Nevertheless, it was with Stewart that Trudi learnt to sail in the fast-running waters of the Torridge, to play at cricket on the sands at Instow and to search for crabs in the rocks at Westward Ho! Though she would always say she had a happy childhood, her lack of close friends made her independent and self-contained.

In 1929 Stewart was accepted for Eton and in August that year Sir Henry and Lady Cynthia returned to England to be present when he joined for his first term. Though Trudi was only eight, they had also taken the opportunity to discuss her future with her headmistress who was pleased with her excellent progress and the promise of academic success, and her name was put down for Cheltenham Ladies' College.

It was while her parents were at Instow, that one morning Trudi overheard some strange, unbelievable news. The memory of that morning would remain with her forever. She had been playing hide and seek with Stewart and concealed in a cupboard in the hall, had heard her mother and grandmother talking. They were speaking of her. Grandmother had said "Gertrude's quite different from Alberta: they're not at all like sisters!" She'd heard her mother reply in a sharp and vindictive voice, "Well they're not sisters! I've never told you before, but Alberta's my child, Gertrude's not! Gertrude's a bastard, the result of a liaison between Henry and that wanton hussy we had as a governess for the children."

Trudi could scarcely believe her ears. What had Mummy said? That she, Trudi, was not her child? Did that mean that though she'd always called her Mummy, she wasn't her mother? Suddenly it made sense. Ever since she could remember she'd never felt loved by her. She'd always known she loved Alberta, but not her! She heard that voice again, "Alberta's my child, Gertrude's not!" Dismayed, she'd crept away to her bedroom. "She says I'm a bastard," she whispered as she climbed the stairs. "Bastard," she said the word again. "What does it mean?" The fishermen always said it, when they were angry, when their nets got tangled, but she'd never asked what it meant. And she'd heard her say, "She's the result of a liaison". What did that mean? She found the door of the bedroom she shared with Alberta and slid inside. She opened her dictionary and flicked quickly through the pages. "Bastard," she read. "Child born out of wedlock," then other meaningless words, "anything spurious, not genuine, non-standard". She shook her head and read on, "So impure as to be practically worthless". She read it again and again. "I'm practically worthless," she sobbed. In her misery she heard noises, footsteps in the hall. Hastily she wiped her eyes and hid below the bed.

"Found you," she heard Stewart's excited voice. "My turn now, no cheating now, count up to a hundred," he shouted as he disappeared through the door.

She nodded in reply as she wondered what "liaison" and "wanton" meant. She searched the dictionary. "Liaison" seemed to have many meanings. "A union or bond of union", she didn't understand what that meant. Then it went on. "An intimacy, usually of an illicit nature". "Oh! It's all so complicated," she cried in despair. And what does "wanton" mean? She found the word. Again, it had so many meanings! She closed the dictionary and in a sudden rage threw it on the floor. Then leaving the room she began an aimless search for Stewart. At first, she didn't hear Bill. Then his words broke into her muddled thoughts.

"You'm lookin' very thoughtful today, Miss Trudi."

"Oh Bill", she cried. "I'm feeling so worthless."

"Worthless y'say? Miss Trudi. Can't think why you'm feelin' like that. You'm clever and bright and when you'm grown up you'll be one of them brainy ladies, a doctor or a lawyer p'raps. What's made 'ee think like that?"

Trudi sobbed. "Oh! I don't know, Bill."

He put a tender arm around her.

"Well, Miss Trudi, 'tis clear somethin''as. Can't 'ee say what 'tis?"

"Well the truth is Mummy, err Lady Cynthia says I'm a bastard! Tell me, what's a bastard?"

"A bastard?" He saw her nod her head as he scratched his. "Well Miss Trudi, 'tain't a nice word for sure. 'Tis a word you use when you'm angry, when somethin's made you mad. You ain't been upsettin''er, 'ave 'ee?"

"Oh! There you are." Stewart's indignant voice interrupted them. "I thought you were meant to be looking for me!"

"Sorry Stewart. I'm afraid I got talking to Bill. Let's stop. It's nearly time for tea anyway."

She always remembered the look of relief on Bill's face as they left him and would never forget the pain that word "bastard" had given her.

Later in the darkness of their room that night she'd asked Alberta what a bastard was. "A bastard," Alberta had said, "is someone whose parents weren't married when he was born."

She remembered she'd replied, "So we're not bastards."

"No, of course not, Mummy and Daddy were married long before we were born. Why are you asking such a stupid question?"

Trudi remembered lying, "Oh! It's just something I've read in a book. The boy in the book's told he's a bastard, the result of his father's liaison with a wanton woman."

"Oh!" Alberta had giggled. "His father must have been unfaithful to his wife and had had a love affair with the woman. What is this book anyway? I don't think you should be reading it!"

That was the day she'd known she was different. Not the daughter of Lady Cynthia Leafe at all, but of some wanton woman. Some woman who had imposed herself on the Leafe family. Some unknown woman, who had come to teach Alberta and Stewart. A wanton woman, a woman the dictionary said was "licentious, unchaste, loose, unrestrained". A woman who had enticed Sir Henry into a liaison, whose bastard product she was.

That was the day she suddenly felt a stranger, a stranger without a family. The day when the need to find herself had spawned, the day when she first experienced an unquenchable thirst to find the mother she never knew and to discover why she had given her daughter away. Now she could understand why it was that Lady Cynthia didn't love her.

When her "parents" had returned to India, she had summoned up courage and finding her grandmother alone in the drawing room had asked her, "Grandmother, please tell me who is my real mother?" Her grandmother's face had stiffened and for a while she was silent, as if not sure what to say. Then she spoke. "What do you mean, girl? Lady Cynthia's your mother! What a stupid question!" Deflated, Trudi had apologised for her stupidity, but as she'd slunk away, she'd known her grandmother had been lying! She knew she'd have to be patient, until some opportunity arose to tackle her father, now half-way across the world in India.

While Stewart had done well enough at Eton to join Sandhurst as an aspiring Army Officer, Trudi had excelled at the Ladies College and her headmistress, supported by her father, had been keen for her to read history at Girton and pursue a career in teaching. Trudi however was ambivalent, preferring some vocation as yet unknown, but one which would be more adventurous.

During her time at Cheltenham, the clouds of war had begun to blow inexorably across the world. Indeed, she'd hardly started at the Ladies College when Italian forces invaded Abyssinia, killing huge numbers with poison gas. And no sooner had the fighting in Africa ended than civil war had broken out in Spain! This had been endlessly reported in the newspapers and on the wireless, but Trudi and her classmates could never understand why the Spaniards were so intent on killing each other! Then there was war in China! Happenings in those distant places had made little impression on Trudi and her peers until the newsreels had shown pictures of the bombing of Shanghai and the Spanish town of Guernica. The terrible damage and loss of life had left her and her friends in no doubt about the horrors of modern war! Yet to the girls of the Ladies' College it seemed that England and her Empire were safe from the fighting and with the nation they rejoiced as Amy Johnston piloted her single seater aeroplane on her record breaking flight to Australia, basked in the glory of winning the Schneider trophy air race, revelled in the success of Fred Perry at Wimbledon and were enthralled by the pomp and ceremony of the coronation of King George VI. The sight of troops from every corner of the vast British Empire parading along the coronation route made them proud to be English. To them the Empire of some four hundred and seventy million people spread across the world, whose lands were shown in red in every atlas, was a great civilising influence in a barbaric world. And Trudi was proud of her father serving as a judge in India, the greatest of all British possessions.

It was when she was sixteen and studying for School Certificate that war suddenly seemed frighteningly close. Having annexed Austria, Adolf Hitler now demanded that the Sudetenland, a province of Czechoslovakia, be ceded to Germany. With his army massed on the frontier, all efforts to dissuade Hitler were proving fruitless and war seemed imminent. Trudi had heard Neville Chamberlain, the Prime Minister addressing the nation on the wireless. "How horrible, fantastic, incredible it is," he had said, "that we should be digging trenches and trying on gas masks here, because of a quarrel in a faraway country, between people of whom we know nothing." Many concurred with him and two days later at a meeting, he and the French Premier agreed with Hitler that the Sudetenland should be transferred to Germany. Neville Chamberlain returned to a relieved nation waving a copy of the agreement and declaring that he had "won peace with honour ...... peace for our time." Though Trudi and her friends never really understood what had been at stake, they like the British public were grateful that war had been averted and thankfully put away their newly acquired gas masks.

But when the time came for her to sit her Higher School Certificate examinations, everyone knew that the peace brokered by Neville Chamberlain would not last. Hitler had begun to demand that the free port of Danzig and the corridor that linked it to Poland be given to Germany. When to many war seemed inevitable Trudi learnt that she had successfully matriculated and had been offered a place at Girton to read history. In a dilemma, she wondered whether to accept the offer and go up to Cambridge or to indulge her implacable desire before war came and visit the country of her birth and find out who she really was. With hope in her heart, she had written to her father seeking his approval to delay joining Girton and to spend a year in India. To her relief he had agreed.

Now as she watched the shore mooring lines being cast off and heard the turn of the propellers, all thoughts of war vanished. A new unknown chapter was opening in her life one which she hoped would lead to the truth.

Chapter 2

A s she sat on the balcony of her hotel room waiting for him to come, memories of the voyage filled her thoughts. She remembered staying on deck as the ship had eased out of her berth, fascinated by the red-sailed barges, the ships and the tugs and relishing those last views of England. It had been a seminal moment; at last she was on her way to India. Now having arrived in this fabled land she was impressed by its architecture, its crowded streets, its vibrant colours, the noise and its dark handsome people with their silky black hair and flashing eyes.

She laughed; her brother Stewart had teased her about sharing a cabin with a missionary, and she had indeed been worried, but Nicola hadn't been one of those prim, humourless women with the strictest of morals. She'd been warm and friendly, a girl about the same age as herself, with flowing blonde hair, smiling blue eyes and a peach-like complexion. Her father owned a fleet of tramp steamers and the family lived in a grand house in ten acres near Ormskirk. She'd told Trudi she was very conscious of being born with a silver spoon in her mouth! Embarrassed by her family's affluence, she'd always wanted to help the poor. When she'd told her parents of her desire to become a missionary, they'd been shocked and had tried to stop her, but she'd been adamant and finally they had reluctantly agreed. In her delight and excitement she'd approached the Methodists and they had suggested she could join their Mission in Calcutta. As an aspiring missionary, she'd wanted to travel second class and had been upset when her father had insisted she should have a first class berth, but she was grateful to be sharing a cabin with Trudi, and as they had got to know each other, Trudi had grown very fond of her. She greatly admired Nicola's commitment, but now in India she couldn't help worrying about her. She herself would be safe in a fine house, surrounded by servants, but Nicola, where would she live, in some refuge for poor beggars? Nicola made her feel very privileged!

She chuckled as she remembered how unsure she and Nicola had been about what to wear on that first night, when everyone was excused dressing for dinner. As they'd unpacked their trunks, they'd agonised over what dress to choose! Nicola had selected a simple turquoise dress with a discreet neckline and calf length hem, yet its very modesty had seemed to accentuate her tiny waist and the curve of her breasts. How ravishing she'd looked! By contrast her own dress had been as exciting as an old school gym slip! When they had found their table, Mr Gerald Bentley had risen to introduce himself. He was an Inspector of Canals, returning to Patna in Bihar with his wife Sheila. He'd asked where they were bound. Nicola had replied "Calcutta, where I am to join the Methodist Mission". Her reply had momentarily stopped the conversation and Trudi, breaking the silence had said "And I'm going to Allahabad, where my father is a High Court Judge." Nicola's answer had clearly unsettled him, but Trudi's had moved the conversation onto more familiar territory. "Ah," he'd exclaimed, "Your father must be His Honour Sir Henry Leafe?" When she'd concurred, he'd added with a roguish smile "So, he's one of the Heaven Born!" The phrase had meant nothing to her and she'd smiled graciously, yet somehow it had irritated her. His pseudo reverence had rankled!

However, the arrival of Edward Birley-Smith followed shortly by Richard Hooper had put her at ease. Richard, the older of the two, made a striking figure. He was tall, certainly over six feet with an upright manly figure. He wore a pale linen suit with a blue polka dot tie and had a matching handkerchief in his breast pocket. Half hidden by a bushy beard, his face was complemented by well groomed black hair. An engaging smile lit up his face as he told them he was a naval Lieutenant travelling to Colombo to join *H.M.S. Strongbow*, a destroyer. Edward looked much younger. He was a newly commissioned Second Lieutenant hoping to join the Ghurkhas after a year with the Royal West Kents. His grey suit sat comfortably on a stocky figure a little over five feet tall and beneath close shorn hair, he sported a moustache. He seemed the very model of a young Army officer! When they took their places, Richard next to Trudi and Edward next to Nicola, the table was complete.

Ever since her schooldays Trudi had kept a diary and there had been plenty to write about in the *Ranpura*. She glanced idly through her writings.

Tuesday 22nd August 1939. Am beginning to feel at home in this huge ship and am starting to find my way around. I spent most of today on deck watching ships and the coast going by. This afternoon we passed the Isle of Wight and saw a huge battleship accompanied by four smaller ships. Richard told me it was the Nelson with an escort of destroyers. She looked very powerful with her huge guns. I told him I'd be terrified if she was an enemy ship, but Richard said he doubted she was a match for the Bismarck, Germany's latest battleship. It seems he is very impressed with the new German navy.

She remembered how delighted she'd been to have Richard on their table. He was so handsome, intelligent and easy to talk to. She couldn't help admiring him! She read on:

Tomorrow we enter the Bay of Biscay and strong winds are forecast!

Wednesday 23rd August 1939 I was awoken early this morning by the ship's motion and dressing hurriedly I went on deck. I thought I'd found my sea legs, but I was mistaken, it was so difficult to walk! The forecast had been right, it was blowing hard and the sea was really rough, but though she rolled and pitched the Ranpura seemed to treat the wind and sea with disdain. Sadly poor Nicola was terribly sick and spent the day in bed. Luckily the motion doesn't seem to bother me, one of the few it appears as the dining room was almost deserted. I spent some time with Richard who regaled me with tales of the storms he'd been through in his last ship the Cairo, which he tells me is a cruiser.

She recalled how attractive he looked when he laughed, with those "crow's feet" forming around his eyes.

There was no sign of Mr and Mrs Bentley either. Dinner was abandoned and we had informal supper, where I met some new people. One, Giles Gallagher, was particularly nice and paid me great attention.

She laughed; it had been rather good for Richard to have some competition!

I found out later, he is married and that his wife Jane was suffering from seasickness and confined to bed. He is returning after his first home leave, having served five years as an Assistant District Officer. Now, he tells me, he will have his own District. He also had heard of Father and told me he too was proud to serve in the Indian Civil Service. When I plucked up courage and asked him why my father had been called one of the "Heaven Born", he laughed and told me he was "Heaven Born" too! All the ICS have that sobriquet he told me. It's because the rest of them, even the Army, are jealous of their status, since the ICS take precedence at all functions. Well, I knew Father was important and has been knighted, but I never thought he was more than a mere mortal!

She smiled to herself and turned the page. She'd liked Giles. She read on:

<u>Friday 25th August 1939</u> Early this morning I was on deck as we passed Gibraltar. What an impressive sight that great rock makes! Thankfully it's British and guards the entrance to the Mediterranean, which Mr Mussolini likes to call "Mare Nostrum"! However I don't think the Royal Navy agrees with him! Richard says our Mediterranean Fleet would have little difficulty in dealing with the Wops*! I just hope they'll never be put to the test! The sea is kind now and Nicola is up and about once more. This evening, with the deck relatively still, we danced and danced. We Stripped the Willow, did the Military Two Step and the Gay Gordons and danced several Eightsomes! Edward and Nicola were with us and so were Giles and Jane who dance beautifully.

She remembered the brief call they had made at Marseilles. No one had been able to go ashore; they had only called to collect the passengers who had come by train to avoid the possibility of bad weather in the Bay.

With them they had brought English newspapers. Though two days old, they were eagerly received, but they gave distressing news. Pictures of Jews seeking to escape persecution in Germany filled the pages and they learnt how Josef Goebbels, the Nazi Minister of Propaganda, was fanning the anti-Polish campaign by claiming that German citizens in the corridor were being attacked and their houses set alight by the Poles, a report strenuously denied by the Polish Government. And there was trouble at home. The Irish Republican Army was continuing its bombing campaign in London, Manchester and the

Midlands. Their latest bomb had killed five in Coventry. In a more sombre mood the *Ranpura* and her company continued their voyage.

She turned another page:

Wednesday 30th August 1939 This morning we had our first glimpse of Malta, the base for our Mediterranean Fleet. As we got near we could see warships and among them was the Barham, a battleship which Richard told me flew the Flag of the Commander-in-Chief. To me she looked rather old-fashioned and not nearly as impressive as the Nelson, but Richard told me she had fought with distinction at Jutland in the Great War.

The Captain is trying hard to keep us up to date with the situation in Europe and today he said the problem of Danzig and the Polish Corridor seems to have reached a stalemate. We are all praying for peace.

Thursday 31st August

At dinner tonight the Captain told us he'd heard that German tanks supported by dive bombers had thundered across the Polish border, that Warsaw had been bombed and that at home the evacuation of children from cities to areas thought to be safe from air attack had begun. The news shocked us all and everyone is worried that we shall be drawn into this dreadful conflict. Nicola and I went to the ship's chapel to pray for peace and found it full!

Saturday 2nd September 1939. We are now in the Red Sea and it's getting hotter! We heard today that the Poles are putting up a gallant fight, but they are being overwhelmed by Germany's tanks and bombers. Pressure is being put on Hitler to stop, but few believe it will succeed. It's all very frightening but everyone is putting on a brave face.

Our voyage will soon be over and we'll be parting from all the friends we've made. Richard tells me he will be catching a boat to Colombo, so we may never see each other again. I am feeling very sad.

As she read this her eyes filled with tears. That time had arrived. Tonight would be their last together! Only now did she realise how much she loved him; loved his happy smiling nature, his intelligence, his handsome manly figure. And he loved her too. How would she survive without him? She fumbled for her handkerchief and wiping away her tears, read on:

Sunday 3ʳᵈ September 1939 Our Sunday service led by the Captain has never been so well attended. We prayed for a peaceful solution to the Polish problem, many including dear Richard feeling ashamed of the way we abandoned the Czechs. They say war is now inevitable. Their prediction seemed about to be come true when a message was passed around that the Captain would address us over the broadcast system at three o'clock. Rumours began to circulate; one that war had been declared, another that Hitler had at last seen sense and had withdrawn from Poland, and a third that the ship was to be diverted to South Africa! I didn't know what to believe, but Richard said we should stop all this rumour-mongering and wait for the Captain to tell us what he knew. When the Captain finally spoke, he told us he'd received a wireless message informing him that today at 1115 British Summer Time, the Prime Minister had spoken to the nation over the wireless and had announced that an ultimatum had been given to Herr Hitler that if he did not stop all aggressive action against Poland and begin to withdraw his forces by 11am a state of war would exist between our two countries. Mr Chamberlain then went on to say "No such undertaking has been received and consequently this country is at war with Germany." Though in our heart of hearts most of us knew that war had indeed been inevitable, the declaration stunned us all and no one spoke. The older ones were perhaps recalling the horrors of the Great War, while in my mind's eye I saw those terrifying newsreels of the bombing of Guernica and Shanghai! The future seemed too frightening to contemplate! But then as the buzz of conversation began again there came another announcement asking us to go to our lifeboat stations for lifeboat drill. There we were told that though it was unlikely we would be attacked by German U-boats or surface raiders it was necessary to black the ship out at sunset. Stewards would therefore begin pulling curtains over in the public rooms and closing deadlights in our cabins before sunset and no upper deck lighting would be switched on. With the porthole closed and blacked out our cabin became so hot I was sure we wouldn't sleep and many like Nicola and me gave up and sought the coolness of the night on deck. There I found Richard and with our eyes accustomed to the dark we marvelled at the stars set like diamonds in the velvet sky and dreamed of what we would do together, and as dear old Bill would say, "built castles in the air"!

She remembered that as the days passed and Bombay drew ever nearer, everyone strangely came to accept that we were at war. Indeed, many seemed relieved that at last England and France had stopped giving in to Hitler, some even declaring that now we had stood up to Hitler, the war would be over by Christmas! But then news came to remind everyone that the conflict was not merely confined to Poland. The liner *Athenia* bound for Montreal had been sunk on the very evening that war had been declared. A U-boat had torpedoed her and she had gone down with most of her company. Everyone was shocked and frightened too, some convinced that U-boats were lying in wait for the *Ranpura*!

She turned over another page.

Wednesday 6th September 1939 Tonight we had our Fancy Dress Ball.

She smiled inwardly. The fancy dress ball! She'd hated the idea of finding a suitable costume to wear, but Nicola assured her everyone felt like that. "We used to have fancy dress parties at home and they were always a giggle," she'd said. The ship had a special shop they were told, where they could hire fancy dress costumes and she and Nicola had gone early hoping there would still be plenty to choose from; but finding something that appealed was difficult. Feeling more than a little self-conscious she had finally settled for a nurse's uniform. It wasn't terribly original but it fitted and she didn't want to appear flamboyant. Nicola of course had shown her good taste and had selected a simple Tudor dress and headpiece. She had looked stunning!

She read on:

I had been dreading it and when finally I was dressed I looked at myself in the mirror and felt a fool, but Nicola, divine in her simple Tudor outfit, told me I looked fine.

She said "What's more you've chosen a very patriotic costume!" I giggled at her stupid remark and felt more at ease. We tarried a little, not wanting to be the first to arrive and when we got there, we found it full. So full in fact that we had difficulty in finding Richard and Edward! But then I heard a voice calling "Nurse, Nurse" and looking round I saw this Sikh gentleman. It was Richard of course; his black beard and turquoise turban making him look every inch a Sikh! Edward was wearing a Victorian tweed suit and a deerstalker's hat and kept saying "Well my dear Watson". Frankly I was mystified, but Richard whispered "He's Sherlock Holmes!"

She smiled as she remembered the prize giving. A young girl, clearly an extrovert, had won the ladies' prize. She had worn a scanty dress and had repeatedly performed her version of the Turkish belly dance. The men of course had loved it! She had rather hoped that Richard might win a prize too, but it wasn't to be, instead a rather unconvincing "Arab Sheikh" was the winner.

She turned another page. It was yesterday's entry:

Friday 8ᵗʰ September 1939 Tomorrow we arrive at Bombay and I spent all morning packing and then unpacking to retrieve what I needed for the last dinner! Nicola has been looking forward to joining her mission in Calcutta, but is very worried about her father, whose offices in Liverpool she feels are likely to be bombed. I'm glad my grandparents are in Instow, where surely they will be safe. I gave Nicola my Allahabad address and Nicola gave me the Mission's and I have promised to visit her if I can. I tucked her address away in my bag without reading it, but later I discovered she had written "Thank you Trudi for your love and companionship. Praise God and when you are lonely and afraid, remember Psalm 56v4 "In God I trust: I will not be afraid. What can mortal man do to me?" Now I feel ashamed for the times I thought she was rather too pious. How I wish I could have some of her faith!

She laid down the diary. Nicola had been a strange cabin mate! Lively and fun-loving but nevertheless one who took her faith seriously, reading her well- thumbed bible in the morning and saying her prayers every night. She seemed to carry the cares of the poor on her shoulders and would brook no criticism of them. Trudi recalled that when she'd voiced her admiration for the great empire over which England held sway and for the Colonial officers who so nobly fought corruption and struggled to bring the benefits of civilisation to the colonies, Nicola had frowned. "But Trudi dear, what right do we have to rule over these poor people?" She had talked about rich England exploiting poor India, about the resentment of the educated Indians who were denied any meaningful role in the government of their country and of her admiration for Mahatma Gandhi, who one day she was certain, would achieve independence for India. She had been so persuasive in her argument; challenging Trudi's long held views about the glory of the empire. But then she smiled to herself. Soon she would have the opportunity to judge how right Nicola was! She continued to read:

Everyone has been making their farewells. Norman and Sheila Bentley were particularly charming and gave me their card too and said I should call on them if ever I visited Patna.

Our last tea dance today had us dancing the Eightsome and my favourite, Strip the Willow. Richard and I were with Giles and Jane. He told me that his District Office is in Hardoi, North of Lucknow, not far from Allahabad and that I must come and visit them.

After dinner which was more formal than usual, the Captain proposed the health of His Majesty and the success of his forces in the battle against the Nazis. Then we all sang "God Save the King" and then "Auld Lang Syne" before seeking the coolness on deck. Richard became very affectionate and told me he loves me. I realise I love him too! But what the future holds for us we could not say! All I know is that life without him will be empty.

That morning she had gone on deck to watch the ship enter Bombay and had been greeted by Richard. "How are you, dearest?" Their imminent parting had made her feel weepy, but she managed to hide the tears that threatened and trying to smile had replied, "The better for seeing you, Richard dear".

They'd found a place at the rail and studied the scene in silence. "I'll write." He was the first to speak. She nodded. "Will we ever meet again with this dreadful war?"

"We will, Trudi dearest, somehow. I know we will."

His confidence encouraged her. "They say it'll be over by Christmas."

She'd felt his arm slide around her waist. He shouldn't do that in broad daylight! But then she'd smiled to herself, there was a war on! She put hers around his too!

"I'll be staying at the transit camp for a couple of days, waiting for my ship to Colombo. I suppose you'll be going onto Allahabad straight away, or will you?" he added hopefully.

"No," she spoke brightly. "My train goes tomorrow. I'm spending the night at the Taj Mahal."

"Oh! How splendid! Shall I see you? Perhaps we could have dinner together?"

She gave his waist a squeeze. "Oh! What fun that would be!"

Chapter 3

·················

It was no good, she couldn't sleep! She'd lain there tossing and turning under her mosquito net for what seemed hours. She got up, slipped her dressing gown over her shoulders and went onto the veranda. The moon was fading, the sky lightening and in the east, she could see the first rays of the sun. It would soon be day. As she settled in her cane chair the memories that had disturbed her sleep came flooding back. She could see him still, there in the hotel foyer with the Victoria waiting. Her eyes filled with tears as she remembered that last evening together. They'd talked so confidently about the future, he telling her how much he loved her, and how happy she made him. He'd taken her in his arms and kissed her tenderly. Then he was gone. On an impulse she searched hurriedly for her handbag and opening it found the dinner menu on which he'd written his address; HMS Strongbow, c/o GPO Ships, Singapore. Finding that precious menu made her feel a little happier. They'd promised to write, why shouldn't she write now?

Hurriedly she found pen and paper and as she began to write she tried to recall his face. She could picture his smart naval uniform, but his features were blurred. She could see that beard of his, but try as she might her mind's eye seemed unable to bring his features into focus. A tear fell onto the paper. Hastily she wiped it away. Would he remember her face? She must send him a photograph of herself and hope he would send her one of him. She'd had one taken before going up to Girton for that interview. She'd kept a copy. Where could it be? Rummaging through her papers she found it. She studied it carefully. Though not beautiful like Nicola's, hers was a friendly face with blue smiling eyes. She examined it more carefully. Was it a quirk of the moment or did she really have that intriguing twist of the lips? Feeling pleased she turned it over and wrote "To dearest Richard with all my love – Trudi". Then she began:

Justice House
Hastings Road
Allahabad
United Provinces

September 12, 1939

Dearest Richard

I will never forget that wonderful evening we had together in the Taj. Will we ever have another like it? Pray God we will, though where and when will it be in this terrible war? Till then I shall have to rely on the happy memories of our time together on the Ranpura. They will have to keep me going until that happy day when you hold me in your arms again. I must confess I was so upset at your going that I recall little of leaving the Taj; I just followed my Chaprassi* and allowed him to put me safely on my train. Luckily, I found that I was sharing a compartment with Giles and Jane Callaghan who succeeded in cheering me up a little. They are a very warm, kind and welcoming couple and have reminded me of their invitation to visit them. They even proposed I should join them when they tour his district in November. I would enjoy that, but I shall have to ask Father!

I hope all is well with you and that you will arrive at Colombo without mishap. I shall always pray that the Lord will watch over you and your destroyer and keep you safe.

Now once again I am in Allahabad with my mother and father. Having seen so little of each other in the past, we are almost like strangers, but I have been made welcome.

When I arrived, I recognised my dear Ayah* straight away and she is making a great fuss of me.

She remembered how all the staff had been lined up to welcome her as she arrived. There must have been about fourteen of them. The *Khitmagar**, the cook and the others were strangers, but her beloved Ayah was still there, a little older, greyer and somewhat fatter too, but with a well remembered smiling face. She had whispered the words of their favourite nursery rhyme *"Talli, talli bad ja baba"** and without thinking she, Trudi had laughingly replied *"Ucha roti schat banaya"**. Ayah had chuckled. "I look after you Missy baba", she'd said. And she had recognised her *Syce** too, he who had so patiently walked or trotted alongside her while she learnt to ride her pony.

Now I am back I realise how much I have missed India. I was never so spoiled in England. India is surely in my blood.

She read what she had written; there seemed no more to say. It told of her love for him, what was more important than that? But as she folded the letter her eyes fell on the sentence *"having seen so little of each other in the past, we are almost like strangers"*. That was true. At the station she hadn't recognised Lady Cynthia and by the unmistakable query in her voice, when Lady Cynthia had said "Gertrude?" it was clear she hadn't recognised her either! Lady Cynthia had made no more than an intelligent guess; Trudi being the only unaccompanied English girl to alight from the train! And their conversation in the car had merely been polite enquiries about the journey and their respective health. When at last, after being shown her room, she had joined Lady Cynthia for tea she'd had a chance to study this woman who pretended to be her mother. How elegant she was, not wisp of hair was out of place and despite the clammy heat there was no sign of perspiration on her well made-up face. Her every movement, even that of pouring the tea seemed to emphasise her status, that of a sophisticated, highly cultured wife of a Knight. After a few predictable questions about her voyage and whom she had met, Lady Cynthia had spoken about life in Allahabad, of the different strands of society with whom an English girl should mix and not mix and how she should behave with those of higher standing. While Trudi had listened politely, she couldn't help remembering what she had heard when hiding in that cupboard; "Alberta's my child, Gertrude's not!" But nevertheless, despite the obvious lack of empathy between them, she determined to try to like this strange woman, if only for her father's sake.

Her father? Her childhood memories of him portrayed a remote silent figure, one she now felt uneasy about meeting. But later that evening he'd welcomed her with a hug, and then holding her at arms length, had studied her face for what had seemed an age, before saying "Gertrude my dear, you are beautiful". His look had been so intense; she had felt that mentally, he was devouring her! Had he been seeing her mother's face, not hers? When he'd released her, he told her how proud he was that she had gained a place at Girton and how pleased he was to welcome her to India. A year in India he said would open her eyes to the Empire's great civilising influence, an influence which someday would result in India being welcomed as an independent member of the Commonwealth. Then he'd smiled. "But you must enjoy yourself too. Enjoy the parties and the dancing and the riding." It had been a strange homecoming!

The opening of the door disturbed her musing. It was *Ayah**. "Here's your *cha*, missy baba**." Following her was a young girl laden with hot water and towels for her bath. This was to be her morning routine and when dressed she would meet Lady Cynthia in the coolness of the garden for breakfast, where Father on return from his morning ride, would join them. While he was keen that Trudi should improve her riding, Lady Cynthia was determined that she should learn and follow proper etiquette. She had had calling cards for "Miss Gertrude Henrietta Leafe" made and she told Gertrude that, without being seen she should put these into the calling boxes of the important people in Allahabad. She listed His Excellency the Governor, his Chief of Staff, the District Commissioner, the Chief of Police, the Colonel of the local regiment, the Chief Medical Officer and others.

"I will accompany you," she said. "It's a task we must undertake with some decorum. It must be completed by Saturday week when your father and I have arranged a dinner party to launch you into our local society."

With the forthcoming dinner party in mind, Lady Cynthia inspected Trudi's wardrobe. She was not impressed. Shaking her head despairingly, she declared her wardrobe to be quite inadequate for a girl of her standing. So hasty arrangements were made for Mr Aziz, the derzi* to visit. He came the next day to measure her, accompanied by his assistant laden with rolls of material. Lady Cynthia surveyed them with practised eyes, and dismissing Trudi's preferences, selected the material for two evening gowns. Her first choice, a verdant fabric with a discreet and irregular pattern of autumn leaves, did nothing to enthuse Trudi, but she accepted it. However, when Trudi suggested that the second, a cream damask-like material, would look pleasing if offset by a lemon sash, Lady Cynthia had reluctantly agreed.

"Mr Aziz," Lady Cynthia spoke authoritatively. "We shall need Miss Leafe's evening gowns by Thursday at the latest".

Mr Aziz nodded slavishly. "Memsahib, if Miss Leafe will kindly allow me to come for a fitting tomorrow, I will have them ready and will deliver them by noon on Thursday."

Lady Cynthia smiled graciously. "That will be fine, Mr Aziz." Then turning to Trudi, she put on her spectacles and inspected her closely.

"Gertrude, your hair; we simply must do something about that. You look like a country girl!" Though put out by her curt manner Trudi acquiesced demurely.

"And how's your dancing?" Lady Cynthia continued, removing her spectacles. "I suppose you dance that stupid modern fox trot, but can you Strip the Willow and dance an Eightsome?"

Trudi assured her she could. "And what about the Military Two Step and the Gay Gordons?"

Trudi confirmed she could dance them too, but Lady Cynthia seemed unconvinced.

"Perhaps I should ask Major White to supper on Thursday. I'm sure he'll be free. He's an excellent dancer; he'll give you some polish. He did wonders with Alberta."

Trudi's new gowns arrived on time and for the dinner and she chose the green with its autumnal foliage, the one Lady Cynthia had insisted upon. Now wearing it and with her hair arranged as Lady Cynthia had proposed she felt like a middle-aged matron as she made her way onto the veranda. Lady Cynthia was already there, looking her elegant self, her silver hair carefully groomed and complimented by a gown of pale sapphire silk. A long rope of pearls hung around her slender neck and as she fanned her face with a beautifully carved ivory fan, the diamonds in her rings sparkled regally. She inspected Trudi with a critical eye.

"Turn around, girl. Yes," she nodded in approval, "that gown looks well on you, and your hair looks better, but" she gave her another analytical look. "Perhaps a bun might be more suitable for Saturday."

Thankfully before Lady Cynthia could comment further, Sir Henry joined them. He was wearing a dinner jacket and black tie. He smiled at Trudi.

"You're looking quite beautiful, my dear."

Playfully she curtsied. "Thank you for your compliment, Your Honour."

Lady Cynthia groaned. "We'll have to get you curtseying with more elegance, Gertrude". Then with a practised smile on her lips she turned towards the door as the Khitmagar, resplendent in his livery, led Major White into their presence. Long passed over for promotion to half-colonel and now the Officer-in-Charge of the Regimental Depot in the Fort, Major White made a magnificent sight in his mess dress, a scarlet bumfreezer bedecked with medal ribbons, a golden cummerbund and blue lightning conductor trousers. Sir Henry greeted him with a firm handshake

"How good of you to come at such short notice, my dear Gordon."

"Not all, it's my great pleasure," Major White replied. Then bowing discreetly, he took Lady Cynthia's outstretched hand and kissing it, told her how well she looked. Lady Cynthia accepted his compliment with a gracious smile.

"Gordon, let me introduce my daughter Gertrude. She's just arrived for the season." Sir Henry broke in. "It'll be a long season I'm afraid, now we're at war again."

As sherry for the two ladies and *chota pegs** for Sir Henry and the Major arrived they discussed the fate of Poland and the arrival of the *B.E.F.** in France.

"That," the Major said, "should take some pressure off the Poles."

Further discussion was interrupted by the arrival of the Khitmagar, who bowing respectfully announced. "Sahib, dinner is served." Thanking him, Sir Henry led the party into the dining room, where the four of them did little justice to the magnificence of the room, with its gleaming mahogany table graced with silver cutlery bearing Sir Henry's new Coat of Arms, two silver candelabra and a large silver bust of Clive of India. The table would always be set like this, Trudi knew, even when Sir Henry and Lady Cynthia dined alone!

When Sir Henry had said Grace, they took their seats and as they ate, the conversation centred on the disturbance in Delhi the previous day.

"Was it the usual clash between Hindu and Moslem?" Lady Cynthia asked in a bored voice, "It doesn't take much to set them at each other's throats these days!"

Major White agreed. "It's the usual fight about the proposed plans for self government."

Lady Cynthia interjected. "Self government! That's a dream! They're just not ready for it."

"Well," Sir Henry broke in. "Whether they're ready or not, the Viceroy has postponed all discussions about giving more power to Congress until the war is over."

The Indians' desire for self-government and how it was to be achieved was usually one of the main topics of conversation, but now it was replaced by the war in Europe and the rumour that the Second Hampshires, garrisoned in the Military Lines, would be sent back to England.

"It's very likely," Major White prophesied, "And no doubt some Indian battalions will go with them too."

Lady Cynthia had had enough of the war, so with a determined look in her eye, she changed the subject. "I do hope the Governor's ball will still be held, war or no war! It's such a good opportunity to introduce all those here for the season." The Governor's ball was the social highlight of the year and soon they were reminiscing about last year's. It had been the best for many a year, they all agreed. By now the pudding had been eaten and the port passed, and conversation tailed off as Sir Henry stood for the Royal toast. He raised his glass. "Ladies and Gentlemen, the King Emperor." Standing, they all replied, "The King Emperor," before sipping their port. During her time in the *Ranpura* Trudi had grown fond of port and was savouring its bouquet and its rounded sweetness, when before she could finish her glass,

Lady Cynthia was on her feet telling the men not to be too long and leading her into the drawing room.

"Major White has work to do," she reminded them as she left and soon, in obedience to her summons, Trudi's dancing lesson began. Though with just four of them, it was difficult to dance an Eightsome or to Strip the Willow, Lady Cynthia with characteristic determination drove them on, until to everyone's relief Major White declared Trudi to be a competent dancer.

Chapter 4

A yah had arrived with her morning tea and hot water. Trudi stretched and savoured the warm sweet drink as Ayah busied herself with the bath. When all was ready. she lowered herself into the hip bath and with her knees almost touching her chin, Ayah began washing her. When she had first arrived Ayah's ministrations had disconcerted her, but Lady Cynthia would not countenance any change in the morning routine for she assured her it had long been the custom for the sahib and memsahib to be bathed and dressed by their ayah or bearer. So, Trudi had reluctantly accepted the custom but now found Ayah's gentle massaging relaxing.

"Ayah," she paused as Ayah soaped her back. "Do you know what happened to my governess? You remember Miss Nichols, don't you?"

"Oh! Yes, Missy baba. I remember her. She was very strict with you and made you work so hard. She never liked me you know. She said I spoilt you!" She chuckled. "Perhaps I did, you were always my favourite."

"Oh! Dear Ayah, you did spoil me too, you gave me a very happy childhood."

Ayah smiled as Trudi continued. "Miss Nichols must have left when Lady Cynthia took me to England. Where did she go?"

"She didn't stay in Allahabad, Missy. I heard she went to an Army memsahib in Lucknow."

"Oh! Did she? I've often wondered what happened to her. Was she Stewart's governess too?"

"Well Missy, she was for a little while. Miss Nichols came just after you were born."

"Oh! I didn't know that. So, who was Stewart's governess before her?"

Ayah didn't reply and began singing one of her old lullabies. She seemed flustered and scrubbed Trudi's back a little harder. Trudi shook herself and began singing softly with her. It seemed to put Ayah at ease. With her bathing finished she stepped into the huge white towel Ayah held out for her. Thanking her, she asked her directly, "Who was Stewart's governess before Miss Nichols? Please tell me."

"Missy, I forget."

"Please Ayah; tell me what you know about her."

"Oh! Missy it's a long time ago. I don't remember much."

She let Ayah dry and dress her. She didn't believe her for a moment. She was sure she hadn't forgotten; that she knew Lady Cynthia wasn't her mother. Had she been sworn to silence? Trudi changed the subject. "We must hurry," she said. "I'm riding with Father."

At a practice ride recently under the watchful eye of the Syce she'd managed a canter, but her riding was still very rusty; no one rode much in Instow, most people sailed! Yet her father had told her that even as a four-year-old, before she had left for England, she had sat easily on her pony and had learnt to trot and canter! Thankfully with Dusty, the gentle and responsive pony she now rode, her confidence was returning and on the first morning when, with her father, she had ridden to the *maidan** and back, he had been pleased with her progress. Yet he'd made it clear that she still had much to do and that she must ride regularly. And so it became a routine for her to ride with him each day. She loved the coolness of the morning, the sights and sounds, even the smells; they were the essence of the country of her birth, but though they rode together, her father rarely spoke; it seemed there was some hidden barrier between them! Yet he was her only kith and kin, the only one whose blood flowed through her veins, the only one who knew the truth about her mother. Often, she tried to visualize her father as a young man, a young man with an elegant wife, yet a young man in love with a pretty English governess, a young man who had sired the bastard child that Lady Cynthia had said she was! Yet how could she ask him about the governess she believed to be her mother, when he was always so silent and reticent? What was her name? Where did she come from? Was she pretty? What happened to her? Why did he abandon her? Was she still alive? Finding answers to these questions had become an obsession!

It was Saturday. Everyone was busy preparing for the dinner that night. The candelabra, the bust of Clive and the silver cutlery had been polished, the table laid and the Khitmagar, having borrowed additional staff from neighbouring houses, was busy instructing them in their duties. Lady Cynthia having cast an expert eye over the preparations was seated at her writing table studying the Warrant of Precedence, the Blue Book. This was a vital tool for any hostess arranging a seating plan. It listed all offices of the Raj in order of precedence. Heading the list was The Viceroy himself, followed in order of seniority by the Governors of the Provinces. Next came the Indian Political Service followed by the "Heaven Born", the ICS. The Army came next and then the Indian Police and so on. Wives took the precedence of their husbands. Etiquette demanded that guests must be seated in the correct order of precedence, so arranging a seating plan was extremely important as great insult and recrimination could result if someone was seated below his or her proper station! Lady Cynthia however was much practised in the art and studied the list of guests with equanimity. The most senior guests were Archibald Bailey CB, IOM, Chief of the Provincial Secretariat and his lady, Prudence. She placed him on Sir Henry's right with Prudence opposite. Then she placed the Collector, Sir Stewart Woolgar OBE, the next senior, on her right with Lady Caroline opposite him. Then came Colonel Hubert Swanson MC and his lady, Mrs Rachel Swanson, followed by the District Superintendent of Police, Frederick Pritchard CGM and his lady, Joyce. Next were the District Medical Officer Dr Hamish MacPherson and his lady, Iris, then the MacPherson girl Rebecca, and Philip Brodie, an Assistant Secretary and finally Major Dennis White and Gertrude. All sixteen (she had wanted sixteen, just enough for two eightsomes) were seated in the order given in the Blue Book. Then sending for the Khitmagar she gave him her plan to be displayed in the hall, and place cards for the table. As he bowed and withdrew, the *Bobajee** appeared. He'd come to report all was well with the *burra-khana**, assuring her the vegetables were fresh and the lambs had just been killed. "It is lamb I hope, not that tough goat you produced last time," she retorted. The Bobajee sighed, "They are fine young lambs. Their meat will be tender and sweet, I promise you Memsahib."

Doubtfully she thanked and dismissed him. All seemed well; Henry she knew would organise the wine with the bearer. Now it was almost time for luncheon, but Lady Cynthia had another duty. "Come Gertrude," she beckoned her. "Help me arrange the flowers. It's an art all ladies need to acquire." As they worked Lady Cynthia took the opportunity to ensure Gertrudel knew what would be expected of her at this her first dinner party. She asked her if she was nervous. "I remember I was quite terrified at my first dinner," she added. Trudi admitted to being a little anxious.

"Well Gertrude, there's really no need to be, but you must observe proper etiquette. I noticed when Major White was with us on Thursday you seemed unsure of the form when we drank the Royal Toast. So let me give you a few tips on what you should do and not do. Firstly, when you're introduced, you simply must remember everyone's name and rank. It's extremely bad form to forget a guest's name and rank and heaven forbid you get it wrong! So, study the seating plan well beforehand and memorize the names and ranks of our guests. Of course, you already know Major White. I shall ask him to escort you into the dining room and lead you to your place. Please wait for him to come to you. Don't go to him, that's not what a lady does! And remember we don't take our seats until Sir Henry has said Grace. And when you're seated, it's important that you make conversation. You must talk first to the gentleman on your right. That will be Philip Brodie; he's a bachelor in his late thirties and an Assistant Secretary. Then you should address Chief Superintendent Pritchard on your left. But be careful not to interrupt his conversation with Mrs Cameron, she'll be on his left. Keep the conversation going as best you can; and remember it's extremely bad form for a lady to change the subject. She paused. "Do you have any questions, Gertrude?" Certain she'd made everything crystal clear, Lady Cynthia expected none. Trudi shook her head, "No, Mamma, thank you". She knew she'd never remember everything, but Lady Cynthia's diktat had irritated her.

"Good," Lady Cynthia gave her a gracious smile. "Now when we've finished the last course Sir Henry will take the stopper out of the Port Decanter and pass it to the guest on his left." Again, she described the routine for the Royal Toast. Then she continued, "When the ladies have finished their port and, Gertrude, don't linger over yours, I will stand and lead them into the drawing room. The men always join us later. Is all that clear? It's all very simple really!"

Trudi found it difficult to rest that afternoon. She feared she'd make some terrible gaffe and knew Lady Cynthia would be watching her with a critical eye. As indeed Lady Cynthia had. The dinner had been an ordeal!

Chapter 5

· · · · · · · · · · · · · · · · · ·

A t last, she could climb into bed, but sleep eluded her, the events of the evening dominating her thoughts. The etiquette at dinner had been quite inhibiting and she realised she'd hardly learnt a thing about the policeman who'd sat on her left. It was perfectly clear he was a man of some importance, but could he not have made a little more effort to respond to her arduous efforts at conversation? Often, she had lapsed into silence awaiting an opportunity to talk to Philip Brodie on her right. But he had Mrs Iris MacPherson on his right and she, clearly as ardent a devotee to proper etiquette as Lady Cynthia, had excelled in her duty by talking endlessly to him. When Trudi had managed to catch his ear, he had been courteous and responsive. He admitted he too was Heaven Born though with a grin he'd said his mother always told him he was born in a bungalow in Nagpur! His father had been a District officer but he, for the past three years, had worked in the Secretariat at Government House. He told her he hoped one day to have a district of his own, but whether he would get one before India became independent, he couldn't say. "So," he'd said with sigh, "I'll probably be desk-bound forever!"

Sitting opposite Trudi had been Major White. His was a familiar face, but she found him to be a dull uninspiring person and it had been only too easy to follow Lady Cynthia's advice not to speak across the table! Indeed, it was only when he escorted her to the table that they had spoken and then the conversation had been restricted to enquiries about her dancing!

The dinner with its many courses had seemed endless and she'd been delighted when at last the decanter had appeared on her right. Then remembering to fill her glass carefully to within half an inch of its brim, as Lady Cynthia had instructed, she waited to toast the King Emperor, before withdrawing with the other ladies.

In the drawing room she'd managed to find a seat next to Rebecca, a girl of her own age who had come out only a few months before. She enjoyed tennis and croquet and they had agreed to play tennis together and Rebecca had promised to explain the mysteries of croquet.

When the men appeared, the dancing began. Major White was in her party for the first dance but to her delight Philip Brodie asked her to be his partner for the Military Two Step. Able then to talk to him without interruption from Mrs MacPherson, she'd found he had a dry wit which he used to advantage when talking about those whom he found vain or comical. He mentioned his boss, Mr Archibald Bailey, and told her he had clearly been disappointed only to have been appointed C.B. in the Birthday Honours instead of the C.M.G. he'd so confidently expected! He'd seen she was puzzled. "C.B.," he'd told her, "Stands for Companion of the Order of the Bath, and C.M.G. a higher order, for Companion of the Order of St Michael and St George." Then he'd grinned wickedly, "But of course C.M.G. really means Call Me God, which is what he expects us to do! Mind you he'd prefer a K.C.M.G. – Kindly Call Me God and his ultimate aim no doubt, is to be advanced to G.C.M.G. – God Calls Me God!" She'd giggled; she found his disdain for pomp refreshing. When she'd told him how difficult it had been to talk to him at dinner, he'd given her a wry smile. "Once Iris MacPherson gets into her stride, she's quite unstoppable! And her conversation is so inconsequential, yet one daren't doze off. If you should answer yes, when she expects a no, she gives you the most frightful look!" He sighed "I'm afraid Allahabad has many like her!" He seemed interested in her plans to read history at Girton. "Ah! University," he'd exclaimed, "it's a wonderful time of life."

His company she reflected had been the one enjoyable ingredient in an otherwise dreary evening, when she had tried so diligently to abide by the etiquette which seemed to rule Lady Cynthia's life. And while she had, she'd noticed with irritation that some of the senior guests had not. Lady Cynthia had emphasised that etiquette demanded that guests should depart no later that half past ten, but all should wait for the most senior guests to leave first. Yet when that magic hour had finally arrived, Mr Archibald Bailey and his lady Prudence had been deep in conversation with her usually taciturn father and had not left until nearly eleven o'clock. She giggled to herself; Philip Brodie would surely tell her Mr Archibald Bailey had probably been waiting for her father to call him God! The memory of his dry humour helped her relax and soon the familiar sounds of the cicadas and bullfrogs lulled her to sleep.

In the morning she'd wakened still in a rebellious mood, Ayah's cheerful welcome and her morning ride on Dusty had helped restore her spirits. Then Lady Cynthia held a post-mortem, "So that, Gertrude, you may learn from experience how to behave in a manner expected of the daughter of the Chief Justice". Her pomp and arrogance had irritated her, but she'd managed to control her anger. She simply could not understand why intelligent people took such trivial rules so seriously, but later in a more reflective mood, she remembered Lady Cynthia had told her, "One has to respect one's betters. That's what makes our servants respect and obey us. We maintain our prestige by showing respect for our betters and our code of etiquette helps us do that."

Thankfully it being Sunday, the post-mortem had to be curtailed. Matins beckoned and still ruffled, Trudi accompanied Sir Henry and Lady Cynthia to the Cathedral. As their car drew near, she marvelled at the quintessential Englishness of the building. Its Gothic lines were admirable and its size impressive. It made her feel proud to be English, proud that her forbears had brought the Gospel to India, that they had also brought civilisation to this great land, that they had managed and were still working to wean so many natives from the strange idols they still worshipped. She'd seen carvings of their weird gods; one called Ganesh had an elephant head and another Durga, had ten arms! She couldn't understand what sort of God these strange figures represented. Her musing was interrupted by the sound of music and in the distance, she saw a column of troops marching down Muir Road with their Regimental Band leading. The men had a confident swagger in their step and made a fine sight, a sight which seemed to reinforce the natural leadership of the Raj in this backward yet intriguing land.

She heard the double beat of the drum, the signal for the music to stop. She watched the troops halt and turn into line.

"We shan't see the Hampshires here much longer." Sir Henry remarked. "Gordon tells me they're off home shortly. They'll be in France by Christmas, I expect."

Turning, he led Lady Cynthia and Trudi towards the Cathedral and pausing by the doors they watched the Colonel review his troops. "I hear they'll be replaced by an Indian battalion," Sir Henry said as he ushered his party inside.

As Trudi studied the building, admiring its lofty arches and great stained windows, a thought struck her. "I may have been here before. Could this be where I was baptised?" She made a mental note to ask to see the Baptism records. They should name her mother. She looked for the font, where her mother could have held her before handing her to the Priest to be named. It was behind her, by the great West Door. She turned in her pew to get a better view; but she seemed to have upset Lady Cynthia who hissed, "Do stop fidgeting, Gertrude!" Obediently she turned around, closing her eyes to control her anger. Then forgetting her taskmaster, she cast her eyes around the chancel, admiring the elaborately carved Rood Screen that separated the chancel from the nave. Above it hung a painting of the crucifixion and through the screen she could see the High Altar and the organ pipes along the North wall.

"If it wasn't for the heat," she thought, "I could be in my own cathedral in Truro!"

She felt very much at home, even the kneelers were embroidered like those at Instow, though these were dedicated to British Regiments; her kneeler remembered the Devonshire Regiment, another the Durham Light Infantry. Easing herself back onto her pew, she studied the dusty red flag hanging from its pole on the South wall. Lady Cynthia noticed her interest.

"Those are the colours of the 93rd Highlanders who fought so bravely at Lucknow during the mutiny."

Hobnail boots coming down the aisle prevented her from saying more. Turning, Trudi saw soldiers placing their rifles still with bayonets fixed, in racks along the walls, before sliding into their pews.

"Ever since the mutiny, which began at evensong one Sunday," Lady Cynthia whispered, "British troops have always brought their rifles into church."

Again, she was interrupted, this time by the organ and the singing of the choristers as they led the Priest down the nave and into the chancel. When the choir had passed, Lady Cynthia whispered, "Gertrude, you must read and inform yourself about the mutiny. Then you'll understand why we worry about our safety when the British troops have gone."

It was a service of matins like so many she had attended at Instow, yet different, all being conscious of the danger facing their families at home now war had been declared and feeling for the troops soon to be fighting the Nazis. The final bars of the hymn subsided, and she heard the familiar words,

"Dearly beloved brethren, the Scripture moveth us in sundry places to acknowledge and confess our manifold sins and wickedness; and that......", the voice tailed off as her thoughts wandered.

In her mind's eye she saw the troops laughing and joking as they climbed the gangway to board their troopship. Though they were destined for the war in France, they were cheerful; they were on their way home to Blighty. How would she get home, she wondered? She'd planned to spend no more than six months in India before going up to Cambridge, but already the regular sailing of passenger ships to England had been disrupted. Some said it would become ever more difficult to get home now liners were being converted into troopships! Would she be stranded here until the war was over? She shook herself; she must concentrate on the service. She heard the Priest,

"Wherefore let us beseech Him to grant us true repentance that those things............" Again, her thoughts wandered. In England men were being conscripted into the forces and women were volunteering to serve alongside them. If she ever managed to get home, should she defer her university course she wondered, and join the Wrens? Her future seemed so unsure, yet one thing was becoming more and more certain, she was trapped in India living a life she was finding trivial and pointless! She heard the others saying The Lord's Prayer; hastily she joined them. The first lesson she knew well, about the killing of Goliath by the boy David with a stone shot from his sling. But she could remember little of the sermon, except the Priest exhorting them to put their faith in God as David had, and assuring them that I Ie would help them defeat Hitler and his Nazis.

They left with the words of the last hymn ringing in her ears:

"Stand up, stand up for Jesus,

The strife will not be long:

This day the noise of battle,

The next the victor's song.

As they filed out of church and watched the troops march off with their confident swagger, Trudi wondered how many would be left to sing the "victor's song" when the war was over.

Chapter 6

•••••••••••••••••

S unday had been a long day, but at last Trudi was able to seek the seclusion
of her own room. Shaking off her hot sweaty clothes and slipping into
her night dress she sank into her chair on the veranda to enjoy the cool
evening breeze. It was a beautiful night with a full moon. Reflecting on the
day's events she reached for the diary she had neglected recently. She recalled
Lady Cynthia telling her how important it was to remember the names of
one's guests and how she always kept the seating plan for the dinners she
hosted. Then she would file it away in her bureau.

"By doing that, I never forget the names and ranks of my guests. That's
what you should do, Gertrude."

Feeling rebellious as she did so often in Lady Cynthia's presence, she had
remained silent; though to herself, she'd muttered "I shall do no such thing! I
shall have no difficulty in remembering those I like!" She liked Rebecca, she
was her age and she hoped they would play tennis and ride together. And
though he was a terrible bore, she found Major White harmless enough and
he did have a kind heart. Then there was Philip Brodie. He was easy to talk
to and his dry wit amused her. He too seemed to dislike the pomp the others
seemed to revere. She had enjoyed being with him and he'd seemed to like
her too! She smiled as she thought how well they had danced together and
what a fine figure he'd cut. But suddenly she felt guilty; she was forgetting
her beloved Richard. Hastily she put all thoughts of the dinner behind her

and picking up her pen began to write to him about her visit to the Cathedral and the events of the morning which had so clearly demonstrated the power and glory of the Raj. Moving inside where the light was better she continued:

After the service we went to the club, where once again we met those who had been with us in church. Father was soon deep in conversation with Mr Bailey, the Governor's Chief of Staff. They were discussing the recent disturbances in Delhi. I heard him telling father that the Congress Party was being difficult because the Viceroy had declared war on Germany without consulting them. He was sure the Congress Party was behind the recent riots. But both he and Father supported the Viceroy. "It's within the powers granted to him by the Government of India Act", I heard Father say. The Chief of Staff nodded, "That half-naked fakir Gandhi has been stirring things up, helped by that left wing rebel Chandra Subhas Bose."

Lady Cynthia had been with them but had contributed little to the conversation, though whenever she did, her attitude towards Mr Bailey was noticeably reverential, quite unlike the regal manner she adopts when talking to lesser mortals! I was keen to slip away as I'd seen Rebecca and I wanted to organise some tennis with her, but Lady Cynthia dragged me off to meet Major White.

`"Dennis dear," she gave him a charming smile; "you must talk to Gertrude and introduce her to some of your friends." With that she wandered off. I thought he was rather hidebound and sure enough he seemed unable to find anyone of my age to talk to. His conversation is always so stilted and all he did was to ask me if I was enjoying India, and how my dancing was coming along and such like. It makes me wonder whether he has any interests or if there is any spark of adventure in him. And he's always so terribly courteous and correct. I'm sure that if I'd ever let him bed me, he'd write me a formal thank you letter the next day! Thankfully I saw the Dean nearby and excusing myself I approached him. "Father," I said. He turned, his blue eyes examining me closely. "You're Sir Henry's daughter Gertrude, aren't you?" I smiled in acknowledgement and thanked him for his perceptive sermon. We chatted inconsequentially for a minute or two and then I grasped the nettle. "Father," I said. "I believe I was baptized here in August 1921, but sadly I've lost my Baptism card and I'm ashamed to say I don't know who my godparents are. I've wanted to know who they are as long as I can remember and now I'm here in Allahabad I'd like to find out." He looked puzzled and asked me why I didn't ask my parents. Well, I'd foreseen such a question, so I was prepared. I told him I'd been sent home to England shortly after my fourth birthday and that I was

ashamed to say I just didn't know my parents well enough to ask them and in any case I feared my ignorance might upset them. He gave me a quizzical look, but then he seemed to accept my story. So, taking a deep breath, I asked whether the cathedral would have some record of my baptism. "Yes of course," he replied. "All churches keep a Register of Baptism and the names of your godparents will be shown there." When I asked whether I'd be allowed to see the register, he said I could and has agreed to see me on Wednesday.

She put her pen down. Godparents, she laughed inwardly. I don't mind who they are, not even if Major White was one of them! It's my mother's name; that's what I want to see. It must be there!

Wednesday came at last. As she was leaving, Lady Cynthia had reminded her of their luncheon engagement at the club and how she wanted to introduce her to her bridge friends. "You must start playing bridge regularly, Gertrude, and we must get you settled into a suitable group." Then she had asked what she had planned to do that morning. Wishing to keep her visit to the Cathedral a secret, she had said quite untruthfully, that she would be riding with Rebecca. Later fearing her deceit might be uncovered, she had called at Rebecca's house to seek her support in the deception, but to her dismay she'd not been there. Worried, but knowing there was nothing she could do, she'd arrived early for her appointment with the Dean and had passed the time examining the brass wall plaques. Due to the constant polishing many of the inscriptions were difficult to read, but one more legible that the others caught her eye:

"To the Glory of God
And in memory of
Edward George Napier-Smith, I.C.S
Slain by Mutineers
at Allahabad April 18th 1857
"And thus dying thou shalt die greatly"

With her eyes now better adjusted to the gloom she found another:

"In loving memory of
Lylie Muriel Struthers
And her children Suzie, Violet, Jonathan and Andrew

Who perished at Allahabad in the fires lit by the Mutineers
April 19th 1857
REQUIEM ETERNAM DONA ET DOMINE"

Yet a third read:

"In memory of
Major Edwin Spencer Gledwyne-Jones
Of the South Wales Borderers
And a Companion of the Distinguished Service Order
Killed by the Mutineers at Lucknow
June 15th 1857
In tempore vesperi erit lux"

"Good Morning Miss Leafe".

Thoughts of the Mutiny were swept from her mind as she turned to see the Dean, the Very Reverend Ronald Pearce, smiling at her. "Now let's find those godparents of yours!" Leading her into the vestry he unlocked a cupboard and brought out a pile of dusty registers. Casting aside the Wedding Register, "We don't have so many of these nowadays", he mumbled, "Nor these, happily," as he put the Register of Burials back. "Ah! Here we are," he opened the Baptism Register. "Now what year was it?"

"1921. I was born on the 24th August, so I presume I was baptised in August or September."

"1921 you say", he hunted through a stack of registers. "Ah! Here it is. August eh?" He saw her nod. "Here's the 18th, it'll be the next page. Oh!" He looked puzzled. "We're into September now! September 2nd entry number 241. He turned back a page. "We're back in August 18th again, entry number 240."

He unfolded a snow- white handkerchief and mopped his forehead. "Well, it's clear you weren't baptised in August. What about September?" With Trudi looking over his shoulder he leafed slowly through the entries for September, October, November and December. Then after searching through the register for 1922 without success, he gave her a searching look. "Miss Leafe could it be that you were baptised in another church? A Garrison church perhaps? You are sure you have been baptised?"

She hadn't known how to answer him. Her birth had always been shrouded in mystery and now it seemed her baptism was too. She told him she'd always believed she'd been baptised. "Perhaps you're right Father, maybe I was baptised in another church!" She'd thanked him profusely and left to find a quiet pew to ponder whether she would ever find her mother. But strangely she found herself thinking not of her mother, but of Lady Cynthia and in a rare moment of charity, could understand how humiliated and deeply hurt she must have felt when she learnt of her husband's adultery and how hateful it must have been for her to have "that bastard child" foisted on her. But then she wondered had Lady Cynthia contrived out of spite, to stop her being baptised? And to appease her, had her father complied with her wishes?

Puzzled, she rose and leaving the cathedral strolled through the close, its tranquillity easing her frustration. As she relaxed a headstone caught her eye. It was the cherub that had attracted her. It had been so beautifully carved. She looked closer. It was the grave of a Fanny Alberta Durcott. Durcott, the name was unusual, but not her death. "Died in childbirth, April 21st 1904" she read. The curt, dispassionate statement shocked her! It bred a horrid thought! Had her mother suffered the same fate? She'd always hoped one day she'd find her. But could she like Fanny Alberta, be buried here? Had her mother died on 24th August 1921, the day she'd been born? She began to search each headstone looking for that date. There were so many, but with determination she began. Some tributes she found distressing, and some were worn and difficult to read. The latter she ignored telling herself that an inscription carved only eighteen years earlier could not yet be badly eroded. When she found one with the right date, her hopes were raised only to be quickly dashed when she read the name, John Maurice Barber. Discouraged, she realised she had set herself a time-consuming task, but persevering, she completed the row. Next time she would start on the following row.

She arrived for lunch a few minutes late but despite her apology she incurred a disapproving look from Lady Cynthia. As the *boy** arrived with a tray of drinks, she saw Lady Cynthia beckoning Rebecca to come and sit by her. To her horror she heard her ask whether she'd enjoyed her ride with Gertrude that morning. Rebecca looking puzzled, had said she and Gertrude had ridden together yesterday, but this morning she'd gone to the bazaar.

Lady Cynthia hadn't at the time seemed concerned about this discrepancy, but Trudi feared the worst and sure enough on arriving home Lady Cynthia had asked her where she had been that morning.

"I was mistaken, Mamma". She hated calling Lady Cynthia Mamma, but at a time like this, she knew she must. "I called at Rebecca's house, but she was not there." Thankfully, that at least was true. "I got muddled with the dates."

"Hmph!" Lady Cynthia had shaken her head irritably. "Gertrude you must learn to keep your appointments diary properly. It's very bad form to miss appointments or get them muddled." She'd sighed despairingly. "Gertrude, you have such a lot to learn about life out here."

Over lunch the war had been the main topic of conversation, everyone expressing great admiration for the gallant Poles, but while the Germans launched their *Blitzkreig** the papers said the Poles were using tactics of the last war with obsolete weapons. Their cavalry had been mown down without mercy by machine-guns when they had so valiantly charged a force of German tanks.

"What use is the cavalry now?" One of the ladies asked with horror in her voice. "We must never let our Bengal Lancers suffer such a fate!"

All agreed and foresaw the early surrender of the Poles. What would happen then? Some hoped Hitler would want peace, but Lady Cynthia said England could not accept any peace overtures unless Hitler withdrew from Poland and so this dreadful war would continue. News of the sinking of the liner *Athenia* with nearly fifteen hundred people on board hade made the reality of this distant war strike home. Many had children at school in England and relatives too and some had sons in the armed forces. And like them, Trudi worried about Richard. She'd received only one letter from him since they'd parted in Bombay. He'd told her he'd arrived safely in Colombo, had joined his ship and sent his love. She had written twice and now waited desperately for his next letter. When it came the next day, she slipped quietly into her room before opening the envelope. It was dated ten days earlier. She read it eagerly.

Dearest Trudi

I was thrilled to receive your second letter and with it that lovely photograph of you, which smiles at me every time I enter my cabin. It makes me long to see you again.

I am delighted to hear that you have settled safely into life at Allahabad. I love to ride on the moors, when I'm home and I envy you your morning rides on Dusty. I have a friendly farmer who lends me a mount and one day, my love, I'll borrow one for you and together we'll ride over to Postbridge for tea!

Her eyes misted over. If only this war were over, then they could be together. He told her about Chagford, where his parents lived and how he knew she would like it there. Then the letter became more serious as he told her he and his fellow officers, felt quite guilty with the war so far away and wanted desperately to get back home to fight the Germans.

But it won't happen. We in the Strongbow just have to maintain a presence out here, while the battle goes on at home.

He seemed despondent, but she was glad. She wanted him and his ship to be far from danger. She read on.

Though we're so far from any action, I'm sure we'll soon be censoring the crew's letters and no doubt the Captain will be censoring mine! And as I shall want to warn you if we ever come your way, so that dearest, we might arrange to meet, I have devised two code words. Colombo will become "my father's birthday" and Trincomalee "my mother's birthday". So if I write "my father's birthday is the 14th October" it will mean we will be arriving in Colombo on that day. I don't think the censor will twig, but you my dearest will know what I mean!

His ingenious idea made her giggle. How exciting it was to have their very own code and how wonderful it would be to meet him again. As she read on, he told her he would never forget the evening they'd shared in the Taj Mahal and how one day he would take her to dinner in the Gale Face Hotel in Colombo. Then he assured her of his constant love and ended on a cheerful note:

We'll meet again one day, my love. I just know we will, who knows it might be quite soon. Dearest, I long to hold you in my arms again.

Your ever loving Richard

Chapter 7
∙ ∙ ∙ ∙ ∙ ∙ ∙ ∙ ∙ ∙ ∙ ∙ ∙ ∙ ∙ ∙ ∙ ∙

After four days steaming down the Indian coast, Richard was on deck to watch the Colombo pilot climb aboard the *Dilwara* and guide her to her berth. Unlike the *Ranpura*, the *Dilwara* had carried troops, a battalion of Indians bound for Ceylon to replace British troops recalled to fight the war in Europe. He'd shared a table with some of their British officers and had enjoyed their company but had been particularly pleased to meet the only other Naval Officer, Harry Allen, a Paymaster Lieutenant on his way to join the staff of the Base Commander at Trincomalee. He'd given him Trudi's address and had asked him to write to her if ever he heard that the *Strongbow* had been sunk.

Now with the *Dilwara* safely berthed he bade farewell to his new friend and finding a *Tonga**, had set off to join his ship. As it clip-clopped along, he could see her lying alongside in the harbour. Despite her age (she was first commissioned in 1919) she made a pretty sight, with the White Ensign flying proudly at her stern. A thin column of grey smoke rose from her for'ard funnel, and he could see her two single 4 inch guns, one on the fo'c'sle and the second mounted between the funnels; the after gun he knew, had been removed and mine rails fitted so as to give her a minelaying role. He was thrilled to be joining her! Most of his contemporaries were starting their long courses, to specialize in Gunnery, Torpedoes, Signals or Navigation, but he had chosen not to follow that path. He had decided to remain a non-specialist, a "Salt Horse" as it is known, since this would give him an early chance to be First Lieutenant of a destroyer, one of the sleek little ships where everyone knew each other and there could be a real esprit de corps. Of course, he'd dreamed of serving in one of the new "Tribals", but then to be *Number One** of a "Tribal" he knew he'd have to wait until he was a junior Lieutenant Commander. So though the *Strongbow* was small and ancient, he felt proud and lucky to be appointed her First Lieutenant.

The pony slowed to a walk and the tonga drew to a halt alongside. It was then that he realised how tiny she was. At just over 200 feet long, the *Strongbow* was about two thirds the size of a modern destroyer, yet he smiled inwardly, with a speed of 36 knots she could match her younger sisters! As the *tonga wallah** unloaded his trunk and suitcase, he climbed down, dusted his reefer, adjusted his cap and, walking up the gangway, saluted the ship's side and introduced himself, "Lieutenant Hooper, come aboard to join." The Officer of the Day returned his salute. "Welcome aboard, sir. The Captain will be pleased to see you, follow me, sir."

They walked for'ard, the iron deck ringing under their footsteps. Reaching the bridge structure, they ducked under a ladder and entered a small compartment. To port was a closed door. "That's the Wireless Office", the Officer of the Day told him as he knocked on the other door. A voice inside bade them enter, and Lieutenant Commander Henry Newcombe rose with outstretched hand. "Thank you, Fisher," he dismissed the Officer of the Day. "Glad you've arrived, Hooper." Richard studied his new Captain. He was clean shaven with receding ginger hair encircling a shiny pate and under shaggy brows his blue eyes seemed ready for a laugh. Instantly he felt they'd get on well. "Now," Henry Newcombe said after their brief introductions, "You mustn't waste time with me. You must meet Carter, your predecessor, he's off to Bombay tomorrow in the *Dilwara*, so you're in for a quick turnover." He pressed the bell for the Quartermaster. "We'll talk about the ship and what we'll be doing tomorrow."

The turnover was indeed quick! He met the other five officers, Bill Jenner the Pilot, Fred Fisher the Gunner, Derek Griffiths the Torpedo Gunner, Stan Bates the Engineer and young Andrew White, the newly promoted Sub Lieutenant come to earn his Bridge Watch keeping ticket. Then he was shown round the ship and introduced to many of the crew. The day passed in a haze and when Frank Carter finally said, "Well that's about it," he'd decided not to ask any questions, there just wasn't time! He knew he'd cope, though he'd have to learn the peculiarities of the *Strongbow* and earn the respect of the men, then they'd accept his authority. With such thoughts he made his way to his cabin to change for dinner when his predecessor would be "dined out". He slid the door back and surveyed his new home. It was minute, but it was his own. No longer would he be sharing! Besides his bunk, there was a small desk, a chair, a chest and a miniscule wardrobe. Throwing his cap onto the bunk he saw an envelope on his desk. He recognised her writing! Hurriedly he opened it and as he did a photograph fell out. It was her Trudi, just as he remembered her with her smiling eyes and that intriguing twist of her lips. He put it aside as he read her letter. She was safe and enjoying life and assured him of her love. He wanted to reply immediately, but it would soon be dinner and he had to change. He would write before they sailed.

Hastily he changed and went to the wardroom, a diminutive compartment below the quarterdeck. Approaching he could hear laughter and entering found the party in full swing and in no time had been given a pink gin. Frank Carter was the centre of attention. He was clearly well liked, and everyone seemed determined to give him a good send-off. It was a noisy boisterous evening, quiet only when they drank the loyal toast to His Majesty the King. Then the *Old Man** rose to pay tribute to his parting First Lieutenant in a short, humourous speech that showed clearly how much he valued all that Frank had done "to lick this old girl and her crew into shape". Finally, the time came for Frank to depart and as he walked over the gangway and climbed unsteadily into his Tonga, the whole ship's company was there to cheer him on his way. Richard was thankful to retire to his tiny cabin, he'd drunk more than he ought, but those pink gins had been difficult to refuse and then there'd been the wine at dinner and that heavy port. It was past midnight and his bunk called, yet so did his half-unpacked baggage. With a throbbing head he emptied his trunk and squared off his cabin; it had to be tidy in the morning for then it would be his office. Finally, he could do no more and lay sweating on his bunk, but hardly had his aching head touched the pillow than he remembered her photograph. Headache or no headache he just had to find it! A hurried search revealed it, buried under papers on his desk. He grinned, just looking at her made him feel better! He held the photograph at arms length admiring her lovely face, then kissing it gently he propped it up below his open port hole and slipped into a welcome sleep.

Woken by the steward with a welcome cup of tea he dressed hurriedly and arrived on deck in time to meet the *Buffer** and attend the morning muster, the daily ritual for all First Lieutenants, when the men were detailed off for the day's work. The fresh morning breeze and that early cup of tea had helped clear his head and bidding the men to stand at ease he introduced himself, telling them how pleased he was to join the *Strongbow* and that her smart appearance did them great credit. But wanting to emphasise his priorities he ended by saying that while in peacetime the Navy takes great pride in the smartness of her ships and men, in wartime appearances must take second place for it was more important that the *Strongbow* gave a good account of herself when tested by the enemy. Later, after a hurried breakfast, he was on the upper deck again, standing among the mine rails, waiting for the White Ensign to be hoisted in the age-old naval ceremony of Morning Colours. A few minutes later he was joined by the Old Man and they both saluted as the Quartermaster piped "the still" and the Signalman hoisted the ensign. With the ceremony over, the Captain invited him to his cabin and bade him sit down.

"I hope you're getting settled in, Number One. We've got a grand ship's company so we don't have any problems on that score, but it's important that you and I are in the same mind about what might be expected of the *Strongbow*. She's a pretty little ship but I'm afraid with her puny armament she was designed to fight the last war, not this one! That's why, the five of us, the *Scout, Sturdy, Tenedos, Thanet* and the *Strongbow* have been left out here with the four ancient "D class" cruisers of the China Fleet. We wouldn't be much use at home, but here at least we can provide a naval presence. Three of our flotilla are in Hong Kong with the cruisers and we and *Tenedos* are based at Singapore. *Strongbow*, as you know, is fitted as a minelayer, so we'll probably be required to lay defensive minefields if Singapore is threatened. So, Pilot and I need to brush up our navigating skills if we are to lay our mines in the right place. Now what else will we be doing? Well , we'll be spending a lot of time patrolling the Straits, I'm certain of that. We'll be required to stop and search any merchant ships likely to be carrying supplies for the Germans. So, we'll need a well-trained boarding party and if it turns out to be a German ship, we'll be expected to take her as a prize or sink her. So, Number One, our gunnery must be up to scratch and able to deal with such an easy target." He paused. "I doubt if we'll meet any German n. val forces out here, but if we do, well God help us, our two little four-inch guns won't be much help then!" He saw Richard nod then continued "But I think it's very unlikely. However, we could meet a *Q-ship**! And intelligence suggests Q-ships will be armed with six-inch guns, so for us a Q-ship would be one hell of a challenge!"

"Yes." Richard nodded. "She'd be firing at us while out of range of our guns!"

The Old Man was nodding too. "Yes, and I'm afraid our guns wouldn't do a lot of damage anyway. Only our torpedoes could sink her, if we ever got within range! But he paused. "Initially we would keep out of range, shadow her to report her position, so any other forces in the vicinity, perhaps one of our cruisers might come and help us."

"What if there aren't any, sir?"

Henry Newcombe paused to offer Richard a cigarette and take one himself. Richard watched his Captain tapping his thoughtfully on the cigarette case, a ritual which seemed to help him concentrate whenever a difficult decision had to be made.

"Well Number One," he lit their cigarettes and inhaled deeply, "We'd have to do what Nelson expects – we'd have to engage the enemy more closely; after all that's what we're here for!"

The Captain's stark portrayal of what might happen had shaken him, but he was right, that's why they wore the King's uniform!

Well, sir," he smiled weakly, "We must hope we don't meet a Q-ship."

"Aye. Well, Number One we can only do our best, but we must make sure our men are well trained, know how to use their weapons and that the weapons work properly." He leaned towards him. "And that's your responsibility."

For a moment or two the Captain was silent; then stubbing out his cigarette he continued, "We've talked about the surface threat, but what about air attack?"

"Well, Sir, there aren't any German air bases out here and the Germans don't have any Carriers, so air attack must be pretty unlikely."

"Perhaps that's as well," Henry Newcombe agreed. "With our one little AA gun I don't think we'd put up much of a fight, though," he grinned. "I'm led to believe that Able Seaman Dodd has a good aim!"

"What about U-boats, sir?" Richard asked. "Presumably there are none out here."

"Not as far as we know. Their prime target is our Atlantic Convoys, but nevertheless we may be tasked to support the *Durban* or one of her sisters if ever we run a convoy to and from the Cape." He stopped to offer Richard another cigarette. "So, Number One, our role as I see it is to lay minefields, to stop and search Merchant ships, sinking any German ones, and to be prepared for the Q-ship." He smiled, "That should keep us busy!"

A knock on the door interrupted further discussion and in came Stan Bates, the Engineer, his oil-stained white overalls testament to his efforts to get the engines ready for sea. After a fortnight in dock, everything had gone well except for a circulating pump which had begun to leak, spewing water into the bilges. But now Stan had a smile on his face. "I'm pleased to report we've fixed the circulating pump, sir. Seems to be working a treat, but I'd like to give it a good run at full power just to make sure".

It was the news Henry Newcombe had been waiting for and happily he agreed for a trial the next day. "If it's successful, Chief, we'll carry on to Singapore".

Chapter 8
· · · · · · · · · · · · · · · · · ·

S ince that lunch in the club, when Lady Cynthia had so rightly suspected
Trudi of lying, their relationship never cordial at the best of times, had
sunk to a new low. Now seemingly by mutual consent, they did their best
to avoid each other. But Trudi, knowing a passage to England was unlikely
until the war was over decided to curb her rebellious nature and come to
terms with the irritating etiquette upheld so forcibly by Lady Cynthia. And
recalling Lady Cynthia's concern about the departure of the Hampshires and
their replacement by an Indian battalion and how strongly Lady Cynthia
felt that she, Trudi should inform herself about the mutiny, she now decided
to ask her for a book on the subject. It was an October morning and Lady
Cynthia, elegantly dressed as usual, was sitting in the shade of the Acacia
tree. She was reading the newspaper and seemed very agitated.

"What's happened, Mamma?"

"It's the Navy. How could they let it happen?"

"What, Mamma?"

"They've let a U-boat sink the *Royal Oak*! Here, read it for yourself."

In a daring raid two days ago, a German U-boat slipped into the navy's
anchorage at Scapa Flow and sank the battleship H.M.S Royal Oak, a
veteran of the Battle of Jutland. The Navy had not yet completed blocking

the entrance to Kirk Sound and German aerial reconnaissance had spotted this gap in the defences. Lieutenant Commander Prien in U-47 sent to exploit this, slid through the gap and fired seven torpedoes at the *Royal Oak*, sinking her within a few minutes with all but three hundred of her crew. U-47 escaped undamaged.

As she read this terrible news, she saw in her mind's eye her beloved Richard struggling in the water, his destroyer sinking beneath him.

"Oh! Mamma," she exclaimed.

For once Lady Cynthia gave her a sympathetic look. "I suppose you worry about that Naval Lieutenant of yours".

"Yes, I do. How I wish this awful war could be over!"

"Yes," Lady Cynthia sighed. "Like you, I worry too. There's Alberta at Thomas's doing her nursing training right in the middle of London, just opposite the Houses of Parliament. That surely must be a prime target for Hitler's bombs! And now that Stewart's finished at Sandhurst, I expect he'll be off to France soon." She shook her head. "How will this war end? Now the Poles have surrendered everyone expects Hitler to turn on France. I just pray their famous *Maginot Line** will hold".

To comfort her, Trudi told her she'd read it was impregnable. "And in any case," she added "after Poland, Herr Hitler says he seeks no further territorial gains in Europe."

"Do you really believe that?" Lady Cynthia seemed unconvinced.

Trudi didn't know what to believe.

"Well, that's what he said!"

Then remembering why she'd come, she changed the subject and asked Lady Cynthia if she knew of a suitable book for her to read about the Mutiny. Her request seemed to please Lady Cynthia, for to Trudi's surprise she smiled, saying she had one in mind and would find it. And after dinner that evening as good as her word, she handed Trudi the book. Its leather binding showed signs of wear, but its title, tooled in gold lettering, could clearly be read, "An account of the mutinies in the Oudh and the siege of the Lucknow Residency."

"Your father was stationed in Lucknow when he was a junior Judge, so we found it particularly apposite. I have another here." She read its title. "Reminiscences of the Great Mutiny 1857-1859" – you may find it interesting too."

Trudi had thanked her and later in her room had scanned a few pages about Lucknow, but her mind had kept wandering. She'd never known her father and Lady Cynthia had lived in Lucknow. If her father had been in Lucknow, had she been born there? Perhaps just before they moved to Allahabad? Could that explain why she hadn't been baptised in Allahabad? Lady Cynthia would never enlighten her, she knew; on the only occasion her birth had come up in conversation her face had stiffened, and she had changed the subject. Only her father could tell her the truth, but he was always so distant and unresponsive. If she had been born in Lucknow, she might have been baptised there, if so her name and her mother's would surely be in the Register there. She must go to Lucknow and find it, but how could she engineer a visit? If she feigned an interest in the mutiny and the events that took place there, Lady Cynthia would be sure to accompany her; then how could she search that Register? This sudden turn of events presented new opportunities and new problems!

Over the following days she applied herself diligently to the task of learning about the Mutiny. She read the book on Lucknow first, for no better reason than because her father had been a judge there. At school she'd learnt a little about the Mutiny and had been taught that the rebellion was caused by the introduction of new rifles. It had seemed an odd reason for a revolt, but now she learnt that a new cartridge had been introduced and to ease its passage down the barrel of the new rifle, it was greased. But so that the gunpowder within the cartridge could be ignited when the trigger was pulled, the end of the cartridge had to be removed. The Sepoys had to do this with their teeth. But they worried about the grease. What was it made from? The Hindus feared it came from beef fat and the Muslims were certain it came from pork fat! To allow even a smear of beef fat to enter a Hindu's mouth would desecrate the Holy Cow he so revered and allowed to roam unmolested over his land

and crops. So, if it was fat from the cow, how could he a Hindu, possibly bite off the end of the cartridge? To a Moslem the pig was a filthy, unclean animal which the Holy Prophet Mohammed had forbidden him to eat. If a Moslem tasted grease from the pig when he bit the cartridge he would flout the Holy Prophet's teaching, be defiled and incur his wrath. So, both Hindus and Moslems asked their British officers what fat was used to make the grease, but they couldn't say. Nor did they seem to care and would brook no question or complaint about the new rifles or their cartridges.

So, discontent spread rapidly among both Hindus and Moslems and rumours began to spread that it was a deliberate ploy by the Kaffirs as they called the Christians, to make them contravene their faith and convert to the Kaffir religion. But the British considered it to be merely a storm in a teacup and when at Meerut, Sepoys of the Bengal Light Cavalry rejected both the new rifles and cartridges the British Officers were totally unprepared. They treated their action as a matter of gross indiscipline and the mutineers all eighty-five of them, were ordered to parade before their comrades, their uniforms were torn from their backs, and they were thrown into prison. Such savage treatment was too much for their compatriots to bear and on the following day Sunday 10th May 1857, when their officers and their families were celebrating Evensong in the Garrison Church, the Sepoys declared a "Holy War against the Kaffirs". Mounting their horses they galloped to the gaol, broke open the gates and set their comrades free. Others entered the church and falling on the British, killed the officers, their wives and children in a terrible blood bath.

From Meerut the mutineers rushed to Delhi where they slaughtered every European in sight. There in the historic capital of the Mughal Empire, they sought the Leadership of the aged *Bahadur** Shah Zafar, the last of the Mughals. The British had made him their puppet and had given him the honorary title of "King of Delhi" together with a pension, but despite this the mutineers persuaded him to sign a proclamation issued in his name, calling all Indians to unite against British rule. This it was hoped would become a manifesto for Indian independence.

At Kanpur, later known as Cawnpore, the mutineers laid siege to the British now huddled inside the barracks. Initially about a thousand men, women and children were incarcerated there, but after a siege lasting many weeks only a hundred or so survived though starving with many sick or wounded. In an apparent act of mercy, the mutineers offered a truce, promising women and children safe passage to Allahabad. But as the women and children boarded the boats, Sepoys on the banks of the river, raked them with rifle fire. Somehow about a hundred and twenty survived this massacre, but before two weeks were out, all had been killed or had died of disease or starvation.

The mutiny spread to Lucknow too, where the British community and those Indian troops that remained loyal, took refuge in the thirty-three acres of the *Residency**. Hastily turned into a fortress with trenches, ramparts and booby traps, the Residency suffered constant attack by cannon and rifle fire, its walls often breached by Indian Sappers. Though many perished the British held out doggedly for nearly three months until at last a relief force managed to break through to evacuate the women and children leaving the men behind to hold on as best, they could. Six months later Lucknow was finally relieved, but by then less than half of those originally besieged remained alive.

Reading about these savage events a mere eighty years ago, Trudi could well understand why the Hampshires had brought their rifles into church and why Lady Cynthia was so concerned about their replacement by Indian troops. Yet she herself had never felt frightened in the presence of Indian people, indeed she felt affection for many of them, especially the servants. But while understanding how difficult it was for the British to forgive the savagery at Kanpur and Lucknow, she discovered to her horror that the British had been as barbaric in their retribution as the Sepoys had been in their rebellion. At Kanpur before being executed, captured mutineers had been made to lick blood from the stained garments of their British victims and pork or beef had been stuffed down their throats! Everywhere mutineers were left hanging on gibbets, while at Lucknow Sepoys were bayoneted on sight, some even being shot from field guns!

How the country had survived such brutal savagery she couldn't understand. Maybe its very vastness had helped, for the distant states may have largely been unaware of the mutiny. But in the Central Provinces where the mutiny had taken place, how could the carnage ever be forgotten? Yet somehow it seemed it had and once more the British and Indians appeared to live together in peace and only forty years after the Mutiny, Sepoys had marched with pride through London at the Jubilee of their Queen Empress while in the Great War, * many had fought in the trenches and had died for the King Emperor!

Chapter 9
· · · · · · · · · · · · · · · · ·

S he had taken to her bed two days ago. Delhi belly had struck, though
not Lady Cynthia or her father. Their constitution had become inured to
such minor infections, but she had suffered terribly, feeling weak and scarcely
eating anything. But today she'd managed to keep a dry biscuit and her
morning tea down and now with a shawl about her shoulders she sat on the
veranda reflecting on her first six months in Allahabad. The constant round
of lunches and dinner parties had kept her busy enough, though she never
enjoyed them, but now at last, Lady Cynthia seemed satisfied that she was
conforming properly to the prescribed etiquette and even her post-mortems
after bridge were becoming less critical. But neither liked each other. Nor did
she have a close relationship with her father. Her closest friend was Rebecca,
though they only had their love of riding and tennis in common, but she
had introduced her to the few other girls of their age and had taught her
the mysteries of croquet. And now that all the young men had gone off to
war, they had to make do with the middle-aged bachelors like Major White
for male company. She chuckled; the others were jealous of her, for Philip
Brodie always sought her as a partner for the reels, the waltzes and for the
slow foxtrots that Lady Cynthia so despised! But for all that life without
Richard was empty.

She reached for her diary; she hadn't written anything for several days,
not that there had been anything of interest to record! But browsing through
the pages she remembered that Guy Fawkes Day had gone unnoticed.

"We don't celebrate that here," Lady Cynthia had said with distaste in her voice. "It's too parochial!"

Armistice Day however had been another matter. Everyone had been in their appointed places to watch the Lieutenant Governor lay his wreath on the War Memorial and take the salute as the local Garrison marched by. The Hampshires had been gone for several months and had been replaced by the 6th Rajputana Rifles. The Rajrifs as they were known considered themselves special. They could trace their origin back to the Bombay Sepoys, the first Indian Infantry Unit to be raised by the East India Company. Father told her in a whisper, that they had an honourable history having fought for the King Emperor in France and in Palestine, where they'd been part of General Allenby's force that had recaptured Jerusalem. As they marched briskly by wearing their scarlet tunics, blue shorts and white leggings and holding their turbaned heads high, Trudi could see they were proud of themselves.

With the ending of the parade the Lieutenant Governor led the assembled dignitaries into the Cathedral for the Remembrance Service. The Rajrifs being Hindus did not attend and without the Hampshires the Cathedral was empty save for the few pews filled by the lonely British. The Dean led prayers for those who had fought in the Great War, but most minds were distracted by news of the present war! Poland had capitulated and had been divided between Hitler and Stalin and now with Poland conquered, hostilities in the rest of Europe appeared to have stalled. Only at sea where the Atlantic convoys were at the mercy of the U-boat packs, was the war still being fought. And only a few days ago news had come that the *Rawalpindi* had been sunk. She had been a P & O liner and the many who had sailed in her felt her loss personally. Requisitioned by the Navy, she had been converted into an Armed Merchant Cruiser and put on patrol south of Iceland where she was found by the German battleships *Scharnhorst* and *Gneisenau* and sunk with all hands. Trudi's father had told her she was a sister ship of the *Ranpura*, the ship that had brought her out! Such news made her worry all the more about Richard and the *Strongbow*, though she comforted herself, all the action was in the Atlantic and surely here in the East he must be safe.

The happy times she and Richard had spent in the *Ranpura* were always in her thoughts and often she remembered Giles and Jane and their proposal that she should join them on tour. Recently he had written to remind her and had invited her to join him on his next. The thought of escaping the dreariness of Allahabad and seeing more of India excited her and she had accepted his invitation by return! He'd been delighted and had suggested they met at Lucknow, where they would spend a night in the Carlton Hotel. This, he had said would allow Jane to do some urgent shopping and give him an opportunity to show her the sights. When Trudi told her father he'd been pleased.

"Good. You'll see something of the real India," he'd said and had given her detailed instructions about what she should take and how she should guard against scorpions, snakes and other hazards. He'd told her about rabies too and said she must avoid the local dogs.

"If you're bitten or even licked by one of the *pi-dogs** you must assume it has rabies and get early treatment." And with his advice she had bought mosquito netting, a first aid kit including a bottle of quinine in case she contracted malaria, a pith helmet and other clothing. And when at last the day came for her to leave, her father had insisted on seeing her safely onto the train. The unexpected care, which her hitherto remote father had displayed for her, had been a surprise, so much so that for the first time, she'd felt close to him. Close enough even to ask him about her mother, but as she was about to do so, Lady Cynthia had brusquely interrupted to tell her she really must see the ruins of the Residency, where so many English had been slaughtered in the mutiny.

When the train pulled into Lucknow, the station was crowded but she had recognised Giles and Jane in the distance. When a coolie had shouldered her baggage, Giles led them to his car.

"This is Giles' pride and joy," Jane said with a laugh. Trudi saw Giles give the car a fatherly pat.

"One day we'll be doing our tour in one of these, but not yet. The roads well, they're tracks really, are too rough, so we'll still be riding for a long time yet."

"Good," Trudi declared. "I'd rather be on a pony anyway. I want to see the real India. I want to feel the fresh air, hear the noises, smell the smells," she laughed. "I expect you think I'm rather naïve."

"No, of course not," he smiled. "I've found a mare for you. She's strong and reliable with a good placid nature. Her name is Marigold. I'm sure she'll do you well."

That was the start of a happy and nostalgic evening as they reminisced about their time in the *Ranpura* and made plans for their visit to Lucknow.

The next morning with Giles she'd visited the Residency.

"The English," he said as he parked the car. "Consider the Residency to be the most historic building in Lucknow and there it is, at least what's left of it!" He pointed to the ruins of a red sandstone building with a half-demolished tower. Now only a shell, it had once been large and imposing, set in a great park encircled by high walls. Gazing at the walls still showing damage by cannon fire, Trudi found it hard to visualise this as the battlefield it had once been, where English and Indians alike had suffered such cruel and barbaric deaths. Now with its well manicured lawns it was a scene of peace and tranquillity! Giles pointed to the ruined tower and its mast, from which the Union Jack proudly flew. He told her it had flown there throughout the siege.

"And it has ever since. It's been there day and night, a new one is always hoisted before the old one is hauled down."

Inside the walls they came across a grave. It was that of Sir Henry Lawrence. "He was the Resident, and it was he," Giles explained, "who organised the defence of the Residency." They read his epitaph: "Here lies Henry Lawrence, who tried to do his duty."

Trudi looked shocked, "That hardly does him justice". Giles agreed, "He was one of the first to die."

"Where are the other graves?" she asked.

"Here somewhere, but only Sir Henry's seems to have been marked. But there are many memorial tablets in the church."

"I'd like to see those," she replied.

They drove to St Peter's church, where for some reason the tablets there distressed her more than those in Allahabad. Perhaps visiting the scene of the siege had brought the suffering into greater focus. Troubled by the savagery of both Indians and English, Trudi returned to the hotel in sombre mood, but her spirits were restored when asking Jane what she had been doing, she saw her face erupting into smiles as she confessed she'd been shopping for her new baby.

"I'm expecting," she announced proudly.

"She's pregnant," Trudi muttered to herself as she climbed into bed that night. "How wonderful it must be to conceive!" She imagined Richard's child growing within her, a lovely son, a spitting image of his father! Then thoughts of her mother bearing a rapist's child assailed her. How had she felt, when she knew she was pregnant? Pregnant with an unwanted child! Had she hated that child? Had she hated her? Again, she felt the shock of hearing Lady Cynthia say, "Gertrude's a bastard" and with it that feeling of being worthless. But she assured herself her mother would have loved her and in a moment of fancy saw herself as a child, rushing into the open arms of her adoring mother. At last, they were reunited! But then reality returned. That would never happen! Somehow, she knew her mother had died giving her life.

The next morning, they set off for Hardoi. The weather was kind and at first the road good, but it soon became rutted making driving difficult. Thankfully nearing Hardoi, the road improved and soon they turned into a drive leading to the house, a square low building painted white, which stood in the shade of a huge Catalpa tree. They were welcomed by the bearer and as he organised the servants to take their baggage, Jane beckoned a young native girl. "Trudi, this is Priya, your ayah." and leading her to her room, continued, "Priya will help you unpack, then you must rest before joining us for dinner at seven." The unpacking thankfully did not take long and when Priya had gone Trudi began a long overdue letter to Richard.

District House
Hardoi,
Central Provinces,
India

Sunday 23rd April 1940

Dearest Richard,

Thank you for your last letter. It means so much to me to hear that you are safe and well and though you may be wishing to see some action I pray continually that you and all the crew of the Strongbow may have a thoroughly boring and peaceful time! Am I wicked to want you to be safe?

The war does worry me so. No one I have spoken to can believe that the Danes have given in to Hitler with barely a struggle! And now I hear the Germans are fighting in Norway and everyone is worried about France, though thankfully at the moment the Germans seem unwilling to fight the French perhaps because of their Maginot Line! What will happen if the Germans conquer Norway? We all feel so helpless out here watching the war in Europe unfold. How will it all end?

She put her pen down. She must stop burdening him with her fears. Richard must be worried too! She must be more cheerful.

As you can see, she continued, I am now with Giles and Jane Gallagher at their bungalow in Hardoi and tomorrow we must pack as we set off to tour his district on Tuesday. I'm really looking forward to it, though I hardly know what to expect. I just hope I won't meet any snakes or scorpions! Father says first thing in the morning I must always check my shoes before I put them on. He says scorpions like curling up in them for a quiet snooze!

As she wrote about her coming adventure her pen moved easily over the paper describing her preparations and the advice her father had given her. Then she added:

I treasure the photograph you sent me. It's a very good likeness dearest. Your laughing eyes give me great pleasure and make me feel you are near.

Then closing with her love, she folded the letter, kissed it gently and put it in its envelope.

"Please God," she muttered. "Stop the fighting and let there be peace".

Chapter 10

Tuesday 29ᵗʰ November, she wrote in her diary.

We arrived in Bawan, the first village of the tour, a little after four o'clock and how thankful I was! Marigold my pony has been very good, but we had been riding for nearly seven hours with only a few short breaks to ease our aching limbs. Giles assures me that after a few days we'll be accustomed to long hours in the saddle. I do hope he's right!

Monday had been a day of great activity and early the next morning the advance party, as Giles called them, had left. Tents, chairs, tables, *charpoys**, their personal baggage, his desk and papers had all been loaded onto bullock carts, together with food for them and the animals. The bullock carts were to go ahead of them and set up camp outside the first village, ready for Giles, when he arrived. He laughed when Trudi had expressed her admiration for such good planning.

"It's not original thinking, I assure you," he said, "District Officers have been doing this since time immemorial."

Later Trudi had been introduced to Marigold, a handsome bay with expressive eyes and a quiet temperament. She was a little bigger than Dusty her own pony, but when Marigold allowed her to mount without fuss Trudi knew they would make a good pair.

The following morning they'd set off for Bawan, accompanied by the Syce and two Indian Policemen, one a *Halvidar**. As they broke into a canter to waken the horses, Trudi thought how important they must look, with their Police escort and their well-groomed horses and so it seemed, for as they passed, people turned to offer their *salaams**. The Eastern sky was still pink when they entered the town already full with people come to shop from stalls laden with fruit and vegetables, carcasses of lamb, silver fish, spices, bolts of cloth and silk for saris. And here and there in dimly lit workshops Trudi could see craftsmen sitting cross legged beating brass into trays, working wood, turning clay into pots or sitting hunched over sewing machines, and everywhere the Holy Brahmin Cows wondered unmolested.

So began a long, weary ride in the hot sun. After three hours they had stopped in the shade of a clump of trees to relax and water the horses. The rest was welcomed, but Trudi found it made it all the more difficult to get started again! Both she and Jane, stiff and saddle sore, were greatly relieved when at last they heard Giles say

"Not far now. I can see the tents."

Soon their eager eyes had found them too, two triangular shapes nestling among the trees which slowly grew as they plodded on, into the tents they expected. When at last they'd arrived, Trudi was amazed to see how well ordered everything was; it was as if the camp had been there for a week or more! The Bearer welcomed them, and they sank gratefully into waiting chairs to drink the warm sweet tea he produced. Then Giles suggested they should rest before dinner and as if by magic, Priya had appeared to lead her to her quarters, a small area of the tent discreetly curtained off. When Priya had finished helping her unpack, she'd heard voices and peeping through the curtain had seen Giles talking to an Indian. Wearing a loose red turban and a baggy yellow shirt over a long white *longhi**, she could tell he was a man of some importance, for Giles and he were in deep discussion. Later Jane told her he, the *Pradham**, the Head of the Village had come to welcome Giles and burden him with his problems!

Her bed with its mosquito net neatly rigged appealed, but she couldn't rest, her diary called.

I've been getting very excited about seeing the "Real India" and once the last few buildings of Hardoi had receded I became only too aware how vast it really is! The land is flat, the plain seems endless, and one can see for miles. Occasionally we came across a few tumbledown huts, and sometimes in the distance we saw the smoke of a train. We rode through two tiny villages, mere collections of thatched huts with dogs barking and a few scrawny chickens scattering before our horses. We saw no adults other than a few women teaching children in the shade of the trees,; the others we presumed were working in the fields. The vultures we spied make a wonderful sight as they circle effortlessly on their great wings, but when they spot a dead animal, they become ruthless scavengers. We stopped for a while to watch them fighting over the carcass of a deer and delving into its body to emerge with its entrails, their heads and necks covered in blood. When they are gliding high in the sky they are things of beauty, but near a carcass vultures become the most disgusting scavengers!

Our camp is quite magnificent; I'm quite sure I shall be happy here. Our tent, the larger of the two, is really big, not much smaller than Father's stables at home! And inside it's pleasantly cool with carpets laid over straw on the ground. Giles and Jane have their own sleeping quarters and I have mine, which is well furnished with bed, table and chair and a canvas wardrobe for my clothes. Opposite my little room is the dining area with a dining table and chairs, so I haven't far to go for dinner! Giles has his office at the far end, complete with a knee-hole desk and has a clerk to look after all his files.

She put her pen down, she really must rest! Woken from her slumbers by Priya bringing hot water, she washed and dressed and went to join her hosts. Jane was wearing a beautiful silk gown, with a pronounced flair that served to hide her fast-swelling form, while Giles wore a dinner jacket. Over a simple meal of roast lamb and crisp vegetables, Giles told them he would be busy tomorrow but insisted they should have a quiet day in camp after their long ride and after they had drunk the King Emperor's health they retired to their beds.

This was to be their daily routine, with Giles leaving early to attend to the problems of the villagers and she and Jane relaxing in camp. Jane however was always busy with her sewing and embroidery and often spoke about her unborn baby. Finding a good Ayah for him would be her first priority, she told Trudi, while Giles was concerned with his education.

"We'd like to send him to Harrow, where Giles was educated," she said, "But we'll have to find him a good prep school first." Then she laughed,

"But that's a long time ahead, thank heaven. I shall hate it when we have to send him back to England!" The difficulty of finding a governess for his early years (Trudi was always amused by her certainty that her unborn child would be a boy) worried her.

"He won't need one for three years or so, but if this war continues, it's going to be hard to find a good English governess." Then she'd laughed. "If you can't get a ship home Trudi, we might ask you, you'd make an excellent one!"

Trudi had laughed at her amusing suggestion. She had no desire to be committed to a job. She hoped to see more of India, its native people, its princely palaces, the new Capital buildings at Delhi, the hill stations and she was fascinated by its animals and birds. She'd been captivated by the kites she'd seen soaring overhead on graceful wings, their forked tails constantly moving to direct their flight. The pair of collared doves that strutted around their camp, the tame hoopoe, which always raised its crest when it landed as if giving thanks for a safe arrival, and the busy myna birds were no strangers to her. Unlike the one Jane called a red-whiskered bulbul. It made a striking sight, with its black cap, prominent crest and bright red plumage. Yet another unfamiliar bird had caught her eye. It had a rapid darting flight and hid among the foliage. When its green wings and scarlet breast caught the sun, it sparkled like some jewel! Trudi wondered whether it was some sort of sunbird, but Jane, having found her bird book declared it to be a rubycheek. Trudi, intrigued by its name, studied it carefully whenever she could and finally exclaimed, "Yes, it really does have ruby cheeks. It's well named!"

She also loved watching the water buffalos, which, after the day's work, wallowed so contentedly in the ponds, but it was the *Sadhu** sitting cross legged under a great peepul tree, with his beard and long flowing hair, his face daubed red that had made her feel she was beginning to see the real India.

Each evening after dinner Giles would tell them about his day's work, often how he'd had to deal with disputes about land, having to measure plots and usually finding for the aggrieved tenants. He told them about the local money lender, who'd been charging interest rates, higher than that allowed by law. But in another village, he'd refused to be involved in a dispute, when the *Harijans**, the untouchables, had threatened to strike for better pay. "I told the Pradhan it wasn't for m and that he should get the *Brahmin** to adjudicate; he with the *janeo** was the best one to sort out that quarrel!" But both had been shocked when he'd told them about the cremation of a Brahmin on the riverbank. In former times at a cremation, it had been the custom for the widow to commit suttee. Suttee, he'd reminded them required the widow to throw herself onto her husband's burning pyre, so she could join him in the next world. This wicked act had been outlawed as long ago as 1829, but it was still thought to take place. She remembered Jane asking in an agonised voice, "But the Brahmin's wife didn't commit suttee, did she?"

"No," Giles had suddenly looked serious. "In the event she didn't, but her daughter claims the dead man's brother tried to force her into the flames. I've therefore had to remand him in custody to stand trial before a judge in Lucknow."

It had indeed been a curious, enthralling tour. As she later wrote in her diary:

On the tour with Giles and Jane, I have seen a different India, an immense, immutable country, a country baked by an unforgiving sun, yet caressed at night by a tender and merciful moon. A land inhabited by gentle hardworking people who certainly in the Hardoi District, seem to hold Giles, their District Officer in great respect as he settles their problems with an almost fatherly love. In his district at least, they seem content with their lot, for at the surgeries when I was helping Jane, I never heard them moaning or complaining and was struck by the fortitude with which they bore their infirmities and ailments. Unlike their urban brothers and sisters, they seem happy to live under the protection of the Raj. But I do worry about and sympathise with the poor Harijans, the untouchables, they are so victimised by the caste system. Sadly, we appear unable to do anything about that. It seems to be an integral part of Hinduism, which apart from the caste system, Hindhu seems to be a gentle and liberal religion.

Chapter 11

"Dearly beloved, forasmuch as all men are conceived and born in sin ...." The voice of the Priest faded as her mind wandered. It had been seven months since she'd said goodbye to Giles and Jane after that wonderful tour. On her return, Allahabad had seemed crowded and noisy and again the etiquette, that so dominated their lives, had irritated her. But she'd been delighted to find those letters from Richard. How she'd devoured them! But now that they were being censored, there was little real news, but he'd told her what she longed to hear, that he loved her, that he missed her, that he couldn't wait to see her again, but despite her hopes there had been no mention of either his mother or father's birthday.

Her life had relapsed once more into a routine of riding, tennis and croquet by day and dinner, dancing or bridge in the evenings. It all seemed so trivial when men like Richard were fighting to defend the freedom, they'd always taken for granted. The so-called "Phoney War" on the Western Front had proved a temporary delusion; now the Nazis seemed about to overrun Belgium. France would surely be the next target, though they seemed confident their Maginot Line would hold. If it did, many believed a long stalemate would be inevitable, like that of the Great War. But if it didn't hold, would France go the same way as Poland? People had begun to ask, if that happened how could Britain continue alone? Such thoughts were too terrible to contemplate!

More Indian troops were being sent to England to join the B.E.F. and for want of something better to do to show support for the war effort, the Allahabad hospital had begun training volunteers in First Aid. She and Rebecca had attended the courses, though no one could see how or when their newly acquired skills would be put to use.

She shook herself, she must stop her mind wandering; she was here in St Peter's church at Lucknow, to be a Godmother to the son Jane had borne for Giles. She followed the other Godparents to the font to join Jane with her son dressed in his lace christening robe. Finding her place in the Prayer Book, she dutifully answered the questions asked by the Priest, then watched him take the child in his arms, sprinkle holy water on his head and proclaim, "Harold Percival, I baptize thee in the Name of the Father and of the Son and of the Holy Ghost. Amen."

Like her, everyone smiled as Harold Percival, untroubled by the water, burbled happily and was restored to his mother's welcoming arms. Jane looked radiant. And so, she should, thought Trudi, now she was the mother of the son she'd always wanted. Seeing her so happy made her envious. Jane's life seemed so complete, blessed by a loving husband and now a healthy son. What more could any woman want? She sighed. How she wished Richard could be with her. They had had such a short time together, only a fleeting moment it seemed. Would they ever be man and wife, like Giles and Jane? And would they, like Jane and Giles start a family? "One day, one day," she muttered; now it always seemed that way!

She followed the others into the vestry and watching the Priest sign the register, wondered if her name was buried in some earlier one. When Jane had asked her to be a godmother, she had readily agreed. Not only had she been thrilled but also delighted as it gave her the excuse, she wanted to visit Lucknow again. On her last visit either James or Jean had always been with her, and it had been impossible to visit the church to search the Register of Baptisms. But now on her own, nothing could stop her and as the guests departed, she'd lingered behind and catching the Priest's eye, had asked whether she could see him privately the next day .He'd seemed rather surprised but had agreed and when she'd met him as arranged, she had repeated her story about finding the names of her godparents. He'd accepted her explanation without a quibble and asked when she was baptised. Trying hard to conceal her excitement, she'd told him as she was born in August 1921 so it could have been at the end of August or possibly in September that year.

He found the register. "Your surname is Leafe?"

She nodded. "Yes, my full name is Gertrude Henrietta Leafe".

He leafed through the pages. "Ah! Here we are. Gertrude Henrietta Leafe, entry number 43, Date of Birth 24th August 1921, that's the right date?" She'd nodded eagerly. "Well Miss Leafe, you were baptised on 5th September 1921. Father's name Henry Alexander Leafe; Mother's name Ruby Eliza Hughes, Oh!" He paused. "Your parents were not married?"

"No, I fear not," Trudi replied as she savoured the name Ruby.

The Priest continued "Address 3, Henry Kavanagh Road, Lucknow, Father's Occupation Judge, Oh!" He exclaimed, "One of the Heaven Born!" Again, she nodded. He started again, "Mother's Occupation, Governess, Godparents, Leslie Roberts, Alice Roberts and Jennifer Dobson." He looked at Trudi. "Well, there you are. Would you like some paper to record the details?"

"Please," Trudi struggled to suppress her tears. At last, she'd found her mother. Her mother Ruby Eliza Hughes; as she repeated the name, she remembered that enchanting little bird she'd seen at Bawan, with its dazzling green wings and bright red breast. Its name was Rubycheek. She wiped a tear from her eye. Was her mother Ruby as enchanting? Lost in thoughts, she stopped copying the details. Was she the result, she asked herself, of a secret passionate love affair or, she shuddered, of a brutal rape?

"Are you feeling unwell, Miss Leafe?" The voice of the Priest broke into her thoughts.

"I'm, I'm fine, fine, thank you. Finding my past has been rather moving."

He smiled encouragingly and thanking him for his kindness she hastily completed her notes. Then finding a pew on which to sit and contemplate, she repeated her mother's name, Ruby Eliza Hughes. Could she still be alive? If she was she'd be in her forties, still an active woman. Or like poor Fanny Alberta Durcott, had she also died in childbirth? She slipped onto her knees. "Dear Heavenly Father, thank you for helping me to find my mother Ruby and thank you for giving me this precious gift of life through her. And, Father, please let it be that my mother Ruby is alive and well and that someday we will be re-united. That, dear Father would make me so happy. Amen, Amen, Amen."

Of a sudden she felt close to her mother and in the stillness of the church sat enjoying her proximity. She was sure she was intelligent and clever, but was she happy? Was she slim and pretty? Were they lovers? The questions seemed endless. She rose; now she must do what she'd been dreading. Walking through the gravestones she searched diligently for her mother's name, Ruby Eliza Hughes. It was slow work, but after an hour or so only one long row remained. By now she dared hope she would find no headstone bearing her mother's name; that her mother might still be alive. But then her growing hopes were mercilessly dashed. She stooped to read the epitaph:

"Sacred to the memory of Ruby Eliza Hughes
Born 18th May 1895
Died in childbirth 24th August 1921
May she Rest in Peace and Rise in Glory"

The finality of the words hit her. She sank onto a nearby bench, feelings of guilt overcoming her. Had she in the moment of birth robbed her mother of life? Was her life worth so much that her mother had to die for her? She stood by the headstone and read the epitaph once again. "Forgive me, Mother. Please, God let her be at rest with you in your heavenly kingdom." She stood in silence for a moment then wiping her tears away, she left. "Ruby Eliza Hughes," she repeated the name as she walked. Was she Welsh? Hughes, was surely a Welsh name. She would ask her father, he must know. And where did her mother's parents live? Finding her had raised so many questions. She made a list of them in the hotel that evening and in the train to Allahabad studied them, adding more and deleting some. How would her father react, she wondered, when he found she knew his guilty secret? Surely he couldn't deny it. If he did, she'd show him the copy she'd made of the baptism record!

Her eagerness to confront him increased as Allahabad grew nearer, but when the Tonga clip-clopped up the drive and stopped by the main door, she knew she'd have to be patient. She must find the right time to approach him!

"Welcome home, Memsahib Gertrude." The Khitmagar organised a servant to take her bags. "Lady Cynthia is in the garden having tea. She asks that you join her."

With a heavy heart she found her. "Hello, Mamma, I'm back." She gave what she hoped, was a friendly smile. Lady Cynthia seemed not to notice her; she was reading the Times of India.

"I've just arrived from Lucknow," Trudi repeated.

Lady Cynthia looked up from her paper. "Well, sit down, girl. Have you heard the news? It's most dreadful. Our Army's been cut off. Here read it for yourself."

NAVY SENT TO EVACUATE BEF

Dover 27th May 1940

From his headquarters in Dover Vice Admiral Bertram Ramsey is organising the emergency evacuation of British and French troops from the beaches of Dunkirk some 70 miles away. Allied forces are holding a 30 mile stretch of coastline centred on Dunkirk and running from Gravelines in the west to Nieuport in the east. Inland the front reaches almost to Lille, where six French divisions are surrounded by seven German. At Dover, Admiral Ramsay has put together a vast fleet of small ships including pleasure steamers, fishing boats, tugs and private yachts to help the navy extract our men from Dunkirk where they are gathering as others fight a rearguard action to delay the German advance. Admiral Ramsay believes he has two days before the Germans overrun the beachhead and reckons he might succeed in rescuing forty five thousand men.

She could scarcely believe what she read; the French and British armies were surrounded!

"There's talk of France suing for peace!" Lady Cynthia interrupted her.

"But I thought they were safe behind their Maginot Line!"

"So did they," Lady Cynthia scoffed. "They didn't reckon on the Germans cutting through Belgium did they?"

Over the next few days no one could talk about anything but the withdrawal of the Army from Dunkirk. Listening eagerly to the wireless they heard that despite the heavy loss of shipping and constant air attack the number of soldiers rescued from the beaches rose steadily day by day Later they were to learn that after seven days when the evacuation was ended, nearly three hundred and forty thousand men had been rescued, in what the Prime Minister called "a miracle of deliverance". While Sir Henry and Lady Cynthia waited anxiously to hear news of their son Stewart, the papers reported German tanks racing towards Paris and it seemed merely a matter of time before France capitulated. When it did, Neville Chamberlain was forced to resign as Prime Minister and Winston Churchill was elected in his place. With the nation facing the imminent threat of invasion, he addressed the nation. "We shall go on to the end. We shall fight on the beaches, we shall fight on the landing grounds, we shall fight in the fields and in the streets, we shall fight in the hills; we shall never surrender. And even if – which I do not for a moment believe – this land or a large part of it were subjugated and starving, then our Empire beyond the seas, armed and guarded by the British Fleet, would carry on the struggle until in God's good time the New World, with all its power and might, steps forth to the rescue and the liberation of the Old."

While Churchill's speech inspired all who heard it, the picture he painted of "our Empire beyond the seas carrying on the struggle" alarmed the English in far-away India. Alone now, with her troops in disarray, their heavy weapons left behind in France, how could England resist Hitler's all-powerful army? A successful German invasion of England now seemed much more than a mere possibility! Yet here in India, what could they do? Everyone felt powerless to help. All they could do was to pray and worry.

Though eventually Sir Henry and Lady Cynthia learnt their son Stewart was safe, they still worried about Alberta in London and about Sir Henry's parents in Instow. So reluctantly Trudi knew it was not the time to approach her father about Ruby. Nor could she over the next few months, when the German Luftwaffe launched its bombing raids on England in preparation for the invasion. The "Battle of Britain" and the daily tally of German and

British aircraft shot down engrossed everyone, especially when German losses regularly began to exceed the British. And when on the 15ᵗʰ September sixty-one German aircraft were destroyed for the loss of only twenty-nine British, the turning point of the battle had come and Hitler, denied the air superiority he needed, gave orders to postpone the invasion. But then he vented his anger by bombing London and other major cities, believing that by demoralising the civilian population he would force Britain to sue for peace. But British morale did not crack and despite the huge number of casualties, the country withstood the "Blitz" and fought on alone. Now with invasion unlikely, at least until the spring, tensions eased and at last Trudi felt the day had come to ask her father about Ruby. But at breakfast that day, while she was inwardly rehearsing the questions she would ask, Lady Cynthia looked up from the letter she was reading.

"Gertrude," she said. "Cousin Catherine tells me she's looking for a governess for her four year old. She says with the war, it's so difficult to find one. She wonders whether you would be interested. It seems a splendid opportunity for you to do something useful, now you're stuck out here until the war's over. What do you think?"

"She's looking for a governess?" Trudi tried desperately to remember who Cousin Catherine was. "Tell me where does she live?"

For once Lady Cynthia seemed to understand her ignorance. "Well, Gertrude, she's my second cousin once removed, so we're not very close and I wouldn't expect you to know much about her. She's married to Hamish, a tea planter in Ceylon, and four year old Jamie is their only son. She's now in her late thirties, so Jamie may be their only child."

As Trudi mulled over the proposal, she remembered how Jane had joked about one day asking her to be a governess for Harold Percival and how she was sure she'd make an excellent one! The more she thought about it, the more attractive it became. It would allow her to escape from Lady Cynthia and the petty restrictions of life in Allahabad and give her something useful to do. And, she thought happily, if she received a letter from Richard with one of those important dates, Trincomalee and Colombo would be so much closer. It seemed a heaven-sent opportunity. "Yes," she replied. "It sounds an excellent idea. Please tell her I'm willing."

The thought of leaving Allahabad became a further incentive to tackle her father and that evening when she found him alone on the veranda she approached him.

"Father," she said. "It's a lovely evening." He turned to look at her. "Yes, Gertrude. We've a harvest moon tonight." For a while neither spoke as they admired the garden bathed in the soft moonlight. Then Sir Henry broke the silence. "Lady Cynthia tells me you're off to Ceylon to work for Cousin Catherine."

"Yes Father, it's time I did something useful!"

"Well, we'll miss you, but you're right. We can't have you wasting your talents here."

"Can I get you another chota peg, Father?"

"Oh! That's kind of you. Why don't you pour one for yourself?" She saw an unexpected twinkle in his eye. "You might like it, you know!"

She smiled. "Perhaps I will." Pleased to find him in such a good mood, she filled the glasses and sat beside him.

"Let's drink to your future in Ceylon." Gently they touched glasses and sipped the whisky. The first sip took her breath away, but she found its flavour pleasing and it gave her courage.

"Father I've known for a very long time that Lady Cynthia is not my mother." He showed no reaction; he made no reply.

"When I was in Lucknow," she continued. "I found my mother's grave. It's in St Peter's churchyard and reads 'Sacred to the memory of Ruby Eliza Hughes died in childbirth 24th August 1921.' Father, please tell me about my mother."

He sipped his whisky, then he took a deep breath. "Your mother," he paused as if lost for words. "Your mother was the most enchanting, captivating ...."

Dinner is served, Sahib." The Khitmagar burst into their conversation.

Chapter 12

. . . .

When the Khitmagar had interrupted them, Sir Henry had seen a
flash of anger cross Gertrude's face, but he'd been thankful; it had
given him time to consider how and what he would tell her. Memories of
Ruby had haunted him ever since her death, though as the years went by
they'd begun to fade. But now Gertrude's questions had brought them into
sharp focus! How was he to answer her? Over dinner he could think of
nothing else. Twice he'd earned Cynthia's displeasure for not responding to
her endless chatter! How had Gertrude found her mother's name? And her
grave? Surely Cynthia would never have told her! Or could she have done
so out of spite? It wouldn't be beyond her! She could be vindictive, he knew
well. He often wondered why he ever married her! She'd been beautiful in
her day and she was a handsome woman now, but she'd always been self-
seeking, ambitious, aware of and keen to improve her status. Inwardly he
grinned; as a *box-wallah's** daughter she'd done well enough, marrying into
the I.C.S.! She was cold too, always had been! How he wondered, had they
managed to produce two children? They'd shared a bed only for the first few
years of marriage, then she'd wanted single beds and now they had separate
rooms! Oh! It had long been a dreary, loveless marriage!

Then Ruby had arrived! How young, how beautiful, how enchanting she
was! He'd been unable to keep his eyes off her, loving it when he saw her face
light up as she smiled and watching her supple body move so gracefully as
she played with Stewart. Just the sight of her had given him a long-forgotten

desire! Involuntarily he shook his head; he must stop dreaming! What was he going to say to Gertrude? Over coffee he'd asked her to join him in the library for a game of chess. She'd agreed and as he'd hoped Cynthia had left, going with the air of a neglected wife.

Trudi watched him set out the chessmen. He seemed hesitant, confused. "The Queen should be on the King's left," she reminded him. No doubt like her, he was thinking of Ruby. She left him to his thoughts, she wouldn't hustle him; he was clearly moved. He would tell her tonight!

"It's your move," he said. She moved a pawn. He offered her a cigarette, politely she declined. He lit his and inhaled deeply. Gertrude's voice broke into his thoughts. "Please tell me about my mother."

"Your mother?" He saw her nod. "Your mother Ruby came to us as governess to Stewart. Stewart loved her and so did everyone, except Lady Cynthia. She said she was weak with Stewart, that she indulged him, that she neglected to teach him how to behave and she hated her Welsh accent!"

"So my mother was Welsh?"

"Yes. Her parents lived in Brecon, her father was a teacher." Her interruption had upset his spiel. He tried to re-marshal his thoughts, but the memory of Ruby's smiling face distracted him. "She was enchanting," he heard himself saying. He moved a pawn. "It was her father," he continued hurriedly, "He suggested she became a governess."

"Did you love her?"

Her direct question startled him. "Did I love her?" For a moment he seemed lost, as if in a dream. "Did I love her? Yes, everyone loved her, and I did too! How could one not love her? Only Cynthia seemed to be immune!"

He tapped the ash from his cigarette. "When first she came, I just couldn't help watching her. Just to look at her gave me pleasure seeing her, made me happy! Perhaps at times I did ogle her, but it was no more than that! But then as she became the object of Cynthia's endless criticism, I began to feel for her and admire the way she responded. She never stood up to Cynthia or argued with her, as I would have done. She must have been upset, but she never showed it! She had such a happy, buoyant nature; she never seemed down at heart."

He lit another cigarette, he knew he was lying! He had seen her distressed, tearful and frightened. On that evening, that never-to-be-forgotten evening when she'd told him she was pregnant! He heard Gertrude's voice.

"So Father, you only admired her?"

"Yes, at first, it was only admiration." She saw his eyes soften. "Then," he inhaled deeply. "Then occasionally, I found I could say something to make her laugh and those soft red lips of hers would open and her blue eyes sparkle. Then my spirits would lift." He shook his head. "It was a heady experience, one I wanted again and again!"

Suddenly she saw her father as a tender lover, a man captivated by his beloved.

"You loved her, didn't you?" He nodded thoughtfully but said nothing.

"Did she return your love?"

"No. I don't think she ever knew how much I cared for her."

"That must have made you sad."

"Yes." He said pensively. "But it was just as well. I had Cynthia and the children to think about. So," he made a face, "I lived in a make-belief world, a world where we were lovers."

"But Father dear," she hesitated; she'd never called him dear before! His tale of love had saddened her. "Father dear, were you never lovers?" Again, she hesitated. "What about me?"

He sighed. "It was Ruby's birthday, her twenty-fifth. Cynthia had been upset by the attention we'd paid her and had gone to bed in a sulk. Ruby followed shortly afterwards, and I was left alone. Suddenly I had an idea. It excited me, I just couldn't ignore it! I would take a bottle of champagne to he, and we would drink to her birthday. With a pounding heart I knocked on her door. She opened it, her blonde hair unpinned and cascading over her shoulders. It made her look so young, so innocent, so beautiful!" He hesitated; his eyes had a far-away look as if he could see her! Then with a sigh he continued, "She smiled and asked me what I wanted. I raised the bottle and muttered something about celebrating her birthday. She laughed and said she wasn't dressed to celebrate, but when I suggested we could drink to her happiness on the veranda, she giggled and said, 'Why not?' She laughed when the cork popped and I saw her red lips open and those blue eyes of hers sparkle and," he shook his head helplessly, "I was bewitched."

He paused as if re-living the moment, then he grinned, "But you know, the noise of the cork worried me. I was frightened Cynthia would hear, but then," he chuckled, "I persuaded myself her room was too far away. So, I relaxed and filled the glasses. I remember I said rather foolishly, 'Ladies and gentlemen, please be upstanding and drink to our Lady from Wales.' It made her laugh again and my spirits rose. Then we drank to her future happiness and as she laughed, I was ecstatic!" He paused. He heard Gertrude urging him to continue.

"I remember I toasted many stupid things, just to make her laugh!" He paused he could see her again!

"Gertrude," he spoke softly now, "I was mesmerised by her; my make-belief world was suddenly real. I remember we were standing looking out into the soft moonlight. We were so close her presence was overwhelming! I slid my arm around her waist. She turned towards me, and we kissed." He stopped. He couldn't tell her what really had happened, how she'd pushed him away and with a smile had suggested he should go. But he didn't go, did he? The bottle wasn't empty, so he proposed they should drink one last toast a toast to her friend Rufus the dog. That made her laugh again, made her giggle! The drink was beginning to affect her and as he filled the glasses, she walked unsteadily towards the bed and sat clumsily on the edge. Then they were lying together! He always told himself it had been an accident, that fearing she might slip onto the floor, he'd gone to help her, that somehow, he'd fallen onto her. He shut his eyes and stroked his forehead.

"Father are you alright?" He saw her looking at him, waiting for him to continue.

"I'm sorry, Gertrude. I'm finding this a little painful."

She smiled sympathetically. "Yes, Father, I can see you are, but please, please do go on."

He needed time to think. This wasn't going the way he'd hoped. He offered her a brandy, but she refused. He refilled his glass and lifting it to his nose smelt its comforting bouquet. "Well, Gertrude, I have to admit that kiss unleashed my passion and hers too, for we made love." He twirled the balloon; then sipped the warm brandy. It hadn't been like that at all! He'd forced himself on her and though she'd struggled and kept saying 'No, no,' he'd had his way. That was the truth! He'd always tried to convince himself she'd been a willing partner, but he knew she hadn't. The brutal truth was he'd raped her!

Her voice broke into his thoughts. "Did you become lovers?"

"No." The way he'd involuntarily shaken his head made her certain he'd been denied what he craved.

Did you tell Lady Cynthia she was pregnant?"

He winced. She'd make a good Prosecuting Council! Those damned questions of hers were making him feel a prisoner in the dock! He took another swig of brandy; he'd ignore her question; he'd tell the story his way!

"When it became obvious that Ruby was pregnant, Cynthia in her usual obdurate way demanded to know who the father was. When Ruby refused to say, Cynthia became ever more furious and began calling her names.

"Gertrude, I'm sure you can imagine what they might be." He saw her nod. "Did you tell Lady Cynthia you were the father?"

"Yes of course. When I saw how she was treating Ruby, of course I told her!"

"What did she say?"

"Well, she flew into a rage. She wanted to dismiss Ruby instantly and threatened to sue for divorce. But I didn't take her threat of divorce seriously.

She had far more to lose than I! I would suffer the stigma of divorce, which could harm my career as a Judge, but she? Well other than me, she had no means of support, so she'd have to go back to her box-wallah parents!" He paused; a sardonic grin creased his face. "Unless of course Major White would have her, then they could dance their eightsomes all day long!" He hesitated for a moment as if enjoying the spectacle, then he continued,

"And as for Ruby, I adamantly refused to dismiss her. I said we'd keep her till the baby was born and then two or three months later, we would send her home to Wales. Cynthia didn't like it, but she knew she'd have to accept my decision."

"My poor Mother, her last months must have been horrible."

"Yes, I'm afraid they were." He was silent for a moment, then he lit another cigarette. "As the months went by Ruby became a different person, no longer the happy, smiling girl she'd been, but silent and introverted. It became difficult to make any meaningful contact with her. Only with Stewart did she have any rapport. When we crossed paths, she hardly recognised me and made little attempt to respond to my anxious enquiries about her health. Cynthia of course was quite abominable. One day I overheard her telling her she was no better than a bit of *black velvet** from the *cages** and on another day she called her a *rum-johni**! She gave poor Ruby a horrible time."

He looked at his glass, it was empty. He felt the same way too! He poured himself another brandy. "When her time came, it was soon obvious it would be a difficult delivery. The midwife said it was a breach and we sent for the doctor. He came and was with her for an age. When he came out, he told us he'd managed to save the baby, but not Ruby." He saw tears in Gertrude's eyes. He wished he could weep too; it might help relieve his guilt.

Gertrude wiped her tears away. "What happened to me?"

He sighed deeply. "Cynthia wanted to get rid of you at any cost, but I was adamant. You were my daughter, and you would be part of my family, so you were baptised and we formally adopted you."

Chapter 13

S itting on her favourite chair under the deodar tree, Trudi took in the
beauty of the garden with its roses and hydrangeas. It was so different
from her father's in Allahabad, tortured by the sun or inundated by the
monsoon. Here in Nuwara Eliya the air was always fresh and the temperature
agreeable. It was truly a heavenly place, where one could enjoy log fires and
sleep untroubled by mosquitoes. As she revelled in her good fortune, she
thought of her father. How he'd changed since that evening they'd talked
about her mother! No longer was he the distant, taciturn father-figure; now
he seemed to notice her, to be interested in her, even affectionate. He'd said
he would miss her! But Lady Cynthia had remained as cold as ever and
it was only too clear she was pleased to see her go. The morning after her
father's confession, she'd found Lady Cynthia alone in the garden. It was
the opportunity she'd waited for so long.

"May I join you, Lady Cynthia?"

She'd glanced at her, a questioning look in her eye. "Why the formality,
Gertrude?"

"Well, Lady Cynthia, I can no longer call you Mamma. You see, though
I'm Sir Henry's daughter, we both know I am not yours."

Lady Cynthia's face had hardened.

"So, you know about his filthy affair with that wanton woman. She'd only been with us a month or two before he started ogling her! And then a few months later she was pregnant. When I tackled him, he couldn't deny it. I should have divorced him there and then. Most wives would have! But the disgrace of the whole sordid affair stopped me. I wanted to get rid of her immediately, but Henry was adamant, he said we must keep her till you were born. Then he promised to dismiss her and send her home. Well, the girl died in childbirth, so he didn't have to."

She sighed as if her anger had been vented; then she looked directly at Gertrude. "And I was left with her baby; with you!"

Despite her hostile manner, Trudi felt some sympathy for her.

"I'm sorry. I can understand how upset you must have been. I must have been a constant reminder of Father's infidelity. Please forgive me for that." She paused, "And Lady Cynthia, I must thank you for taking me into your family and treating me as your daughter."

Lady Cynthia gave her a cold smile but said nothing.

Now their sham relationship had at last been recognised, Trudi felt it was as well she was leaving. Perhaps time might help heal their antagonism, but how she wished she could have known her real mother, the young, the beautiful, the enchanting woman who'd submitted to his desires. But that champagne troubled her. He'd said the drink had affected her! Had it? If so, had she really consented? That question had begun to nag. Had he forced himself on her? She closed her eyes in horror. That would have been rape! Now as she toyed with the ring on her finger, she determined to put the thought behind her.

On the evening before she left, Father had asked her to join him in the library. Was he about to tell her more about her mother, she'd wondered? He gave her a tender look as she joined him. "Trudi, I want you to have this." He held out a ring, a golden signet ring.

"It was your mother's. I gave it to her a few months before you were born." He began to look distressed. "I hoped she'd accept it as a token of my love and," he paused, "my great concern."

"That was kind of you, Father, what did my mother say?"

"She thanked me but said no more!" He closed his eyes, as if to blot out a painful memory.

"I like to think she was touched!" He sighed. "Since her birthday she'd hardly spoken a word to me and I wanted her to know how I felt for her, that," he was silent for a moment, "that I loved her."

She saw tears in his eyes. He turned away clearly upset. Then he gave half a smile, "Look," his voice was brighter now, "these are her initials. I had them engraved on the ring, can you see?"

She had seen them; R. E. H. inscribed in copper plate – Ruby Eliza Hughes!

"I want you to have it; I know she'd like that."

She slipped the ring on her finger; it fitted perfectly! She'd held out her hand to admire it and told him it was beautiful. Then she too had been unable to hold back the tears. Her mother had worn it! Her mother's finger had felt its encircling message of love. Her mother was near that message of love now a message to her long lost daughter!

As she sat in the garden of Oliphant House, she fingered it. It was the first tangible link she'd ever had with her mother. It gave her a feeling of belonging, a feeling she'd never had before, a feeling that she had a mother who really loved her!

"Miss Gertrude." Her thoughts were rudely interrupted by Jamie standing in front of her. "Let's play Snakes and Ladders."

She smiled. "Of course, Jamie what a good idea!"

It was a game she'd taught him only a week or so ago and now he always seemed to win!

"I suppose you'll beat me again!"

"Yes," he laughed as he shook the dice. "Double six," he cried triumphantly. He shook again. "Four and three, only seven!" He climbed the first ladder and reached the second without mishap.

"It's your turn now," he gave her the dice. She put the cup to her lips, muttered a secret spell, gave it a shake and emptied the dice onto the board. As usual her secret spell had failed!

"Three and five, that's only eight!" Jamie looked at her. "Bad luck!"

While she struggled up the first ladder only to slide down the nearest snake, he climbed unhindered almost to the last ladder; then he met a snake! Now it seemed possible she might beat him. She wondered whether he'd be upset. But no! "It's time you had some luck," he laughed.

He's such a happy child, she thought; she'd grown very fond of him. They started another game and while he shook the dice and moved his counter up the ladders, she realised she was happy here, the happiest she'd ever been. Life in Nuwara Eliya had taken a new and satisfying turn. To be a governess like her mother delighted her; she hoped her mother would be pleased.

"I've won," Jamie exclaimed happily. "Shall we have one more game?" "Yes," she laughed, "but I'm going to win this time. I've got a new spell for the dice."

"Ah! A new spell, eh!" Hamish was standing there. "Mummy says it's time for bed, Jamie, but finish your game and don't let Miss Gertrude beat you!"

Jamie laughed; the game didn't take long. He avoided every snake and raced up all the ladders and had won, before she'd hardly started!

"Well done. Don't forget to thank Miss Gertrude!" Hamish reminded him as he led him away.

She watched them go. They made a lovely pair! He was such a nice man, keen to make her feel at home. Within a few days of her arrival, he'd taken her to the yard, when the workforce was gathered for the morning muster. He'd said she ought to know something about life on the Oliphant Tea Estate. As he gave the workers their jobs for the day, she'd been impressed by the way he spoke to them in their own Tamil tongue and when the workers had departed for their tasks, Hamish had suggested they walk through the lines where the workers lived and see the estate school where the children busy at their slates, sat cross legged on the ground in the shadow of the trees. Finally, he announced, "It's time for breakfast" and they headed back to the house. As they passed the estate garage, a turbaned Sikh, salaamed.

"This is Yuvraj Singh," Hamish told her. "Yuvraj drives the estate lorry."

"And the motor car, *Durisani**, when *Duri** allows," Yuvraj said, then added, "It's an honour to meet you Durisani." Her "Thank you Yuvraj" made him smile and she saw two gold teeth shining in the depths of his jet-black beard. That beard and turban of his reminded her of Richard; of Richard dressed in that stupid Sikh costume on the *Ranpura*.

"If only we could be together," she sighed inwardly. "When will I see him again?" Eighteen long months had passed since they'd been together. Would that long awaited letter announcing the birthday of his father or mother ever arrive? She'd sent him her new address, but it had been a long time before his next letter came, then three had arrived, two redirected from Allahabad and one addressed to Oliphant Estate. He was still fretting at being in the Far East so far from action, though she was eternally grateful! In his last letter he'd been subdued, writing about the loss of the *Hood*. She'd already heard about it on the wireless. The *Hood*, the pride of the nation, the battlecruiser which only two years ago had taken the heir to the crown on a tour of the Empire, had been hit by a salvo from the German battleship *Bismarck*. A massive explosion had followed and within minutes the *Hood* had disappeared beneath the waves with all but three of her crew. Her loss had shaken the nation and the Navy had assembled a huge fleet to search the empty wastes of the Atlantic for the *Bismarck* and her consort the *Prinz Eugen*... After three days, *Bismarck* had been found and after a brave fight sunk. Of the *Prinz Eugen* there'd been no trace.

But his next letter had been more cheerful, though like everyone he knew that despite the sinking of the Bismarck and the Army's successes in North Africa, Britain now stood alone against the might of Hitler.

Chapter 14

Richard reached for the pile of letters to be censored. It was a task he disliked, but it had to be done. He hated intruding into the men's private affairs and rarely made any deletions; the *Strongbow* was having a very quiet war! He sighed, the first was from young Harris. His letters, written to the girl he'd married a month or so before he'd left home, always pulled at his heart strings. How the poor fellow longed to see the daughter his wife had borne so recently! Then there was Petty Officer Allen; his mother had been widowed a month or so ago and now she was ill herself! He shook his head sorrowfully. These letters made him know his men better than he could have expected! Yet despite that, he couldn't sympathise with them, for that would break the censor's code of confidentiality.

He heard a knock on the door. It was the Quartermaster. "Cap'n says will you have a word with him, sir?" He thanked him, tidied his desk and went.

"Take a seat, Number One." He took the cigarette offered and watched the Captain tap his thoughtfully on his cigarette case. "Something's up!" he thought. Having lit their cigarettes, the Old Man inhaled deeply and held out a copy of the "Straits Times". "Read this," he pointed to the headline.

JAPANESE TROOPS ENTER FRENCH INDOCHINA

With the agreement of the Petain regime, Japanese troops have entered the Vichy French colony, which Japan now declares to be its Protectorate. And

Japanese troops are reported to have entered Cambodia too, taking up positions close to the border with Thailand. Furthermore, Japanese battleships and aircraft carriers have been sighted off French Indochina and are thought to be making for the Vichy French naval base in Camranh Bay. These deployments must surely be the preparatory movements for the invasion of Malaya and Thailand.

"That's serious!" For the first time since the outbreak of war, Richard felt scared. "If the Japs really mean business, sir" he hesitated, "how can we cope with those battleships and carriers of theirs? All we have is four elderly light cruisers and five ancient destroyers!"

"The editor clearly agrees with you, Number One! Read what he says."

He found the editorial:

Japan, with its army encamped on our doorstep, threatens our very existence here in Singapore and Malaya. Is His Majesty's Government taking this threat seriously? Does it know how many warships and aeroplanes we have to defend ourselves? The answer, if it doesn't know, is precious few and those we have are ancient and no match for the modern ships and aircraft Japan possesses! We in Singapore know that, and there can be no doubt that the Japanese know it too! Alarm bells are ringing! His Majesty's Government must act now. Reinforcements for both the Navy and the Air Force are urgently needed and must be sent and sent quickly.

Phew! That's a pretty tough line he's taking, sir, but it's so true. I wonder he was allowed to print it!"

"Well, perhaps the censor only read the main article! But he's right. It looks as if our quiet war may soon be coming to an end."

Richard nodded.

"Well sir, let's hope we get those reinforcements before the fighting starts, otherwise," he shook his head, he could say no more. The future looked very frightening. He changed the subject. "Is there any thing else, sir?"

"Yes, Number One. As you know, Chief's having trouble with that damned circulating pump again, and we're also overdue for our annual docking." He saw Richard nod.

"Well," Henry smiled. "Apparently, they can't dock us here, so we're to go to Colombo. That'll make a nice change!"

"To Colombo, sir?"

Henry grinned, "Yes, Colombo. You seem mighty pleased."

"Well, as you say, sir, it'll make a nice change from Singapore! When are we going?"

"Well, our docking is planned for Monday 27th August, so I'm planning to arrive on Friday 24th."

"So, we'll be in Colombo a week or two?"

"A week, maybe ten days; it depends. But keep it under your hat for the time being. I'll tell the Ship's Company as soon as I can."

He just couldn't stop grinning as he made his way back to his cabin! He felt he was walking on air! He'd see her in three weeks time! But he stopped for a moment; whose birthday was Colombo? Was it Mum's or Dad's? He had to get it right! He'd made a note of it somewhere! His elation turned to panic as he hurried to his cabin. Where was that note? How could he forget that! Then it all came back. He reached for her photograph and slipped it out of its frame. There it was, written on the back: C-Dad, T-Mum. He chuckled, now he remembered he'd put them in alphabetical order Colombo with D and Trinco with M!

Hastily he found pen and paper. If only he could write "Dearest, I've got great news. I'm coming to Colombo," but of course he couldn't. Instead, as usual he began by telling her how much he missed her and how he longed to see her again. Then he wrote about the monsoon which they all hoped would soon be coming to an end. It was the sort of letter he always wrote, so the Captain, when he read it, would suspect nothing. Then he felt he could tell her his great news.

I keep thinking of my Dad these days, for it will be his birthday on 24th August, when he will be sixty-two. Dear Dad, he's always been conscious of his age. I remember he hated the thought of becoming forty and on his fortieth birthday, he kept on saying he was only thirty-nine! He was only joking of course, but my mother who actually was forty at the time, got quite red in the face as she asked him how he had the gall to pretend he was younger than her! It's been a family joke ever since!

He read the paragraph again. Would she see he was suggesting the Galle Face hotel? How else could he do it without raising the Old Man's suspicions? He could think of no other way. Well, if she wasn't there, he'd ring all the hotels in Colombo. He'd find her somehow! Excitedly he finished the letter. He'd give it to the Old Man before lunch so he could censor it, then it would be landed with all the other mail in the morning. He'd be seeing her in just a few weeks' time, he could think of nothing else. He'd see her on the 24th. Suddenly he remembered the 24th was her birthday! He'd have to take her a present. He'd buy something today!

He took one of the rickshaws waiting on the jetty. "Take me to the shops," he said. He wanted a jewellers, but what should he buy her? The shop window was full; rings, bracelets, brooches, silver tankards, sporting trophies, the choice seemed endless.

"I'm looking for a necklace," he said. An array of necklaces appeared. One with a crucifix took his fancy, but wasn't that the sort of thing she might already have? A string of pearls caught his eye. All women he knew liked pearls, but they were very expensive! One could almost buy a diamond ring for that price! A ring! Yes, a ring, that's what he'd buy! He'd buy an engagement ring! Why hadn't he thought of that before? Of course, that's what he'd buy her. He loved her and wanted to spend his whole life with her. He so often dreamt of them being man and wife. Yes, he'd ask her be his wife. If he didn't ask her now, with the war on, it might be a long time before he could. Yes, that's what he'd do; he'd pop the question and pray she'd say yes! "Could I see some rings please?"

"Wedding rings sahib?"

"No, no, I want an engagement ring."

"Diamonds, or rubies or sapphires, sahib? Shall I bring a selection?"

Richard nodded. What should he choose? He chuckled; he'd never bought an engagement ring before! A huge selection arrived. He liked the rings with three diamonds; they were like his mother's. He examined the first one. The price tag worried him; he put it down. One with smaller diamonds looked more suited to his pocket. Yes, but maybe she'd prefer two diamonds and a sapphire. He found one and held it at arms length. The diamonds sparkled nicely, and they set off the sapphire beautifully.

"I'll have that one please."

"Thank you, sahib. Do you know the size of memsahib's finger?"

"Oh! No. I don't." He looked at his fingers for inspiration! How did hers compare with his?

"Might I suggest sahib, that memsahib's wedding finger is likely to be the same size as your little finger?"

"Do you think so?"

"Well sahib, we often find that to be the case, but if the ring is too small or too large, I can easily adjust it."

He tried the ring on his little finger. It fitted well, not too loose, not too tight.

"Right, I'll have it please."

He watched the jeweller put the ring in its little box, and asking him to gift wrap it, paid the bill and left. The deed was done, but would she say yes? That question was to torment him all the way to Colombo!

Trudi, unaware of the *Strongbow's* intended visit to Colombo was at last beginning to come to terms with his absence. Though she dearly wanted to see him, like all the other wives and sweethearts separated from their men by this wretched war, she knew she had to be patient; that she had to make the best of things. And she wasn't unhappy here. And in the afternoons when she wasn't teaching, she enjoyed riding her pony Ginger along the lanes and pathways of the estate. But for all that, without Richard, she was only half alive. Only his letters made her truly happy. When she read them she felt he was close, but when they were read the emptiness returned and she would wait impatiently for the next! One had come this morning, but it wasn't until after lunch that she could open it in the privacy of her room. It was comforting to hear of his love for her and she laughed about the silly things he said about the monsoon. Then as she read on, her heart nearly stopped!

"I keep thinking of my Dad these days, for it will be his birthday on 24ᵗʰ August, when he will be sixty-two." His father's birthday! That was the code she'd waited for so long! But was that Colombo or Trincomalee? Excitedly she read on but found it hard to concentrate. Why was he telling her about his father's fortieth birthday? His mother had been upset that he had the gall to pretend he was younger than she? Why was he telling her all this? Did it mean anything? If so what? She was mystified! She found her diary and searching found the page she wanted. There she had written; *Exciting letter from Richard. C is Dad, T is Mum.* She remembered how thrilled she'd been to have their very own code and how careful she had been not to reveal its meaning. But now she knew for certain it was Colombo. And on the 24ᵗʰ, only five days away! Heavens she thought, I must ask Catherine to let me go to him, but where will I stay. She read that strange paragraph again. Why did his mother get red in the face? Was that some sort of coded message? 'And he had the gall to say he was only 39?' Red, face, gall, 39? Were they clues? Was it some sort of anagram? She wrote the words down several times putting them in a different order. 39, gall, face, Red - gall face. Was that it? She repeated the words gall face. She'd heard of the Galle Face Hotel in Colombo. Was he suggesting they meet there?

She hastened to find Catherine, to tell her the news. She was very understanding and immediately said "of course you must go." Thanking her profusely she asked if she could use the phone to book a hotel. "Certainly, try the Galle Face," Catherine smiled. "It'll be very suitable and I'm sure Hamish will let you use the car."

Thanking her again she went into the hall, picked up the phone and wound the handle. There was a buzzing noise, then "Good afternoon Nuwara Eliya exchange".

"Hello, hello," she said excitedly, "Can you connect me with the Galle Face Hotel in Colombo please?"

"Do you know the number?" the voice asked. When she admitted she didn't, the voice promised to find it and ring back. It seemed an age, but then she heard a voice "Galle Face Hotel reception" and in no time she had booked a room and was delighted to learn it had a sea view.

When it was done, she wanted to shriek for joy, but trying to control her excitement she hurried back to her room to write to Richard. He probably wouldn't get it before they met, but she had to tell him how thrilled and happy she was!

Chapter 15

He gave the windscreen a final polish, adjusted his turban, buttoned up his linen suit and opened the driver's door.

"Yuvraj Singh, you love that car more than me." He heard Jasvinder's sulky voice.

"Wife, you are talking nonsense, the Duri hates a dirty car." Perhaps though, she was right, for sometimes he did! His parents had found her for him. The daughter of a retired *Subadar** of the 1ˢᵗ Sikhs, she'd come with a sizeable dowry and obediently he'd married her. But she'd never roused him and though he'd done his duty by her, she had yet to bear him a son or even a daughter!

He flicked a piece of dust from his sleeve.

"Where are you going in your smart uniform?" she asked.

He revved the engine, slipped it into gear and released the handbrake.

"The Duri wants me to take Durisani Gertrude to Colombo."

Ah! Durisani Gertrude, he saw her in his mind's eye. She was different from Jasvinder, so different, different from all the women on the estate. That blonde hair of hers and those blue eyes thrilled him every time he saw her, saw Indira, as he'd come to call her. Unlike Sikh and Tamil women, she never hid her hair under a *chuni** but let it flow as nature surely intended. Nor did she seem unafraid to show the shape of her body! When he saw Indira, he admired her shapely legs and his eyes were always drawn to those breasts of hers, whose contours were so often outlined by her blouse. He shook his head. She was beautiful, she excited him!

The gravel crunched under the wheels as he turned unto the drive. He drew up by the porch and as usual the *Appu** gave him a scornful look. He was jealous of him; he coveted his smart uniform and envied him driving the Duri's plush new Rover. He ignored him; the Appu had a very high opinion of himself and expected everyone to kowtow to him. Well, he wouldn't, the Appu was no better than a harijan. He busied himself loading the baggage. Then he saw her. Oh! How radiant she looked with those sparkling blue eyes of hers! When she smiled her red lips revealed teeth like pearls! He felt his heart quicken. Why was she so happy? Was she going to meet someone special, some man, some lucky man? As she made her farewells, he waited ready to open the rear door for her. That Indira would sit in the front with him had only been a dream, but as she settled into her seat, he consoled himself; he would be able to see her in the mirror.

"To Colombo, Durisani?"

Yuvraj's voice broke into her thoughts.

"Yes, Yuvraj, to Colombo please; to the Galle Face Hotel."

His eyes met hers in the mirror, brown eyes like Richard's but eyes that lacked the warmth and affection of his. She averted hers and slid nearer the window to hide from his. She wanted nothing to distract her from her memories of the days she'd shared with Richard on the *Ranpura*. On that last day she'd asked him whether they'd ever meet again. He's replied with conviction, "We will, Trudi dearest, somehow I know we will." His certainty had stayed with her, giving her hope when she yearned for him. And now his prophecy was coming true! Tomorrow, she'd see him, and he'd hold her in his arms again. Lost in her dreams, the countryside slid by unnoticed, but a sudden thought brought her back to reality. His present, did she have it with her? Hastily she rummaged through her handbag. Ah! There it was! With a relieved sigh she opened the box and took out one of the cufflinks. Would he like them, she wondered? Deciding what to give him had been difficult, but then she'd seen these gold ones and had had his initials R.D.H. - Richard David Hooper - engraved on them. Feeling happier, she noticed that the scenery had begun to change. The coolness of the hills had been left behind and the humidity of the valley floor had begun to wrap itself around her.

"Open the windows, Durisani." She heard Yuvraj and saw his brown eyes in the mirror again. Like the humidity they troubled her, once more she slid out of his vision. The road was beginning to twist through the trees now, surely that would keep his eyes busy! But as they reached the paddy, the bends ended and while she watched the water buffalos wallowing in the mud, he kept watching her and again she moved to avoid his prying eyes. Then *atap** huts lining the road gave her hope that the journey would soon end, and she saw the first signs of Colombo.

"Ah! Durisani, Colombo is a beautiful city." She saw his eyes in the mirror again.

"Is this your first visit, Durisani?"

"Yes, Yuvraj." Avoiding his eyes, she said no more.

It's a fine city, Durisani, with grand old buildings."

When she made no reply, he lapsed into silence for a while, the increasing traffic demanding his attention. He began to use the horn.

"These Sinhalese, they just don't care. They cross without looking; they think they own the road!" He scowled and passing a rickshaw used the horn again.

"Be Careful if you use one of them, Durisani. Choose one pulled by a Tamil, he won't cheat you!"

"Thank you, Yuvraj, I'll remember that." She saw a smile light up his eyes.

"We'll see the sea soon Durisani; the harbour is right behind these *godowns**. You can see ship's masts over the roofs."

She saw them and many more as they drove on and through gaps in the buildings, she caught an occasional glimpse of a steamer. Is this where his ship would be, she wondered.

"And there ahead of us is the Fort and on the left the Pettah bazaar," she heard his voice again. "Durisani, you can buy everything there, fish, meat and vegetables, pots and pans, silks and diamonds and sapphires, anything you want."

Despite herself she began to soften towards him. "Yuvraj, you're a mine of information." His eyes caught hers. They seemed pleased!

"How far is it to the Galle Face?"

"Not far now, Durisani. We'll soon be passing Slave Island on the left and opposite is Galle Face Green. The hotel is on the seashore at the end of the Green."

They drove on in silence, she taking in the view, and he saddened that their journey was soon to end.

Then she saw the hotel. Painted white and perched by itself on the cliff, it clearly had a fine view of the sea. 'How wonderful,' she thought, 'I'll see his ship arriving!'

Yuvraj drew the car to a halt under the porch, "Here we are, Durisani."

A uniformed Tamil came to open the car door. "Welcome to the Galle Face Durisani." He led her to the hotel doors, but before entering she hesitated. Though Yuvraj had troubled her with his constant spying, she must thank him. She turned. He stood there watching her intently. As she spoke their eyes met, his clearly portraying his desire for her! Hastily she thanked him, and pushing the revolving doors fled inside. There away from those searching eyes, she felt safe and with a feeling of relief followed the porter to the lift.

"Your room, Durisani, is on the first floor. It has a balcony overlooking the sea. I hope it will please you."

As he opened the door and stood aside for her to enter, she knew it would, if only for its fine view of the sea. She would see him soon! Happily, she tipped him and surveyed the room. Even from the bed, with its English chintz bedspread matching the curtains, she could see the sea! She threw her handbag onto an easy chair and went onto the balcony. There were plenty of ships and boats to be seen and she could hear the surf breaking on the beach below. She studied the horizon. Tomorrow she'd see his ship!

"Morning sir", the middle watchman offered Richard a cigarette as he arrived on the bridge for the morning watch. With a mug of *Ki** they studied the chart together; then he was alone except for the signalman and the lookout. It was a balmy night with a full moon. He scanned the horizon, he could see nothing, but that didn't mean they had the sea to themselves. There could be a darkened ship out there sailing without lights, like the *Strongbow* herself. "Keep you eyes peeled, lads" he said. He studied the chart again and finding the dividers measured the distance to Colombo. Four hundred and twenty miles; at their present speed they'd arrive on time. He was excited, tomorrow he'd see her! In his mind's eye he saw her enticing red lips and those blue eyes of hers. He shook his head to wake himself from his dream, he must concentrate; he was on watch!

He heard a whistle. It was one of the voice pipes. "Bridge," he shouted. A faint voice replied.

"Engine Room here, we've had to stop the starboard engine sir; the circulating pump's playing up. I've sent for the Engineer Officer."

"Oh damn!" he muttered. He called the Captain. With only the port engine the ship had slowed down. He reckoned they were making only about eight or nine knots. He made a mental calculation. Now they'd arrive on Saturday morning at about eight o'clock at the earliest. Saturday, that was the 25th. Damn! He'd miss her birthday!

"Well, I've been expecting this!" It was the Captain. What speed do you think we're making now?"

"Eight, maybe nine knots, sir. That'll make our *E.T.A.** about oh-eight-double-oh on Saturday at the earliest."

"Ah! There you are Chief. Can you fix it?"

"'Fraid not, sir. All the packing's gone. It's a real dockyard job now!"

"Well we're nearly there and it's a calm night. Can I have more revs on the port engine?"

"Of course, sir. But I don't recommend more than two hundred."

"Well, that should give us twelve knots. What would our E.T.A. be then, Number One?"

He thought for a moment, "About eighteen hundred on Friday."

"Right then, two hundred revs it is. Pilot will give us a better E.T.A. when he's done his *morning stars**."

The ship slowly picked up speed, the Captain retired to his cabin and Richard felt happier. "We might make Colombo on Friday after all," he muttered. "Even if it's as late as eighteen hundred, I can still slip ashore and see her!"

"I'd like breakfast on the balcony please." Trudi told the maid who'd brought her morning tea. It was a bright clear morning and though she didn't know when it was due, she should see his ship. She'd just have to keep on looking for it! Hurriedly she bathed and dressed ready for her vigil. Her breakfast tray arrived and as she ate, she studied the sea before her. There were plenty of local fishing boats close inshore and a few larger ships in the distance, but there was no sign of his ship. Would she recognise it? She really didn't know. She'd never seen it or even a picture of it. All she knew was that it would be grey and small, and it was sure to have some guns. She studied the few ships that passed carefully, but to her eyes none looked like a British destroyer. Lunch came then tea, still with no sign of him. Now she began to worry. What had happened? Surely it hadn't sunk. Had she made a mistake with the code? Could his ship be bound for Trincomalee instead? She fought back her tears and searched her bag for her diary. Hastily she turned the pages until she found the entry she sought. *"exciting letter from Richard. C is Dad. T is Mum"*. She'd known it was Colombo, but nevertheless she breathed a sigh of relief. She looked at her watch and returned to the balcony.

It was nearly six o'clock: it would be dark soon! She began to feel quite weak with worry. There was only one ship out there and that had a red funnel!

It wasn't his! Now disconsolate, she searched listlessly, all the morning's hope ebbing away. Why was life so cruel? She'd never known love before she'd met Richard. Never before had anyone shown her any affection, she'd always been someone they'd had to accept, had to accept because she was her father's bastard daughter. Anger rose within her; she wanted to scream, but with an effort she controlled herself and wiped away her tears. What would she do if she lost him? If she never saw. him again? She shook herself; it was too awful to contemplate. Wearily she went back into the room.

There in the wardrobe was the dress she'd planned to wear for him. She took it out and looked at it. when she chose it she'd been happy and excited; but now............. Angrily she threw it onto the bed; she'd never wear it if anything happened to him! Never! In the mirror she caught a glimpse of her tear-stained face and dishevelled hair. How awful she looked! What would he say if he saw her like this? She hurried to the hand basin, wiped her face with a cold flannel, tidied her hair and re-did her make-up.

Despondently she returned to the balcony. The setting sun had turned the horizon red, but there in the fading light she could see a ship. It was quite close. She studied it carefully. In the twilight she couldn't see whether it was grey or not, but it wasn't very big and surely that pointy thing in the front must be a gun! Could it be the *Strongbow*? Excitedly she watched it and as it came closer, she was sure it must be a destroyer. It looked as if it had a turn of speed, and that pointy thing was definitely a gun. She could feel her heart racing, it must be his ship! She saw it turn into the harbour entrance and then disappear. She wanted to shriek "He's here, he's here at last." Now she was laughing, she was so happy she hardly knew what to do! Then she saw her crumpled dress. She picked it up and shook out the creases and holding it close to her, examined herself in the mirror. Oh! It was a lovely dress, she was sure he'd like it.

"All secure fore and aft, sir." Richard made his customary report to the Captain.

"Thank you, Number One. Will she be here?" he asked with a twinkle in his eye.

"Who, sir?" Richard asked innocently.

"The girl you write all those letters to. Why else have you been so excited ever since I told you we were coming to Colombo?"

Richard laughed, "Well, I hope so!"

"Well, you'd better be off and find out. I'll see you tomorrow at Morning Colours."

She had bathed hastily and put on the dress. She twirled around before the mirror she did like it. She'd hardly finished touching up her make-up when the phone rang.

"Duri Hooper wishes to speak to Durisani." It was him! She heard his voice.

"Dearest, dearest Trudi, is that really you?"

"Yes, yes, darling. Where are you?"

"Dearest, I'm in the foyer." She found him there standing expectantly and threw herself into his arms. She felt giddy with happiness. He led her to a quiet corner on the terrace, kissing her again and again as he told her how much he'd missed her and how much he loved her. How wonderful it was to be with him, all the worries and frustration of the past hours forgotten.

"Dearest," he laughed, "perhaps we should find a table; I think we're becoming a little conspicuous!"

They found one in a secluded corner, and he surprised her by wishing her many happy returns.

"Thank you, thank you dearest," she smiled. "It's so wonderful to be together again and on my birthday too!" He saw her lips twist in that intriguing way as she continued, "I hope I'm not growing old and haggard."

Dearest Trudi," he replied. "You are so beautiful. You'll never look old to me!" He reached for her hand. "I've loved you ever since the first day I saw you and I always will." For a moment he seemed lost for words. Then in a quiet voice he continued. "Trudi dearest, I can't live without you. Please, please be my wife."

Her tender eyes assured him of her love as she whispered, "Yes, yes of course darling, and I can't live without you."

Lost in happiness, they held hands gazing into each other's eyes. Then he remembered the ring.

"This dearest," he said, slipping it onto her finger "is for you. It's to seal our betrothal." He saw her face light up in delight. "Does it fit?" he asked anxiously.

"Yes, perfectly, how clever you are!

He laughed. "Yes, my love you are right I am clever, very clever; clever to have found someone as lovely as you to be my wife!"

They were blissfully happy, lost in themselves, forgetting the war, thinking only of their future together; where they would marry, where they would live and how once this dreadful war was over how they would never be parted. But as the evening slipped by Trudi began to dread his leaving. When finally, she'd dared ask when he had to go, he'd said, "I have to be onboard by seven tomorrow morning."

"Oh! Richard." she smiled blissfully, "we've the whole night. We mustn't waste a second of our precious time together." Then feeling wicked, she'd whispered, "My room's on the first floor, it's number seventeen. Give me ten minutes darling, then come."

He came with a bottle of champagne!

"Darling, we don't need that," she said as they embraced. "You're all I want." She took him by the hand and led him onto the balcony. "I sat here all day watching for your ship, I thought you'd never come!"

"Dearest I was getting desperate too!" He told her about the problem with the engine then he laughed. "But here I am."

"Yes, at last."

He put his arms around her and kissed her again. She could feel his hand creeping nearer her breast and could feel his hardness. Pushing him gently away, she unbuttoned his shirt and kissing him led him to the bed.

"Careful with my dress," she said as he unhooked her.

"Let go fore and aft. Hold on to the fore spring," the Captain ordered, then "Port twenty, slow ahead starboard." Richard heard the propeller turn, saw the spring tighten and watched the stern wind slowly away from the jetty. He was off, Colombo behind him, their blissful time together at an end. Would he ever see her again? Would they ever be man and wife? "God only knows," an inner voice replied. He felt wretched. Being separated from the woman he loved was unbearable. Suddenly he felt angry. If he was doing something worthwhile in this damned war, serving in one of the hard-pressed destroyers in the Med, perhaps he could bear their separation. But he wasn't! His endless patrols in the *Strongbow* had achieved nothing! He'd lost count of the number of ships they'd stopped and searched. And how many had been carrying contraband? Just one! One carrying rice from French Indochina to Algiers! Denying the Germans such vital supplies as that must surely have been a devastating blow to Hitler! He shook his head in anger. If only the *Strongbow* was based at Colombo or even Trincomalee, she could do her useless job there just as well!

Numb, devoid of all feeling, Trudi waited for the car. Was it only six days ago that she'd sat on that balcony watching for him? Yesterday she'd been there too, but then full of misery and despair waiting for that last glimpse of his ship as it carried away the man she loved, the man she'd promised to marry. As the sun had slowly set, she'd watched it grow smaller and the gulf between them grow ever larger. Then the *Strongbow* was gone, lost in the darkness. Now her whole being was empty except for a desperate longing to be with him, to hold him again. Again, she remembered that time on the *Ranpura* when she'd asked him if they'd ever meet again. This time she hadn't dared ask for fear of tempting fate! Yet when he'd embraced her, he'd read her thoughts and had quietly sung "We'll meet again" and kissing her had whispered, "we will, Trudi my love, we will." Then with a quivering chin and tears in his eyes he'd gone, and she had fled to her room. Now she was alone, with only memories to console her. Memories that made her cry and laugh! That first night had been so joyful! Through her tears she looked at her left hand. She wore two rings now, one to remember her mother and one to remember him. But would his like her mother's only serve as a memento of their love? Fiercely she dismissed the thought.

"No, no," she said almost audibly. "There'll be another, a plain gold one, when we marry." The diamonds sparkled, they seemed to agree!

She hadn't seen him on the second day; he'd had duties which kept him onboard, but though he'd telephoned her twice, it had been a long, lonely day. He'd come the next evening and then they'd had two whole days together. How blissful it had been, exploring Colombo, admiring the Old Dutch merchant's houses, bargaining in the bazaar and lunching in the Colombo Club. Then they'd returned to the Galle Face for a siesta – a warm relaxing feeling spread over her – she smiled they'd not had much of a siesta! Then that night like newly-weds, they'd slept together. The following day they'd swum in the sea at Mount Lavinia and in the evening had dined and danced together. That tune they both loved, 'Embrace me, embrace me, you sweet embraceable you,' now returned again and again reminding her how closely he'd held her as they'd shuffled round the floor to its intoxicating melody. That had been their last night together. Despite their efforts it had been a melancholy evening, each dreading the moment of his departure.

Her eyes filled with tears. She wiped them away. She couldn't be seen crying when Yuvraj came.

"Ah! There you are Gertrude."

It was Hamish. "Oh! Hamish, how kind of you to come, I was expecting Yuvraj!"

"Well," he smiled. "I thought I'd come instead. I hope you've had a happy time."

"Yes." She heard the tremor in her voice. "Yes, it's been wonderful, but oh! so short!"

He settled her in the front passenger's seat. He'd thought she'd be tearful. It wouldn't have been right to have sent Yuvraj.

Chapter 16

"Two Singapore Slings, sir?" The barman poured the ingredients into his shaker, added a copious quantity of ice and shook the mixture vigorously before pouring it into the waiting glasses. Then hooking a slice of orange onto the rim and placing a cherry in each glass, he placed the cocktails before of them. "Your Raffles' special, sir," he said with a smile.

"Your health, Number One."

"And yours too, sir."

The bar was crowded, but above the chatter he could hear the band; it was playing their tune; "Embrace me, embrace me, you sweet embraceable you". Memories of those happy days with her came flooding back. Those words affected him so! He wanted to stop his ears. Suddenly he realised the Old Man was speaking. "Sorry sir, I was taken with the music. What did you say?"

"I said, that's a Gershwin tune, isn't it?"

"Yes sir, it's one of my favourites."

"That lot in there seem to like it too," he pointed to the couples shuffling round the floor. "You wouldn't believe we're at war. Don't they know the Russians and Germans are slaughtering each other at Stalingrad and the U-boats are mauling our convoys?" He shook his head despairingly. "They seem to be living in a different world! I expect their biggest hardship is not getting the Tattler sent out anymore! Don't they know the Japs are on their doorstep? Doesn't it cross their tiny minds they could be in the firing line soon?"

"It doesn't look like it." Richard remembered how scared he'd felt, when he'd learnt the Japanese fleet was in Camranh Bay. "They seem to have buried their heads in the sand."

When they had returned on board, Richard began his letter to Trudi, but he'd hardly started when the Quartermaster was at his door. "Captain says he'd like to have a word with you, sir."

He found him sitting at his desk, a glass of whisky in his hand.

"Have a whisky." He handed Richard a glass. "I think our war is about to hot up. Read this."

It was a signal.

SECRET

From Admiralty

To C-in-C China and ships of the China Fleet

Force Zulu consisting of *Prince of Wales, Repulse, Energetic* and *Express,* under the command of Admiral Sir Tom Phillips, now appointed Commander-in Chief Eastern Fleet, has been despatched to Singapore to arrive by early December. *Indomitable* will join force Zulu in the near future."

"Phew!" Richard exclaimed. "That's good news. The *Prince of Wales*! We can certainly do with her fourteen-inch guns and the *Repulse* too."

"Yes, and the *Repulse*." Henry nodded. "She's quite an old lady now, but with her six fifteen-inch and sixteen four-inch guns she still packs quite a punch! And the destroyers *Energetic* and *Express* too. They're twice our size and modern too!"

"Yes, sir, though it's a pity there are only the two of them."

"Yes, but two are better than none! I wonder when the *Indomitable* will join. She's what we really need, a modern aircraft carrier to give us air support. The ancient Brewster Buffalos the RAF have, aren't much of a match for the Zeros the Japs fly!"

"You're right there, sir, though I've heard the RAF boys say the Japs aren't any good in the air. They believe they're all short-sighted, that they all wear specs! D'you think they're right?"

"I can't believe that. But as we haven't got the *Indomitable,* we'll have to hope the RAF are right! And it's good to know we've got a couple of battleships coming our way!"

The news was to remain secret for several weeks and life continued as usual, with *Strongbow* and her sister ship, the *Tenedos,* maintaining their regular anti-contraband patrols. But on the 2nd of December the two ships met the *Prince of Wales*, the *Repulse* and the two escorting destroyers in the Malacca Straits. What a spectacle the great ships made as they glided majestically through the sea, their fourteen and fifteen-inch guns and their arsenal of anti-aircraft weapons reassuring the men in the two destroyers that so happily welcomed them.

"All secure for'ard and aft, sir", Richard made his usual report.

"Thank you, Number One." The Captain looked up from a sheaf of signals and handed him one. "You've got a *pier head jump**!"

CONFIDENTIAL

From C-in-C Eastern Fleet

To *STRONGBOW* information *ENERGETIC*

Lieutenant R D Hooper is to be lent forthwith to *Energetic* as First Lieutenant vice Lieutenant R J Hammond. Lieutenant Hammond has been admitted to Military Hospital for surgery. It is expected he will return to duty within three weeks, when Hooper will return to *Strongbow*.

"It'll be a chance for you to show your worth," Henry Newcombe gave him a fatherly smile. "So off you go, and the best of luck!"

Within an hour he was standing at the bottom of the gangway admiring his new ship. How modern she seemed with her four 4.7-inch guns, eight torpedo tubes and eight 20mm Oerlikon AA guns. Thrilled to serve on such an up-to-date destroyer, yet anxious about his abilities, he adjusted his cap and stepped onboard.

"Lieutenant Hooper come aboard to join," he reported as he saluted. The Quartermaster returned his salute and led him below to his cabin. "Leave your bag, sir. The Captain wants to see you."

Lieutenant Commander Derek Cook welcomed him warmly. "Glad to have you with us, Hooper. Hammond was very ill, appendicitis I hear. We had to land him as soon as we tied up. They'll be operating tomorrow, so he should be alright, but he won't be fit for duty for a couple of weeks or so."

"That's bad luck sir, but I'm pleased to help."

His new Captain asked him about the *Strongbow* and told him what he thought would be required of the *Energetic*. Then he sent for the Navigator.

"Number One, meet Pilot, Charles Maxwell. He'll show you round and introduce you to the others."

With his head reeling from his lightning tour of the ship and meeting so many of the crew, he was glad to retire to his new cabin and unpack. He'd heard the *Prince of Wales* needed emergency repairs and that the rest of Force ZULU would have a few days in harbour for some routine self maintenance. That thankfully would give him time to learn more about the ship, before she went to sea. Feeling more relaxed he found Trudi's picture, kissed it gently and standing it near his bunk, changed ready for dinner. Arriving in the wardroom he found it to be much bigger and better appointed than he'd expected. Indeed everything seemed to be bigger and better in the *Energetic*. And he was aware that, unlike the *Strongbow*, the *Energetic* had seen action right from the start of the war, rescuing survivors from a liner torpedoed by a U-boat and later forming part of the force that had hunted for and sank the *Bismarck*. Even the *Wavy Navy** Sub Lieutenant had seen real action! It made him feel a *makey-learney**!

He thanked Pilot for the pink gin he was offered when he arrived in the wardroom and shortly afterwards the Captain came in.

"A gin, sir?"

"Thank you, Number One, that would do nicely."

The routine of dinner, with him in the chair as President and the Captain on his right, helped to confirm him in his new appointment. It was a lively meal with plenty of banter and by the time the port had been passed and he had proposed the King's health, he had begun to feel that he too, was part of this happy band.

Chapter 17

●●●●●●●●●●●●●●●●●●●

"First Lieutenant, sir." It was Fred Currie, the Officer of the Day.

"Yes, what's up?"

"We've been hearing explosions. There's another. Can you hear it?"

Hastily he pulled on some clothes and went on deck. The southern sky was alight with flashes. What could it be? Was it the long expected Japanese attack? He rushed to the Wardroom and tuned to the BBC. A crackly voice came through "……….. at Pearl Harbour. Many aircraft have been destroyed on the ground and many casualties are expected as a result of this surprise attack."

"Go shake the Captain. Tell him about the explosions and ask him to join me in the Wardroom. The BBC is reporting some sort of attack on Pearl Harbour. Then tell the *PO Tel** to set watch and listen for any signals from C-in-C."

He adjusted the tuning of the wireless. Now he could hear more clearly. "It is now becoming evident that Japanese carrier-borne aircraft have launched a surprise attack on the US Naval Base at Pearl Harbour."

"What are you hearing, Number One?" It was the Captain. "Are they bombing Singapore?"

As he told the Captain, what he'd heard on the BBC, the PO Tel appeared. "Urgent signal from C-in-C, sir. "Suspected Japanese bombers attacking city of Singapore. Repel all aircraft flying over Naval Base."

"Sound Action Stations, Number One."

Amid the jangle of the Alarm bells and the rush of men to their weapons, he could hear gunfire. The *Repulse* moored in the stream, and even the *Prince of Wales* in dry dock, were firing at an aircraft caught in their searchlights. Running to the Oerlikons he told the crews about the suspected Japanese aircraft and ordered them to fire at any planes they saw, but the planes seemed to have disappeared as quickly as they'd come.

He found the Captain. "It seems all over for the moment, sir."

"Yes, Number One, we've had *Air Raid Warning White**. Stand the men down." He looked at his watch. "It's four thirty on Monday 8th December; make sure we record this attack in the Log, and Number One, I want to talk to all officers in the Wardroom immediately after Morning Colours."

There was an expectant hush in the Wardroom as the Captain entered." Please be seated." He lit a cigarette and inhaled deeply. "I want to read you a signal from C-in-C, 'Without any declaration of war, Japanese carrier-borne aircraft today sank four US battleships and damaged or sank fifteen other ships in a surprise attack on the US Naval Base at Pearl Harbour. Last night Japanese bombers also attacked Singapore city, inflicting much damage and many casualties and early this morning an RAF Hudson reported sighting two large convoys escorted by Japanese warships off Indo China. Their destination is not known but as they were steering a westerly course an amphibious landing on Malaya or Siam* cannot be ruled out. Although Britain has not yet declared war on Japan, it can only be a matter of time before it does and accordingly, *Prince of Wales* has been ordered to undock this forenoon and will sail with Force ZULU at 1730 today and provided war has been declared will intercept the Japanese convoys. Officers and *Senior Rates** are to be made aware of these events on a need-to-know basis, but ship's companies are not to be informed until Force ZULU has sailed.'

"Well," the Captain concluded, "this of course is why we've been sent out here! So, everyone, make sure we're ready for the fight. Has anyone got any questions?"

There were questions about the attack on Pearl Harbour and the likely size of the Japanese force, which he could not answer.

Later that morning *Energetic* and *Express* sailed to search for submarines lurking in the Straits. None were found and in the evening they destroyer *Tenedos* led the two capital ships out into the open sea, *Strongbow* remaining behind to lay her mines. As the three destroyers began to form a protective anti-submarine screen around the two battleships, a signal from C-in-C told the force that Britain had declared war on Japan.

Fortune seemed to smile on the British Fleet as it set off, for heavy rain and low clouds reduced visibility to a mile or so, giving welcome cover from the prying eyes of Japanese aircraft. But on the following day in the early evening visibility improved and three aircraft were sighted. They made no attempt to attack, but remained obstinately out of gun fire range, clearly reporting the size, position, course and speed of Force ZULU to Japanese Naval Command.

"Well, Number One," the Captain frowned. "We might have expected they'd find us. They'll be after our blood tomorrow! Pity we don't have the *Indomitable* with us. We'll just have to rely on those RAF Buffalos!"

"Yes, sir, let's hope they're up to it."

The setting sun gave them welcome relief from Japanese eyes, but all knew that come the dawn, they'd come again but then laden with bombs and torpedoes. As Richard considered this frightening prospect, the Captain's voice broke into his thoughts, "Make sure the crew have a good breakfast before dawn action stations Number One. Tomorrow's going to be a long day!"

"The cook's already been warned, sir." He turned to leave the bridge, but seeing the Flagship signalling, waited to see what it was. Finally, the signalman handed the message to the Captain. "We're aborting the mission," he told him. "The RAF can't give us air cover and C in C has decided to return to Singapore, rather than face air attack without fighter protection."

"It's to be a 'fleet in being' then," Richard said.

"Yes, Number One, you could put it that way; maybe it's better to have a fleet which by its mere existence provides a threat, rather than one on the bottom of the South China Sea!"

The night was dark and uneventful, but as dawn broke the first enemy aircraft were sighted. Again, they made no attempt to attack, but their presence was an ominous portent of things to come. The attack came a few minutes after 1100. Eight or nine enemy aircraft appeared high in the sky on the starboard bow. Untroubled by the massive anti-aircraft barrage, they flew without deviation towards their target, the *Repulse*. Richard held his breath as he watched the bombs fall and straddle her, but to his great relief she emerged apparently unscathed. But that was just a prelude, for soon more aircraft were seen diving out of the clouds, to fly at sea level towards the two capital ships. The planes were so low; the destroyers could use their surface guns, against them. But again, the Japanese seemed invulnerable and flew resolutely through the barrage, to release their torpedoes. Watching the *Repulse,* he saw black smoke emerge from her funnels as she accelerated and turned rapidly to port. Her Captain had clearly judged the moment of release, well for the torpedoes passed harmlessly down her side. Relieved, he turned to look at the *Prince of Wales* and saw her execute a similar emergency turn, but she was less fortunate, for a huge explosion followed and he saw flames erupt near her after funnel and yet more by her after turret. Clearly badly damaged, she began to lose speed and list to port. Their mission accomplished the torpedo bombers climbed into the heights and disappeared leaving the *Prince of Wales* turning helplessly in a wide circle. But then like a maddened swarm of hornets more aircraft came, this time clearly determined to sink the *Repulse* which had so skilfully parried their earlier attacks. Once more she turned and avoided their torpedoes. But now aircraft were attacking her from all directions and as she turned to avoid one torpedo, she presented a broadside target for another. Two, maybe three torpedoes struck her. The *Repulse* lurched, her mainmast shook, and she too began to list.

Watching in disbelief, he heard the Captain say, "She's going." Gradually her list increased until at last she capsized, her propellers still turning. Men could be seen clinging onto her red bottom until one by one they slid off into the sea. Now the sky was empty, the guns silent and only the cries of the men in the water could be heard. He ran onto the iron deck ordered the scrambling nets to be lowered and watched the Captain bring the ship skilfully among the men in the sea. As the ship lay rolling in the gentle swell, the survivors began swimming towards them. Some were strong enough to climb the nets unaided, but those who were too weak had to be helped though the oil which covered them, made it difficult. Some fell back exhausted, but eager sailors jumped in to tie ropes around them so they could be hauled onboard.

"Get them aft and hose them down," he told the Buffer. "Then send them below." Still, they came, and still they laboured to save them.

"We've got about three hundred and fifty now and about another twenty still in the water" he shouted to the bridge, where an anxious Captain agonized about the stationary target the *Energetic* was presenting. He need not have worried however, for the bombers had a more valuable target, the *Prince of Wales*. Protected by the other destroyers and still listing, she was once again steering a steady course. But it was clear she was mortally wounded and only a few of her small calibre AA guns were firing. Then there were more explosions as further bombs struck her and she was lost in flames and smoke.

Richard heard the Captain shouting, "Get those last men out of the water as fast as you can. The *Prince of Wales* is sinking."

When there were no more to be rescued, Richard rushed to the bridge to report. The Captain had his binoculars trained on the *Prince of Wales*. "They can't save her," he said. "The *Express* is going alongside her to take off the wounded."

The Japs had had a field day, but still they weren't satisfied, for now he could see planes heading for the *Energetic*. Shouting "Alarm Aircraft starboard" he heard the cracking of the Oerlikons as the Japs strafed them before disappearing. No one had been killed, but some had been wounded and both the bridge and the for'd funnel bore marks of the attack.

Now the *Energetic* had joined the other destroyers standing by the stricken *Prince of Wales*, whose crew were abandoning ship. Men could be seen sliding down her side into the sea, and swimming towards carley floats*. Luckily the sea was calm, but as the great ship finally succumbed and disappeared beneath the surface, great bubbles of air began escaping and the sea became a maelstrom, its whirlpools ready to suck everything into its vortex.

Then all that could be done was to rescue the survivors and seek refuge in Singapore. It was a sad passage home. Richard recalled how proud he'd felt leaving Singapore in company with those two great battleships, but now both were on the bottom, sunk by puny aircraft! Never before had battleships suffered such a humiliating fate! Yet he had to admire those Japanese airmen. They'd flown through that barrage of gunfire with great courage and determination regardless of their losses. But where had the RAF been? They who had complacently underrated the Japanese airmen, believing them to be short-sighted!

Chapter 18

· · · · · · · · · · · · · · · · · · · ·

It was New Year's Eve. Roger Hammond had recovered from his operation and had returned to his duties in the *Energetic*. Unable to re-join the *Strongbow* as she was at sea, Richard had spent two nights in *H.M.S. Terror*, the shore establishment in the Naval Base. Now full to overflowing with survivors from the two sunken battleships, he'd had to share a cabin with two officers rescued from the *Repulse*. They'd recognised him as being from the *Energetic*, the destroyer that had rescued them and at the bar they'd pressed him endlessly for "another gin". Like him, they'd been greatly impressed by the skill and determination of the Japanese airmen. As one of them said,

"The sky was full of Japanese aeroplanes, it was one attack after another, and nothing seemed to stop them!" Everyone was now convinced the day of the battleship was on the wane; that naval air power now reigned supreme.

"Hadn't the Fleet Air Arm shown that at Taranto, when they'd sunk those Italian battleships a year ago?"

"Where are our carriers?" they asked, and how would our ancient Swordfish and the mediocre Fulmar fare against the fast modern aircraft the Japs flew? These questions were on everyone's lips and when all they could hear was news of the endless strategic withdrawals in Malaya, it seemed to them that the Japs were invincible! It was a truly depressing time and Richard was glad to hear that the *Strongbow* had returned. Hurriedly he packed his gear and on re-joining, reported to the Captain.

"Come in." It was Henry Newcombe's familiar voice. "Good to have you back. Have a gin."

He poured out two large measures and handing a glass to Richard, listened with increasing disbelief as Richard told him how the Japanese aircraft had completely overwhelmed the two battleships.

"What a disaster!" Henry Newcombe shook his head despairingly. "Both sunk in a few hours and by aircraft too! It's incredible!"

"How's the minelaying going?" Richard felt he must change the subject. If he could, he wanted to forget that awful defeat.

"We've finished now; laid the last defensive field yesterday and tomorrow our minerails will be removed and replaced by our after four-inch gun. Then we'll be ready for convoy escort duties."

"So, when's our first convoy?"

"Well, we're earmarked to meet and escort a convoy bringing troops from Australia."

Later when *Strongbow* and another destroyer had shepherded the convoy into Keppel Harbour, they learnt that the Japanese had bypassed the causeway linking Singapore with the mainland and had made a successful water-borne landing on the island. When the two destroyers berthed in the Naval Base to refuel, the two Captains were summoned to Naval Headquarters.

"We're off again tomorrow, Number One," the Captain said on his return. "We've got to tow the Australian destroyer *Vendetta* to Palambang."

"Really, sir why?"

"Well, her engines aren't ready, she's only half-way through her refit and they don't want the Japanese to get their hands on her if Singapore should fall!"

As they set of with *Vendetta* in tow and *Jupiter* in company, everyone wondered whether Singapore would still be in British hands when they returned and having delivered their tow safely to Palambang, they hurried back. As they'd feared, Japanese forces were now in control of much of the island and all non-military Europeans were to be evacuated and on the next day the two destroyers set sail convoying the evacuation ships to Batavia. The first day was uneventful, but early on the second their peaceful progress was shaken by a huge explosion. Orange flames and thick black smoke poured from a ship that had clearly been torpedoed, though no submarine had been detected by either escort. But when a second ship was hit *Strongbow* got a submarine contact and held it long enough to attack. Richard watched the throwers hurling the depth charges into the sea. No one spoke; all looked expectantly astern, waiting for the great plumes of water to be thrown up by the exploding charges.

"Starboard thirty." He heard the Captain order as the charges exploded. "Right, a good lookout now everybody: let's see if we've got him."

All eyes scanned the sea for any signs of a hit, but there were none. Then the asdic operator reported, "Possible sub bearing red two oh, nine hundred yards." The hunt was on again and once more the rhythmic ping of the Asdics could be heard as the range decreased.

"Standby depth charges" the Captain shouted, then later, "Fire." Again everyone watched the depth charges being hurled into the sea and waited for the explosions. But again there were no signs of a hit.

"Asdics, can you hear his propellers?" The Captain asked, his binoculars searching the sea astern.

"No sir, but we can hear rumbling noises."

Then as they watched, a great bubble rose from the depths and bursting, spread a blanket of white foam over the surface.

Had they hit the submarine? Had its hull been fractured? The bubble seemed promising! Henry Newcombe was tapping his unlit cigarette on its case.

"Keep listening, Asdics," he said. "He may have pumped air out of a torpedo tube, to fool us!"

"I can see oil, sir," Richard shouted, pleased to be the first to spot it. The slick was getting bigger by the second. He was certain it was oil; it had that rainbow hue.

"I think she's sinking," the Captain muttered as yet more oil appeared. Now he was certain they'd had a kill. "Well done everybody," he grinned as he lit his cigarette.

Everyone was in high spirits, but Richard couldn't help feeling for those poor men trapped in their sinking submarine. Did anyone deserve such a terrible death, he wondered? But remembering the two ships the submarine had just sent to the bottom, he knew they did!

Two days later the remnant of the convoy arrived safely in Batavia, and learnt what to many, had seemed inevitable. On December the 14th, Singapore had surrendered to the Japanese.

The port of Batavia was full of ships and indecision. What was to be done with these vessels crammed with evacuees? With the Japanese army now ashore in Borneo and Eastern Java, it seemed only a matter of time before Batavia would go the same way as Singapore! But while the shore authorities wrestled with the problem of the evacuees, the destroyers refuelled, watered ship and found whatever victuals they could. No one knew what the future held or who was now in charge of what was left of the Allied navies. But then all warships were ordered to assemble in Surabaya, where *Strongbow* and *Jupiter* became part of the new joint fleet. Richard was encouraged to see so many ships. *H.M.S. Exeter,* was there with the Australian cruiser *Perth,* the American cruiser *Houston* and two Dutch cruisers, *Java* and *De Ruyter,* the latter flying the flag of the Fleet Commander, the Dutch Admiral Doorman. In addition to the *Strongbow* and the *Jupiter,* there were two other British destroyers, the *Encounter* and *Energetic* and two Dutch. Four American destroyers were expected to join soon.

Though the fleet looked impressive, it was clear that controlling this multi-national group of ships would prove difficult, so all Commanding Officers were summoned to the flagship for a briefing by the Admiral. Luckily the Dutch had a reasonable command of English and this became the common language. But the four navies all had different signals, codes and operating procedures, making it difficult for the Admiral to communicate and control operations, so it was agreed that control would be exercised by voice on a common radio network, using plain language. If necessary, a preliminary explanation of what was to be done would be made. The possibility that the enemy might intercept their plain language signals was discussed without solution and when news came that a Japanese invasion force was heading for eastern Java, the briefing was hastily terminated, and the fleet sailed at once.

As the force neared the Japanese, four cruisers and dozens of destroyers could be counted. "Lord help, us," Richard heard the Captain exclaim. Then in a defiant note, he continued, "Well we've got five cruisers and six destroyers!"

The loudspeaker crackled. It was a message from the Admiral. A guttural Dutch voice was ordering the cruisers into single file behind "De Ruyter" and the destroyers behind "Kortenaar". The Yeoman of Signals appeared. "He means '*Cruisers Form One*', *Guide* De Ruyter, Destroyers Form One, Guide *Kortenaar*, sir."

The Captain nodded. "Thank you, Yeoman. Officer of the Watch take up station."

The enemy was now only about ten miles distant and soon the leading Japanese cruiser could be seen firing. *Strongbow's* 4 -inch pop-guns, as Richard mentally described her main armament, had a maximum range of four miles, so all they could do was wait with trepidation for the enemy shells to land. The first Japanese salvo fell close to the *Exeter*, whose eight-inch guns spewed a cloud of grey smoke as they returned fire. The American cruiser the *Houston* was firing too, but not the Australian cruiser nor the two Dutch whose smaller guns were out of range. The next Japanese salvo crashed into the *Exeter*. She shuddered and steam poured from her after funnel, followed shortly by thick black smoke. All eyes were on the crippled ship, now losing speed and hauling out of line.

"Starboard thirty," he heard the Captain order. "Yeoman," he called. "Make a signal to *Kortenaar*. 'Am standing by *Exeter*'." As they headed for the crippled ship, the Yeoman shouted "Signal from *Kortenaar*, sir. Your last not approved. Rejoin destroyer force for torpedo attack."

A long plain language message began coming over the radio link, with many requests for repetition. "If only we could use our signal book!" Henry Newcombe exclaimed in exasperation, but eventually it became clear that the Dutch and British destroyers were to attack in two divisions with the Dutch forming one division and the British another. With the *Jupiter* leading the British, they increased speed and raced towards their target. *Strongbow* with her puny armament was "tail end Charlie" following in the wake of *Energetic*. The Japanese cruisers now shifted fire to the other cruisers, apparently leaving their destroyers to deal with the torpedo threat. Fortunately for the Allies, it seemed the Japanese destroyers were having difficulty ranging on their targets for their salvos were falling regularly behind the allied shpss, though near enough to worry "tail end Charlie". But then the Japs found the range and two salvos hit the *Energetic*. *Strongbow* hastily pulled out of line to avoid the stricken vessel, now settling in the water with fires raging about her funnels. The enemy cruisers were getting nearer now, and Richard could see a red pendant with flag nine below it flying from Jupiter's yard arm.

"Execute to follow, sir," the Yeoman shouted, "Turn 90 degrees to starboard in the wake of the next ahead". *Jupiter* hauled the flag signal down and the Yeoman yelled, "Execute, sir."

Richard watched *Jupiter* turn and *Encounter* follow in her wake. Then it was time for *Strongbow* to turn. The Japanese cruiser was getting very close and *Strongbow's* guns now at last within range were firing. Any minute now they'd be launching their torpedoes. He moved to the back of the bridge and shouted "Be ready to fire torpedoes." Derek, the Torpedo Gunner raised his hand in response. The noise of gunfire was almost continuous now and as they sped towards the enemy, he saw *Encounter's* torpedoes hit the water. As she turned away, he went to the back of the bridge to watch *Stronghold's* torpedoes go, but as he did the Japanese cruiser heeled and turned under full helm to starboard. Now she presented an impossible target. Their torpedoes would be wasted if they fired. "Don't fire," he shouted.

Turning to tell the Captain, he heard a burst of rapid gunfire. He ducked and as he did, saw a line of holes, jagged holes cut into the funnel. The Captain lay huddled on the deck.

"I told them not to fire the torpedoes, sir," he shouted. "She was head on we wouldn't have hit her!" The Captain made no reply. He picked himself up, but the Captain made no effort to do the same. Why not? Why doesn't he move, he asked himself? He couldn't go to him now!

"Officer of the Watch," he shouted. "Come hard a starboard. Follow *Encounter*, let's get out of here as fast as we bloody well can."

He went back to the Captain. He hadn't moved! Gently with the help of the lookout he turned him over. Then he saw his face, or what was left of it! The lower half was a bleeding mass of flesh and bone. He laid him down again; there seemed nothing he could do. It was strangely quiet now. 'A' gun could no longer bear and the enemy seemed to have lost interest in firing too. He looked around; there was another body over there. The Yeoman was tending to him.

"Is he alright?" He cursed his stupidity, what a foolish question! He wouldn't be lying there if he was alright!

"He's still breathing, sir, he's been hit in the chest."

Richard nodded in reply, then shouted "Officer of the Watch put someone else on the wheel. Get the *Cox'n** up here quickly."

The Yeoman had been hit too. "It's only my arm, sir," he said stoically.

The rest of the Bridge team, Pilot, the young sub and the lookouts were OK, but what about the rest of the ship's company? He shouted for Fred the Gunner to come to the bridge. "Go round the upper deck and tell me if there are any other casualties or damage and tell Derek to do the same below decks." He also spoke to the Engineer. Thankfully all was well below, but Stan had added "We're getting low on fuel." Richard pressed him to be more exact. "Can't say for sure but I'd say we've about 25% remaining," he said.

It was not good news. They'd have to return to harbour to refuel; he'd have to talk to the Captain. The Cox'n was bending over him. "How is he?" he asked, though the answer was obvious. "First Lieutenant, sir, I'm afraid he's a goner. He must have died instantly."

He looked at the lifeless body of the Captain he'd so admired; he'd learnt so much from him. Now his sightless eyes seemed to be assessing his suitability for command. He looked away; the import of those eyes struck home; he was Captain now! For a moment he felt frightened, the burden so suddenly thrown upon him seemed too much to bear, but then he pulled himself together, he had no choice; he had to take command.

"Thank you, Cox'n," he said. "Have a look at Harris, he's in a bad way and the Yeoman's been hit too." His attention had been focused on the wounded too long; he looked at young Andrew, hunched over the *pelorus**, with his binoculars glued to his eyes scanning the sea ahead. He was doing well, keeping the ship nicely in the *Encounter's* wake.

"Well done, Andrew," he said. The young sub's face relaxed, "Thank you, sir," he replied. He raised his own binoculars and trained them on the enemy cruisers. They seemed to be receding. He examined the one they'd aimed at. Had any torpedoes struck home? It seemed unlikely, he could see no smoke or any sign of damage, yet she'd stopped firing.

He called the Signalman over. "Make a signal to *Jupiter*. "Regret to report death of Lt. Cdr. Newman and Ordinary Seaman Harris due to enemy fire. Lieutenant. Hooper has assumed command."

By the time they re-joined the main force the sun was sinking in a red sky and the enemy was far behind. He'd reverted to Cruising Stations, the men needed to eat and rest. He himself had been on the bridge since dawn, but strangely he didn't feel tired, his mind was too active, thinking about what might happen next and what he would do with the two dead bodies.

The Leading Signalman arrived with a signal. It was from the Admiral informing them that the *Energetic* and *Kortenaar* had been sunk and *Exeter* damaged, but gave no assessment of damage to the enemy. The signal ended with the Admiral's intentions for the next twenty-four hours and instructions for ships to report levels of fuel and ammunition remaining. He read it again, that torpedo attack had resulted in the loss of two destroyers and had achieved nothing! It was depressing news! He sent the signal reporting his fuel and ammunition state, reflecting that the only good thing was that it would soon be dark and there might be a few hours of peace.

Then came a signal telling *Strongbow* to go to Tjilatjap to refuel. Wherever was Tjilatjap? He and Pilot studied the chart. Neither had heard of the place! But at last, they found it. It was on the south coast of Java and dropping out of station the *Strongbow* set course for this strange port. There was no moon, and it was pitch black and though thankful for the cover the darkness gave, he knew conditions were perfect for a collision! But with all eyes searching for the dim outline of the other ships or the silver of their wake he managed to skirt the fleet without incident. Then mercifully he was clear, but only when he could see the flashing of the lighthouse guarding the straits that separated Java from Sumatra, did he allow himself to leave the bridge. In his cabin he searched for the Book of Common Prayer. He'd decided that tomorrow when they were near Tjilatjap and comparatively safe, he'd muster all hands for the burial of Harris and the Captain. By then he'd order their bodies to be sewn up in hammocks ready to be slid over the side. He thumbed through the pages to prepare for their burial,

Sunrise found them in an empty sea close to the shoreline and with speed reduced and lower deck cleared and mustered aft, the ensign was lowered to half mast.

"Ship's Company," he announced, "We are gathered here to make our farewells to our Captain, Lieutenant Commander Henry Newcombe and to our shipmate Ordinary Seaman Peter Harris who both died in the service of our King and Country in action against the Japanese in the Java Sea. Though our torpedo attack was unsuccessful their deaths were not in vain. Their courage and dedication will surely serve as an inspiration for us to renew our efforts to fight on with determination. Now we commit their bodies to the deep, looking for the resurrection of the body and the life of the world to come, through our Lord Jesus Christ. Amen."

Nodding to the Buffer to let the bodies slide into the sea, he concluded with the Lord's Prayer.

Then returning to the bridge, he ordered "Half ahead both engines," and resumed course for Tjilatjap. It was not far now, he'd studied the harbour chart carefully and had discovered the fuelling berth. It was in a difficult corner. He'd hoped that for this, the first time he brought the *Strongbow* alongside, he'd have an easier approach. But it wasn't to be and calming his nerves he ordered "Port Fifteen" to bring her bows round for the jetty. Then he was too busy to be scared and to his relief brought her safely alongside. As he waited for the mooring lines to be finally secured, he scanned the harbour. He could see only one other ship, a Dutch freighter. He read the name on her bow, *Zaanfontein*. She looked modern and fast and was busy loading. But the harbour itself was a scene of destruction. Everywhere there were burnt out cars, lorries and buses. Some were still smouldering. A train was burning too. Then he saw an officer waiting to board and left the bridge to meet him.

"Welcome to Tjilatjap, Captain. I'm the Harbourmaster. You want fuel?" He assured him he did and also a doctor.

"Fine," the Harbourmaster saw Stan the Engineer, standing there in his white overalls.

"You're the Engineer, eh?" Stan nodded. "Good," the Harbourmaster replied. "I will arrange *bunkers**. Now," he turned to Richard, "You've got a wounded man, eh?"

"Yes two in fact, they need proper medical attention. Can you arrange that?"

"Sure. There's a ship's doc in the *Zaanfontein* over there. Leave it to me, but before I go, what news do you have of the battle? We've heard the *De Ruyter* and the *Java* have been sunk and the Admiral's been lost. And we've heard tell that two other cruisers have been sunk too. We just can't believe it! What do you know?"

Richard told him of the fight with the Japanese the day before and of the *Exeter* being damaged and of two destroyers being sunk. "But" he continued, "It's the first I've heard of the Admiral being lost and the *De Ruyter* and *Java* being sunk. And you say the *Houston* and the *Perth* have been sunk as well?"

The Dutchman nodded. "Yes, that's what we've heard!" He paused. "Tell me, what are your orders?"

"To refuel and rejoin."

"Who will you rejoin?"

"Well, after what you've told me, I don't know. Are you sure what you've heard is true?"

"Yes, as sure as anything can be now!"

"Well, I'm sure we need fuel. That can be arranged, can't it?"

"Yes, that's no problem, Captain, but please let me know what your intentions are."

"Yes of course, but do you know how close the Japs are?"

"All we know is that they've landed on the north coast and a general evacuation has been ordered. Five ships left last night for Australia crammed with men, women and children and we've been busy destroying everything of value," he pointed to the smouldering vehicles. "The *Zaanfontein* is the last ship out of here; she's waiting for the last evacuees. She'll be sailing tonight or maybe first thing in the morning," he gave Richard a searching look. "Is it possible you could escort her?"

"I don't know. If Admiral Doorman's lost and most of his fleet with him, I need to find out now who is my boss!"

He watched the Harbourmaster go and sent for the P.O. Tel. "Make a signal to Admiral Combined Striking Force with copies to *Exeter* and *N.O.I.C.** Ceylon. Make it Secret and Urgent. Text begins; Understand cruisers *De Ruyter, Java, Perth Houston* and destroyers *Jupiter, Energetic, Kortenaar* and possibly others have been sunk by Japanese forces and that Admiral Doorman has been lost. Am refuelling at Tjilatjap and have been asked to escort merchant ship *Zaanfontein* now loading with evacuees for Fremantle, Australia. Request instructions."

He watched the P.O. Tel depart and wondered if anyone would answer his signal. And if someone did, who would it be? Might it be *Exeter*? But that seemed unlikely; she'd been badly damaged and for all he knew she could have been sunk too. Could it be N.O.I.C. Ceylon? His heart lifted. Surely, he'd tell him to make for Trinco! In his mind's eye he saw his beloved Trudi, her face smiling, and her arms open waiting to embrace him. Wouldn't it be wonderful to see her again! Yes, he assured himself, they'd tell him to rejoin whatever was left of the Navy in Trincomalee.

He waited anxiously for a reply. It was no good telling the others; he'd let them have a *make and mend**; it could be the last sleep they'd have for some time! When he knew his orders, he'd tell them. He set off for his cabin, thinking happily about Trinco; then realised he was making for his old cabin, the First Lieutenant's! He turned he was Captain now! Reaching his new cabin, he treated himself to a shave, a wash and some clean clothes. Then hearing explosions, he rushed to the bridge. Pilot was there working on his charts. "They've just blown them up," he pointed to two tugs burning fiercely on the other side of the harbour. "And there are more lorrics burning over there."

They were watching the fires when the P.O. Tel arrived with the signal. Eagerly he read it.

"From N.O.I.C. Ceylon to *Strongbow*," he read:

"Until further orders you are under my command. You are to escort *Zaanfontein* and any other evacuation ships from Tjilatjap to Fremantle. I wish you the best of luck."

"Oh!" he muttered. His hopes had been cruelly dashed. Would he ever see her again? He wanted to sob, to cry out, to hide, to escape from this merciless war. But somehow he controlled himself and put on a brave face.

"Well, Pilot, we're off to the bright lights of Fremantle. Get to work on your charts. We'll be escorting the good ship *Zaanfontein* but keep it to yourself for the moment. I'll tell the ship's company later." With that he left and stepping ashore made his way to the Harbourmaster's office.

Chapter 19

· · · · · · · · · · · · · · · · · ·

He'd arrived on the bridge at dawn action stations to find the Officer of the Watch busy receiving reports from men closing up. Pilot was shooting morning stars. Hopefully his fix would confirm their estimated position, some two hundred miles south of Tjilatjap. As the hubbub eased Richard heard the familiar ping of the asdics and glancing astern saw the *Zaanfontein* following nicely in his wake. They'd been at sea for ten hours now, yet it seemed only a moment ago that he'd gone to tell the Harbourmaster he would escort the *Zaanfontein* to Australia. Together they'd boarded the Dutch ship to meet the Master, Captain Adriaan Van Kempen a burly Dutchman, who told him his ship normally sailed with a crew of thirty and a maximum of eleven passengers, but that now he had over eight hundred souls onboard.

"De ship is full, but still dey come!" He'd shrugged his shoulders. "Maybe vee can take another five hundred, but dey'll have to sleep in number four hold, that's de only empty space vee have below decks. But before vee talk anymore you must have a glass of bols!" He reached for the genever and poured out three large measures and passing them their glasses, he raised his.

"To Fremantle!" He took a swig then added "Und a safe passage, eh?"

As the spirit warmed him, Richard surveyed the large well-furnished cabin with its overhead fan revolving slowly and its windscoops pulling a cool breeze through the portholes. What luxury; the Master's quarters were three times as big as *Strongbow's* wardroom and his own cabin was only half the size of Captain Van Kempen's sleeping cabin! He'd enquired about her speed and propulsion.

"Vee 'ave two diesel engines and can do twenty-four knots, but vee usually cruise at twenty," he was told.

"Good," he'd replied, and they'd agreed that the *Zaanfontein* would follow in the wake of the *Strongbow* at twenty knots. They'd also discussed what they would do if they met the enemy.

"If we detect a submarine, I'll hoist flag Sugar," he'd said. "Then please stop following me and alter ninety degrees to port or starboard to keep clear, while I hunt the submarine. Go the opposite way to me please. I will signal instructions if necessary. If we meet a warship, I'll hoist flag William and again please stop following me, turn away from the enemy and get clear at full speed. If I lay a smoke screen, please hide behind it."

The Dutchman had nodded, "Ya, ya," then added "If aircraft attack vee vill shoot vith our guns, vee 'ave four and vee know 'ow to use dem."

Loud explosions had interrupted their discussions. "That's the Army destroying the cranes," the Harbourmaster had told them. "We won't need them anymore! We're the last ship out of Tjilatjap! Soon they'll be blowing up the oil tanks and the last two tugs." He'd looked at Captain Van Kempen, "You'll have to leave without tugs, OK?" The Dutchman had grinned. "Ya, ya, OK, but you'll be my Harbour Pilot, eh?" The Harbourmaster had nodded his agreement and hearing more explosions, they'd gone to the bridge wing and saw smoke and flames belching from the oil depot.

"When will the demolition party finish?" Richard had asked.

The Harbourmaster had shrugged his shoulders, "In two or three hours I expect, then as soon as they're onboard, we can leave."

"Good, then with your agreement, I propose we leave half an hour before sunset. That'll give us ten hours of darkness to cover our departure, so hopefully we'll be well clear before the Japs find we've gone!"

His proposal had been accepted, and so with the sun about to set, and with her crew at action stations, *Strongbow* had slipped and a few minutes later he'd seen *Zaanfontein* leave the jetty and take up her position astern and follow in his wake. He'd taken a final look at the port. The oil tanks were ablaze and above the flames a huge column of black smoke rose into the sky; the demolition party had done a good job!

Now he scanned the sea horizon. He'd told everyone on the bridge to keep their eyes peeled, that whatever they saw must be presumed hostile, until proved otherwise. But they saw nothing except the sun setting in a glorious red sky. Then without a moon it was reassuringly dark, and he'd given orders to revert to cruising stations. It was important that everyone had as much rest as possible. Tomorrow, he feared would be a fine day with clear skies and good visibility, like that happy day he'd enjoyed with his beloved Trudi at Mount Lavinia. For a moment he revelled in those happy memories, but a clear sunny day tomorrow was the last thing he wanted now! He prayed for low clouds to protect the two ships from enemy eyes.

"Indeed Lord," he added, "a good thick fog would be more than welcome."

That night he'd managed to snatch a few hours' sleep, but before sunrise he was on the bridge again. The Officer of the Watch welcomed him with some ki. "Just about to sound Dawn Action Stations, sir," he said as he pressed the Alarm bell. Thanking him, Richard scanned the sea carefully, but there was nothing to be seen, nothing except *Zaanfontein* following dutifully in his wake. And listening to the monotonous transmissions of the Asdics, he could hear no answering ping, no submarine; it seemed they had the sea all to themselves. He sipped his ki gratefully, wondering how long this happy state of affairs would last. Already the sun's yellow disc was climbing over the horizon and despite his prayer a clear day with excellent visibility would soon be upon them.

He sat on the Captain's chair, his chair now. He settled himself more easily and felt in his pocket. He pulled out the cigarette case. It was Henry Newcombe's. He'd taken it from his body. One day he hoped to give it to his widow. He opened it. The cigarettes were still there, held neatly in line by that yellow elastic. He counted seven, seven "Senior Service", the brand he'd always smoked. He could see him now, slowly tapping his unlit cigarette on the case as he pondered some problem! "I could really do with some guidance, sir," he muttered. "What would you do?"

Then as if Henry Newcombe was there to advise him, he'd reconsidered his plans for the threats he might face. It was a useful exercise; it had made him see the dangers more clearly and had helped him revise his plans.

"Thank you, sir," he muttered. He felt a little more confident!

It seemed Lady Luck was sailing with them, for the sea had remained steadfastly empty all day and when the first red tinges in the western sky foretold the safety of darkness, he felt thankful and relieved. But then he heard the cry he'd been dreading.

"Aircraft Red six oh, low."

All eyes scanned the firmament. It was difficult to find it, but then he saw it on the port quarter.

"Sound Action Stations," he ordered. "It has to be a Jap." Anxiously they watched it approach. Now they had a better view. It was a flying boat with four engines.

He leant over the bridge and shouted to 'A' gun. "Can you see that flying boat?" The Gunner assured him he could.

"Well get all guns on it and shoot the bloody thing down!"

The plane was circling them, clearly busy reporting their position. Then it altered towards them. "Port thirty," he ordered, "Bring her round Andrew, and keep the Jap thirty degrees on our port bow." He wanted to present a difficult target, yet allow all guns to bear. He glanced astern; *Zaanfontein* was obediently altering to follow in his wake. 'A' gun opened fire, followed quickly by 'Y' then 'B' gun. Black puffs appeared in the sky as the shells exploded. They were close, but not close enough! Noise of rapid fire pummelled his eardrums; the two-pounder was firing. And looking aft he saw *Zaanfontein* was firing too. Now the Jap was on its bombing run and closing fast. He watched it carefully, then saw the bombs fall, four of them. "Port thirty," he shouted to Andrew, "Aim the ship at the aircraft." The ship had to be the narrowest target. Then all he could do was hold his breath! He never saw the bombs hit the water. Like everyone else he'd flung himself on the deck, finding whatever cover he could. Then the ship was enveloped in a wall of water. Scrambling to his feet he found all the bombs had missed. He couldn't believe it, but it was true, the ship was unharmed.

"Where's that bloody Jap?" he shouted. Then he saw it, disappearing in the darkening sky. He called the Yeoman over, "Make a signal to *Zaanfontein*. Japs know our position, course and speed so expect enemy aircraft or surface ship attack sometime tomorrow. Intend steering two four oh degrees till sunrise to try and put them off the scent. Please continue to follow in my wake."

Another peaceful night followed and at Dawn Action Stations came the welcome sight of clouds, low clouds obscuring the rising sun. "Just what we need," Richard exclaimed as he told the Officer of the Watch to resume the course for Australia. The sky was fast becoming overcast, and visibility deteriorating. Perhaps they could see four or five miles, he couldn't really tell! He wondered whether that ninety-degree alteration had fooled the Japs. He hoped it had, but whether it had or not, he couldn't do it too often, else he might not have enough fuel to reach Australia! But later as the clouds began to thin and the visibility improved, that became the least of his worries. "Keep a good lookout now," he told everyone, "We've only a few of hours of daylight left, then darkness will hide us again."

Bill the Pilot was the first to see it.

"Ship, green two oh, sir, looks like a warship."

He swung his binoculars round and saw it. It was a warship, a huge one.

"Sound Action Stations," he shouted. The enemy ship was broadside on, making no effort to close. "Full ahead both, come 90 degrees to starboard," he ordered. In the unlikely event they hadn't been seen he didn't want to get any closer. But a moment later he saw flashes and then heard the sound of gunfire.

"We've been spotted," he muttered. "Hoist flag William," he shouted. He saw the salvo fall, luckily well short. "Tell the Engine Room to make smoke and the tube's crew to standby torpedoes." Anxiously he waited for the boilers to spew forth their thick black heavy smoke. A second salvo fell, closer this time. Then with black smoke pouring from the funnels he began to lay the screen to hide the *Zaanfontein*. Laying the screen made him an easy broadside target for the Jap, but he had to maintain the course for at least two minutes. By then the screen would be about a mile long, long enough! Those two minutes seemed like two hours, but then at last he could alter course and race directly for the enemy. He told the Cox'n to *weave** fifteen degrees either side of the course. He could only hope his weaving and rapid approach would confuse the Jap. Indeed, it seemed it had for his next salvo was wide. That was comforting, but he knew the Jap would do better next time!

"All guns open fire when within range," he shouted. The enemy's shells were falling with terrifying regularity now, but thankfully behind him. He tried to estimate the range; perhaps four or five miles. 'A' gun could open fire soon, but it would be some time before he could turn to launch torpedoes. Now he could recognise his adversary. It was a heavy cruiser of the *Takao* class, armed with eight-inch guns, *eight* of them! He shuddered; just one of those shells could sink his little ship! The Jap was steering a course about ninety degrees to his own, so all his guns could bear. He was broadside on to the *Strongbow*, a perfect target for torpedoes; a perfect target if only he could survive long enough to get within launching range. Would he? The range seemed to be closing at a snail's pace, but then he heard 'A' gun firing. That cheered him, but as he watched anxiously for the fall of shot another enemy salvo fell close astern. The Jap was getting nearer now, less than a mile away. We might make it!

"Tell the Torpedo Gunner I'll be turning soon," he shouted at young Andrew. "Tell him to fire torpedoes when on target". But it would be an age before they could launch them! They'd been lucky, so far! Would they make it? At last, they were close enough. He shouted down the voicepipe, "Starboard thirty, steer two four oh degrees." Then he yelled "Fire torpedoes when ready," but his voice was lost in the blast, a huge blast that flung him onto the deck. A merciful darkness enveloped him.

Chapter 20

· · · · · · · · · · · · · · · · · · · ·

They'd heard the terrible news about the *Prince of Wales* and the *Repulse* being sunk. Had he been involved in this awful battle? Every day she waited hopefully for the post, but there was never a letter from him. She'd re-read his last one so many times! It was written on the 6th of December and all had seemed well. Now it was nearly Christmas and still there was none! Surely his ship hadn't been sunk too. If it had, wouldn't it have been reported like the others? No, she convinced herself, only those two battleships had been sunk. She sighed; there was never any good news these days. The Japanese had overrun most of Malaya and soon only the Johore Straits would stop them entering Singapore. Hong Kong was besieged, and the Americans had been hit badly too by that surprise attack on Pearl Harbour and now they were fighting the Japs in the Japs in the Philipines. She shook her head in disbelief; the whole world was at war, and everyone was frightened and terrified by the Japanese successes.

There'd been nothing from him again when the post came that morning. Catherine had sympathised and had done her best to reassure her.

"No news is good news," she'd said as she always did, but that hadn't helped, for good news would only come with a letter from Richard. Nowadays the thought of bad news tormented her. Had he been hurt? Or, her heart missed a beat, killed? But would anyone tell her? The Navy would inform his parents, they were his next of kin, but did his parents know how important their son had become to her? Had he told them they were engaged to be married? And if he had, would they remember to tell her? Did they even know her address? And if they did write, it would be ages before she knew; letters from England took so long to come! She felt thoroughly wretched; waiting for his letters had become a torture.

But she wasn't the only one to be worried. Hamish, who'd always laughed about his role in his part-time army, had been ordered to report with his company for a fortnight's exercise. Though he assured Catherine it was just another drill she like the other wives, was certain the Ceylon Planters Rifle Company would one day be mobilised to fight the Japanese. The thought of Hamish under fire was too awful to contemplate! And if he was mobilized, who would look after Jamie and her? And what about the estate? Who would manage that? When a few weeks earlier his father had seen Hamish in his soldier's uniform he'd joked,

"When you go off to war my boy, I'll come and run the estate again."

No doubt he meant well, but the thought of him doing so and living in the bungalow with her and Jamie had been quite unbearable! She'd never liked him; he was a difficult man with a quick temper, and one who believed children should be seen and not heard! Yet with Hamish away the work on the estate was becoming disorganised and without a European in charge she feared the estate would soon deteriorate.

So, when Hamish and his Rifle Company had been mobilized, his father had come and had now made himself thoroughly at home in Catherines's house. That was bad enough but with the Japanese advancing through Malaya and now invading Burma as well, life was becoming ever more frightening and uncertain. And with the men gone off to war she and Catherine, like the other planters' wives had noticed subtle changes in the attitude of the estate workers. Many were noticeably less respectful, making impertinent and derogatory comments about the Army. She'd asked the Appu if he'd heard such talk. At first, he said he'd heard nothing, but after being pressed he'd told her the workers couldn't believe how easily their Asian brothers had put the English to flight! Now many had begun to hold the English in contempt and support for Mahatma Ghandi and his efforts to win independence for India was growing.

As Christmas approached everyone did their best to put their worries behind them and make it a happy occasion for the children, but the Christmas spirit eluded the adults, especially when they learned that Hong Kong had surrendered. No-one could understand why the British and Indian armies they'd so admired were unable to stop the relentless advance of the Japanese. Before the war the Japanese soldier had been portrayed as second-rate, only fit to fight the poorly trained rabble that the Chinese called an army. But now he was being described as almost superhuman, an expert in jungle warfare and one who would rather face death than the shame of surrender. If that was so, the outlook was terrifying. Yet for Trudi, Christmas had brought her the unbelievable joy of receiving three letters from Richard; all had arrived in the same post on Christmas Eve. Hastily she opened the first. It was dated 8th December and was written from *HMS Energetic*. *HMS Energetic?* What did that mean? Had the *Strongbow* been sunk after all? Mystified, yet relieved that he was safe, she read on:

Dearest Trudi

This is a scribbled note to tell you that I am now serving in the destroyer HMS Energetic, a fine modern ship in which I'm thrilled to be the First Lieutenant. Sadly, it's only a temporary appointment as my predecessor has had to be landed for emergency medical treatment, so I am just here until he is fit enough to return to duty. We are shortly sailing for yet another patrol, so I have penned this in haste to remind you my dearest betrothed, that you are constantly in my thoughts.

A warm glow of happiness flowed through her. She read on and when she had finished, she folded the letter carefully and read the others. As she had expected they told her nothing about these mysterious patrols, but just to read his thoughts and dreams of their future together was enough. Retiring to her room she found pen and paper to tell him how relieved she'd been to hear from him again, to blame this wretched post for being so slow and unreliable and to assure him of her continued and undying love for him.

The post was to remain as irregular as ever, though they wrote constantly, their letters often arriving in batches. Richard's last came on Valentine's Day of all days, though it had been written on the 2nd of February. He told her Roger Hammond had been pronounced fit for duty again and had resumed his duties in the *Energetic*, how sad he had been to leave that modern destroyer, but that it was good to be back with his shipmates in the *Strongbow*. Trudi didn't know whether to be pleased or not, all she wanted was that his ship whichever it was, was safe. But that she feared might be a pious hope, for the war against Japan was going from worse to worse. The Americans had now been driven out of the Philippines and the Japanese had landed in the *Dutch East Indies**. Then came unbelievable news. Singapore had fallen! The *Rising Sun** now flew over the island and more than one hundred and thirty thousand British and Empire troops had been taken prisoner. As the Planters and their families digested the news of this the worst British defeat in living memory, the frightening truth struck home. The Japs were on their very doorstep; Ceylon was now in the front line! A month later this was amply confirmed when Japanese aircraft carriers swept into the Bay of Bengal sinking the elderly British carrier *Hermes* and two cruisers. Then their aircraft bombed Colombo. Fears of the Japanese invading Ceylon now began to grow, soon to be heightened, when the new Governor recommended that all European women not engaged in war-work and their children be evacuated to South Africa. Some eagerly took his advice, but Catherine and others did not. Nor did Trudi ever consider leaving; Richard and his ship might yet come to Colombo or Trincomalee!

A week or so later, when Hamish came home for a few days' leave, Catherine and Jamie rushed to greet him and in doing so collided with the postman. Grateful for an excuse to hide her envy, Trudi had rescued him and taken the mail. Again, there was nothing from Richard, but there was a letter for her, from some stranger, whose handwriting she didn't recognise, but controlling her curiosity she waited dutifully to greet Hamish. He kissed her on the cheek and asked for news of Richard, but before she could answer Jamie dragged him away, "Tell us what you've been doing, Daddy."

He told them his Company was employed on guard duties in Colombo and spoke of the damage done in the air raid; of the fires that had taken so long to extinguish. He spoke of the new airfield being built on the Racecourse and how it had proved its worth as a base for the newly arrived Hurricanes, which had shot down many of the Japanese bombers. The news reassured Catherine, who dragged Jamie away and persuaded Hamish to change out of uniform "so you'll look more like the husband I know."

With Hamish gone, Trudi excused herself and stole away to read her strange letter. Did it concern Richard? With a trembling hand she tore the envelope open. It came from the Naval Base at Trincomalee! It was written by a Paymaster Lieutenant Henry Allen. Who was he? she wondered, as she began to read:

Dear Miss Leafe

I haven't had the pleasure of meeting you but we have a mutual friend Richard, Lieutenant Richard David Hooper.

Oh, get on with it, she muttered, what are you telling me?

When we last met, he made me promise to tell you if anything happened to his ship H.M.S. Strongbow Oh my God, she cried. What's happened? *and it is with the greatest regret that I must tell you that having fought a gallant fight against overwhelming odds the Strongbow was sunk by a Japanese cruiser on Monday 2nd March. Sadly, it appears there are no survivors, but if I hear any news of Richard, I will tell you immediately.*

Benumbed she could read no further. Richard was dead! His ship sunk. The vision that had haunted her so often came again. Her beloved Richard floating face down in the sea! Through her tears she could see nothing else, only his lifeless body! How could she live without him, the only one who'd ever shown her any real love? When they were together, he made her feel alive, but without him life was empty, a mere passing of days. She felt numb, paralysed by grief and the void that lay ahead. How long she sat there she had no idea, but when she heard Jamie calling her for lunch, she'd fled. She couldn't bear to be with them, they were happy, they were together again. In her misery she wanted to slink away, to hide; to be alone. Lost in despair she wandered down the drive. A voice disturbed her misery. It was the Syce. "Do you want Acorn, Durisani?"

She nodded automatically and without seeing, watched him saddle the horse and bring him to her. In a dream she allowed him to help her mount and Acorn began to walk the route he knew so well. His motion comforted her. Gently she stroked his neck, "What can I do? How can I live without him?" No one had ever loved her before Richard. He was the only one who had ever shown her real affection and now he was no more, she'd never ever see him again! As the vision of his lifeless body floating in the sea came again, she prayed for death too. She couldn't bear the thought of living without him. She saw the road was running through woods. Could she hang herself? She saw plenty of trees, but she had no rope. As she pondered whether the reins would do, she became aware of Acorn. He was trembling violently. Then she saw the yellow eyes of a leopard. It was in the tree. Acorn shied, turned and raced the way they'd come. The leopard was close behind and Acorn was kicking with his hind legs. "God is answering my prayers," she thought. Then she was thrown.

Chapter 21

· · · · · · · · · · · · · · · · ·

"**H**amish, whatever is the estate van doing in the drive?" Catherine asked her voice full of irritation. "What does Yuvraj think he's doing?"

The van stopped by the porch and Yuvraj opened the passenger door. Then they saw her.

"It's Gertrude!" Hamish hurried to the van. "What's happened?" He helped Yuvraj bring her in.

"Gertrude, are you alright?" He saw blood in her hair and her left eye was swollen, but she said nothing.

"I found her by the side of the road, Duri. She was staggering, wandering around as if she'd had too much to drink."

"How dare you suggest Durisani Gertrude was drunk, Yuvraj," Catherine broke in angrily.

Hamish was examining her eye. "Catherine, he didn't say she was drunk and clearly, she's not. She's been in an accident, look," he lifted back her hair, "her eye's badly swollen and she's hurt her head; we'd better get her to the doctor. Did you see anything else, Yuvraj?"

"Duri, Duri." The Syce came running down the drive. "Acorn's come back without Durisani…….." his voice tailed off. "Oh! She's here, Durisani

Gertrude. Was she thrown, Duri? Something must have happened. Acorn's badly hurt, he's bleeding Duri."

"How's he been hurt? Tell me, Rakesh." The Syce said there were deep gashes on his haunches. He'd managed to calm him and staunch the bleeding, but Acorn was still very nervous. "Something must have attacked him, Duri; he must have bolted and thrown Durisani. Perhaps it was that leopard people have seen!"

"Yes, Rakish, it seems that Durisani Gertrude was thrown."

He asked her. "Is that what happened, Gertrude? Can you remember?"

Gertrude looked at him; she seemed not to have heard. "I saw Richard. I saw Richard. I saw him again," was all she said, then the happiness that had briefly lit up her face faded.

Catherine frowned. "She's obviously badly concussed. We must get her to hospital as quickly as we can. I'll find some bandages for her head."

"Good, I'll get the car; Yuvraj take me to the garage. I'll take Durisani Gertrude to the hospital."

As they drove Hamish asked Yuvraj where he'd found her.

"Just before the five milestone Duri; where the road enters the woods."

"And you say she was wandering around?"

"Yes, Duri, as I said it looked as if she was drunk."

"Did you think she was drunk?"

"Yes, at first Duri, but I soon realised she wasn't. She was dazed, she seemed confused."

"Confused? What made you think that?"

"She kept calling me Richard, Duri."

He didn't tell him she'd flung her arms around him. That his Indira had hugged him and had showered him with kisses! That she had said "Richard you're wearing your funny turban again. Is there another fancy dress ball?"

He saw the look of astonishment on Duri MacDonald's face. "What, what did she call you?"

"Richard, Duri, I don't know why!" In his mind's eye he saw Indira again. She'd kept on calling him Richard and she'd kissed him and said how wonderful it was, but he couldn't tell Duri that!

"Well, Yuvraj, it's clear she's badly concussed." He got into the car. As he engaged gear, he wound down his window. "Thank you for rescuing her. I dread to think what could have happened if you hadn't found her. You did well, Yuvraj."

Yuvrah watched the car disappear then climbed into the back of the van. As he feared there was blood on the floor. He'd not seen the blood in Indira's hair, when he'd found her, when she'd thrown her arms about him and kissed him so passionately. She'd roused him as Jasvinder never did. When he'd found them, her breasts were soft and welcoming and as he'd kissed them her hands had caressed him tenderly. He couldn't remember how they'd got into the back of the van, all he could recall was how compliant and passionate she'd been and afterwards as they'd lain together how she'd said, "Richard darling, I do love you!" It was then that he realised what he'd done. At any moment he'd expected her to scream "You're not Richard", yet she hadn't, she'd just lain there holding him closely and looking serenely happy. But as she held him, he'd wondered desperately when she would realise it was, he not Richard, who'd lain with her. But strangely she never did and somehow, he got her into the passenger seat and finding her handkerchief had wiped the blood from her bleeding forehead. Then, thanking the Gods, he'd driven off.

Satisfying his long-held desire for Indira had been veritably seismic, but as he neared the estate his exhilaration began to fade, to be replaced by a frightening realisation of the consequences. Surely, he tried to convince himself, no one could say he'd raped her; she'd been a willing partner, she'd enticed him, she'd been the instigator! But why had she called him Richard? It puzzled him. She'd called him Richard again and again! Who was this Richard, this Richard with a turban? Was it the fellow she'd gone to Colombo to meet? Whoever he was, she was obviously captivated by him. But why did she think it was Richard, not him? When she woke, when the confusion left her surely, she'd realise it hadn't been Richard. Then she'd know it could only have been him! As he drove, he'd watched her out of the corner of his eye, expecting her to come to her senses at any moment, that she'd know it was him, but she never did! She seemed completely oblivious to everything. It was as if she was sleeping, yet her eyes were open. Could it be that she hadn't been aware of him from the moment he'd found her? That she'd only seen this Richard fellow? Was she as badly concussed as Durisani Catherine suggested? Perhaps she'd never know it was him! He felt a little less worried and went to find a scrubber and a pail of water.

"Where have you been, Yuvraj Singh?" It was Jasvinder. "You're looking worried. Is something wrong?"

"No, Jasvinder dear," he smiled at her and tried to look relaxed. "It's just that I found Durisani Gertrude on the road. We think she was thrown from her horse."

"Oh! is she badly hurt?"

"Duri MacDonald is taking her to hospital. That's all I know."

Yuvraj, is that blood on your collar? Let me have a look. Yes, it is blood. Have you hurt yourself?"

She examined his neck and throat. "I can't see a cut Yuvraj. Where's the blood come from? And look there's some on this fancy turquoise turban of yours!" She scowled at him, "It's not yours is it? Is it hers? It must be hers! Yuvraj, what have you been doing?"

"What have I been doing, wife?" Anger hid his fear. "I've been rescuing Indira, I, I mean uh Durisani Gertrude. She's banged her head, so the blood must be hers!"

"Indira, Indira? Yuvraj what are you saying?"

"Wife, I said Durisani Gertrude." In a fury he strode off to find the scrubber. Now it was all the more important to get rid of the blood where they'd lain. As he scrubbed he cursed himself for that stupid mistake. He'd always called her Indira. Calling her Indira had seemed to make her his and he smirked; for a moment she had been his. But then an inner voice asked,

"What will you say if she says you raped her?" It stopped him in his tracks. "As she surely will," the voice continued. He shuddered, what could he say? Men were imprisoned for rape and if it was a white woman, it could be a life sentence! No jury would ever believe she'd consented. They'd believe he an Indian, had forced himself on this innocent white woman while she was badly concussed. But then a thought offered him hope; if she was concussed, he would say it was merely a dream of hers, a muddled fantasy about her and her lover Richard, played out in her disturbed mind. He would laugh at the absurdity of it all and swear it had never happened, that it was just a flight of fancy! He would insist he had never raped her, that all he'd done was to rescue her and bring her home. He felt better then, but he knew he must stop Jasvinder talking about the blood on his collar. He'd have to be nice to her! Perhaps tonight he'd talk about the baby she wanted so much! Yes, he'd be nice to her, try yet again for that elusive baby!

The van was clean now; he could see no more blood, except some on the passenger's seat. He'd leave that; it would be evidence to show how he'd cared for her and brought her safely home. He set to and washed the bodywork as he usually did after a long trip, then as he stood back to admire his work, he heard Jasvinder.

"What are you doing now, Yuvraj?"

"Wife, you are always impatient. I am cleaning the van. It's my job, that's what Duri Macdonald pays me to do."

She walked around it. "Where's this blood of hers, husband?"

"You want to see her blood? Here, on the passenger's seat? See for yourself!"

She peered in. "Hmph! Are you going to leave it like that – to remind you of your Indira?"

He stifled his anger. "Dearest, I shall clean it in a moment. When I've finished the bodywork; I always clean the inside last!"

She gave him a disbelieving look and turning, stormed off.

He went to fetch another pail of water and saw the Rover returning.

"How is Durisani?" he asked.

"She's safely in hospital now. They've dressed her head and the bleeding has stopped. The doctor says she's badly concussed, that's why she doesn't remember what happened. But he tells me she'll be OK in a week or so."

"That's good Duri, very good."

"I see you've been cleaning the van. Was there much blood?"

"There's some in the cab Duri, on the passenger seat. I was about to clean it when you arrived." Yuvraj opened the door for him to see.

"Oh yes, I see. Well leave it now. Get in the car and show me where you found her. I'll drive."

He drove along the road to Nuwara Eliya. "You said you found her near the five milestone, Yuvraj?"

"Yes, Sahib, where the road goes through the woods."

"Well keep your eyes peeled and tell me where you found her."

He drove on slowly. There was little traffic about, only a few bullock carts and an occasional car. The fivemilestone appeared and disappeared, but Yuvraj said nothing. After a further mile or so Hamish stopped and turned the car. The day was drawing in, it would soon be dark.

"You're sure it was the five milestone?"

"Yes Duri, it must have been before the five milestone. I passed it just as I drove off with her."

"Well. Yuvraj, keep your eyes open, I'll drive slowly." A few minutes later came the cry Hamish was waiting for.

"Duri, it's here I think."

They saw the tall vegetation had been flattened, as if trampled on and on the verge were the undoubted marks of a tyre.

"It could be here," Hamish muttered. Walking back along the way they'd come he saw some broken branches. He inspected them carefully; it looked as if they'd been broken recently. He also saw the tree nearby had lost some of its lower branches. Another had lost some bark and looking closely he found blood. This must be the place. "Yuvraj," he called. "It looks as if she hit this tree. Find a stone or something to mark it."

He left Yuvraj hunting for a stone and wandered back searching for any signs of Acorn bolting. He counted his steps as he went, "Thirteen, fourteen, fifteen, sixteen." Then he saw the verge had been damaged. A deep jagged groove had been cut into it. "That could have been made by the hoof of a horse bolting," he muttered. Was that the mark of Acorn's hoof? They and the wound on Acorn's haunches seemed to indicate that the horse had indeed been attacked and had thrown Gertrude. If that was so, it seemed Yuvraj was the innocent rescuer.

"Well done, Yuvraj, we've seen enough. Let's go home, you drive."

They went home, the car's headlights piloting them through the darkening woods. Catherine met him when he arrived. She held out a piece of paper.

"Come and have a chota peg while I read you this." He sighed, "I need a burra peg!" She led him onto the veranda where he threw himself into his favourite chair.

"First let me tell you what I've discovered." he insisted. "Then we can talk about your piece of paper."

When he'd finished, he sipped his whisky and said "I'm sure that leopard Rakesh was talking about made Acorn bolt and throw Gertrude. Then she must have struck her head on the tree where I saw blood."

Catherine agreed.

"That seems very likely. No doubt she'll tell us exactly what happened when she's better. But now let me tell you about this." She unfolded the paper. "When I returned from the hospital, I went to her room to pack some things for her and found this. It's a letter, a private letter. I didn't want to read it at first, but then I saw it was from the Navy, the Navy at Trincomalee. Well, poor Gertrude hasn't had a letter from Richard for weeks and I wondered if it could be about him. So, I read it. Hamish it's terrible news! His ship's been sunk. The letter says there are no survivors. Here read it for yourself."

Hurriedly he read it. Then he read it again more slowly.

"Poor Gertrude, what are we going to do? She was so happy, so blissfully happy on her way to see him in Colombo. Oh poor girl! I suppose that's why she wanted to get away from us, why she never came to lunch."

Ten days later Trudi was ready to come home. Hamish had returned to Colombo to re-join the Planter's Company, so Yuvraj drove Catherine to the hospital.

Trudi emerged pale and drawn and showed no reaction as Catherine affectionately hugged and kissed her. To Yuvraj's great relief she seemed unaware of his presence.

"Gertrude dear, the Doctor says you should take things easily for a week or two," Catherine reminded her.

"Yes, Catherine, but I must keep myself busy otherwise oh! I don't know, I'll just wallow in my misery." She reached hastily for her handkerchief. "I just don't know how I can live without Richard." She wiped away her tears. "You know his ship has been sunk with all hands?"

Trudi remained distraught and withdrawn over the coming months. Only Jamie, it seemed could lift the dark cloud that hung over her. When she was not with him, she kept to herself, never again wanting to ride Acorn and whenever Catherine suggested they went to the club for a game of tennis she would always politely decline. Nor despite the most delicate and tactful questioning would she reveal what had happened that day when Yuvraj had found her wandering!

It was Jamie who noticed it first. "

Mummy," he said, "You're always telling me I mustn't be greedy, that I mustn't have too much pudding or I'll get fat!" She'd laughed "Jamie, you're not getting fat!"

"No." he replied. "But Miss Gertrude is. Do you think she's being greedy?"

"Jamie, Miss Gertrude's not greedy or fat. You're just imagining it!"

Yet he was right! She'd noticed it too! As the weeks passed her enquiring eyes had seen Gertrude's figure becoming ever more round. Her father-in law had too.

"That girl Gertrude's getting fatter by the day," he'd said as he sipped his whisky. "She ain't pregnant, is she?" Catherine had made some non-committal reply, but he'd continued "The girl's in the family way for sure! Who's the father d'you think?"

Both were mystified. Neither could imagine how Gertrude, still grieving over the loss of her Richard, could have found a man! After all she'd given up riding Acorn and wouldn't even go to the club for a game of tennis! It seemed utterly impossible, yet to everyone's eyes there could be no doubt, she was definitely pregnant. Even Yuvraj to his horror, knew. "Her belly's bigger than Jasvinder's!" he muttered. He could see trouble brewing! Now that Jasvinder was at last pregnant, he hoped it had taken her mind off Indira. But when Jasvinder found that Indira was pregnant too, he knew there'd be a terrible scene. He could hear her now, 'Is that your bastard child your Indira is carrying?' and then the screams and tantrums would follow! And then the thought of being charged with rape returned to haunt him!

But though Trudi seemed unaware of the interest her ever growing belly was rousing, Catherine noticed a gradual transformation coming over her. Slowly her depression and listlessness waned and occasionally she could be seen to smile as if she was enjoying some private dream. Mystified by the absence of her monthly period, Trudi had herself begun to wonder if her rounded stomach could be nurturing a new life. She might have missed two periods, she couldn't be sure. After that accident her memory still played tricks with her! But one morning when she'd felt sick and had put it down to something she'd eaten the night before, she'd had her doubts! And when the sickness returned the next day, she'd begun to wonder whether it could be morning sickness! Then as she surveyed her wardrobe for a loose-,fitting dress, she'd finally accepted that she was indeed pregnant.

'But," she asked herself, "Who is the father? I'm no Mary, this can't be an immaculate conception; a woman needs a man! How, how have I become pregnant?"

It baffled her, it was inexplicable, an enigma. Richard was the only man she'd ever slept with and that was last August, nine months ago! It couldn't be him. Who else could it be? Yet strangely the thought of bearing a child somehow comforted her. After her repeated, but unanswered pleas to the Almighty to let her die and be with Richard, she now began to feel she had some reason to live. If only Richard could be the father! That would be truly wonderful, but it couldn't be! He was dead, lost at sea. Yet that strange dream when she saw her beloved Richard, kept recurring, again and again and he was always wearing that funny turquoise turban he wore for that fancy dress ball. And he was as handsome as ever and though it was only a dream she could vividly remember the tickle of his beard as they kissed and that ecstatic moment when their bodies had become one. That dream seemed as real as any moment they'd shared in Colombo! As she prayed the dream would never fade, a movement within her brought the realisation that she must now be in the fourth month of her pregnancy. Four months! The coincidence was uncanny! Four months ago, Acorn had thrown her. Four months ago, she'd first had that dreamlike experience of being with him, with him wearing that turquoise turban of his! But surely Richard couldn't be the father? She shook her head that would be impossible. It had only been a dream! But how lovely it would be if he was the father! As she thought of holding the child in her arms, an inner voice whispered, "It could be Richard's". It came again but her logical brain dismissed it; it was impossible. But that small voice would not be stilled. "Listen to your heart not your head," it seemed to urge.

Now that Gertrude's pregnancy was beyond dispute Catherine could control her curiosity no longer. She asked as tactfully as she could, who the father was, but Gertrude rebuffed her. "Catherine, I cannot tell you, "That was all she'd said! Her reply had left her dumbfounded! When asked why, Gertrude had simply smiled and left! That evening, when she'd told her father-in-law what Gertrude had said neither could understand why she was being so secretive. Yet again they discussed who might be the father. None of the men they knew seemed likely candidates; indeed, many of them had been away serving in the Planters Company and had been for some time! Her father-in-law had snorted,

"It's some dark horse. Some fellow we don't know. Someone she's ashamed of. She ain't been off the estate on her own lately, has she?"

"No Father, not since she returned from that accident of hers. I've told you; she's always been with me or Jamie."

"That accident of hers, that must have been about four months ago?"

"Yes, it was. Why do you ask?"

"Didn't that self-important Sikh driver of yours bring her home?"

"Yes, Father. What are you suggesting?"

"Well you say he brought her home four months ago and you tell me she's four months pregnant! It makes you think!"

"Father, you're not suggesting she's been having an affair with Yuvraj Singh?"

"No, though I suppose it could be possible. Cynthia de Beaufort-Laurence produced after a liaison with one of her Tamil servants!" He chuckled, "It was hushed up of course, but nonetheless we all knew!"

"Father, I just can't see Gertrude doing a thing like that!"

"Perhaps not, but she was badly concussed when he found her wasn't she?"

"Yes."

"Well, it's possible he raped her, isn't it?"

"Oh! Father how awful! But surely Gertrude would have told us!"

Her father-in-law had shrugged his shoulders. Women always mystified him. They were illogical creatures ruled by their emotions! He said no more and closed the conversation by calling for another peg of whisky.

Her father-in-law's suggestion had alarmed Catherine and made her more reticent about asking Gertrude who was the baby's father. And Gertrude seemed to show none of the signs one might expect of a rape victim, indeed she was growing ever more content, one could say serene!

Trudi was indeed happy, living in her own make-believe world and only rarely disturbed by the impossibility of Richard being the father. When that happened, she would take comfort in the whispered message that told her to listen to her heart not her head.

The doctor having confirmed that she was pregnant, had foreseen a difficult birth.

"You should come to hospital for the delivery," he'd said and had added,

"Don't delay. Come as soon as the labour pains begin."

Catherine was with her when the birth appeared imminent and had immediately sent for the car. When the sound of wheels on the gravel could be heard, she led Gertrude out onto the porch. Trudi saw the car, its rear door held open by Yuvraj. She gasped, how he reminded her of her beloved Richard, with that beard of his and that turban, that turquoise turban. The likeness had startled her, but then the baby moved; it was becoming more and more impatient!

Chapter 22

"It's not Richard's," she shrieked, her face contorted with grief. "It's not his. You've made a mistake. It's not mine!"

The midwife had handed her the infant, wrapped in clean white linen.

"Here he is, Durisani; a beautiful boy with lovely blue eyes!" She'd expected Durisani's face to light up with joy as all mothers' did when they first saw their newborn baby. But a look of horror had spread across hers and she'd shrieked "It's not Richard's," and she'd resolutely refused to hold it or have anything to do with it. Not knowing what to do, she'd taken the baby away to tell the doctor. He'd been surprised to find her still carrying the infant, but he'd listened carefully to all she told him.

"Well," he stroked his chin. "There's been no mistake. You know as well as I do, it's hers. Wait a while then take it back again. When she's calmed down she'll accept it, I'm sure."

When Catherine had arrived an hour later the doctor had asked to see her.

"Mrs MacPherson, Miss Leafe has had a difficult delivery, but she's been blessed with a perfectly healthy boy. However, before you see her, I must tell you she's in a very agitated state and is refusing to have anything to do with the child. She keeps saying there's been a mistake, that it's the wrong child!

But I can assure you there's been no mistake; it most certainly is hers, it's the only child born in the hospital this week! She keeps saying it's not Richard's. Have you any idea why she's behaving like this? Who is this, Richard?"

Catherine told him all she knew about Richard, that he and Gertrude were engaged to be married, that he was in the Navy and had been killed almost a year ago when his ship was sunk by the Japanese.

"Oh! I am sorry. But if he died a year ago, he can't possibly be the father; yet for some reason she seems to think he is!"

Catherine agreed "Yes, we that is my father-in-law and I have known all along that it couldn't possibly be Richard's, but whenever we've asked her who the father is, she'd never tell us!"

"Well Mrs MacPherson please come and see the child. I expect like me you'll be surprised by his colour. He's not pink as one might have expected! He's tawny, definitely tawny; it makes one think his father could be Indian. But tell me what you think."

When she eased the shawl back from the child's face, she'd gasped. There was no doubt, no doubt at all, the child was decidedly tawny, and had jet black hair!

"Yes," she nodded, "He is tawny, very tawny! I'd always thought the father would be one of the young Englishmen learning his trade on the local tea estates but clearly, I was wrong!" She frowned. "But anyway, I just can't think how she became pregnant. Poor Gertrude, she was heartbroken, utterly devastated when she heard of Richard's death and withdrew into a world of her own. She hardly ever left the bungalow and then never alone. So how she could have found a man? How did she become pregnant?"

"Well she did and surely she must know who the father is."

"Maybe, but if it is an Indian, perhaps she's ashamed to name him."

When Gertrude came home, the father's identity still remained a mystery. Whenever Gertrude was asked to name the father, she would become agitated and would adamantly refuse to answer. Nor would she accept the child as hers and would have nothing to do with him. So,

Catherine was left to care for him until one of the new mothers on the estate could be found to act as wet nurse.

Gertrude's rejection of her child clearly irritated Catherine's father-in-law. He became ever more short-tempered.

"Catherine, what's wrong with the girl? He asked angrily over his whisky. "She knows as well as you and I, that this Richard fellow can't possibly be the father. It must be some dark horse, some fellow who's found her fancy!"

"But when Father? As I've told you before, since Richard's death she's rarely left the house, and then always with me."

"Umph; are you sure?"

"Yes Father. She wouldn't even ride Acorn again after that accident!"

"Accident? Oh! That's right. She was thrown by her horse and rescued by that self-important Sikh driver of yours, wasn't she? "

"Yes."

"When was that?"

"Oh! Let me see now. It was some time ago, in March, yes early March. That would be uh, nine months ago! Nine months! Surely it couldn't have happened then! She'd been riding alone; there was no man with her," then she hesitated, "except of course Yuvraj, but she certainly wouldn't have had anything to do with him! All he did, poor man, was to find her badly concussed and bring her home!"

"Mm, that was nine months ago?"

"Yes."

"And she ain't been out of the bungalow on her own since then?"

"No, Father, you know as well as I do how withdrawn she's been and how I had the greatest difficulty in persuading her even to come out with me!"

Umph!" He lapsed into silence. What, he asked himself, was the matter with that stupid girl?

With an angry father-in-law and a withdrawn Gertrude, the atmosphere was becoming increasingly tense and one evening when Gertrude had retired, Catherine's father-in-law had said "Catherine, it's got to be that damned Sikh driver. He found her, didn't he?"

"Yes, I told you so."

He sipped his whisky. "Didn't he say he found her wandering around not knowing where she was or what she was doing?"

"Yes, Father."

"Catherine, I reckon it's him! He got her into the back of his van and raped her, that's what happened. Never did like the man, never felt he could be trusted!"

Father, I can't believe that! Only a fiend would rape a girl as badly injured as Gertrude!" The possibility horrified her. "But, the date's right, I must admit! I suppose it's possible, but if he did rape her, why didn't Gertrude tell us?"

"Yes, Catherine, that's strange, but you said she was badly concussed! Isn't it possible she didn't know what was happening? If she was badly concussed, she could have thought it was some sort of dream."

"Father, do you really think so?"

"Well, it's possible. Else why didn't she accuse him of raping her?"

"I don't know, I just don't know, but I suppose you could be right!" She looked at him thoughtfully. "Come to think of it, I do remember how happy she seemed to be when I bandaged her head. She kept on muttering 'I saw Richard'."

"How d'you mean?"

"Well, when we asked her what had happened, she never told us. She just kept saying she'd seen Richard! We didn't understand what she meant. I was busy dealing with her injury, and I thought she was probably hallucinating."

Suddenly it all seemed to make sense. It must have been Yuvraj. He'd raped her, he was the father!

The next morning father-in-law sent for him.

"Yuvraj Singh, we know you raped Durisani Gertrude; that you found her wandering around after her accident and raped her in your van. Admit it."

Yuvraj hotly denied the accusation, but father-in-law refused to accept his plea of innocence. "I want you, your wife and your bastard son off this estate, or Durisani Gertrude will charge you with rape. I want you gone by this time tomorrow. Do you understand?"

Fear of being found out had haunted Yuvraj ever since that fateful day. Now somehow the Duri knew and was threatening to bring charges unless he went! He had no choice, he must go, otherwise trial and imprisonment beckoned!

The Appu, who happened to be in the passageway, had happily heard the Duri dismissing his adversary and news of Yuvraj's imminent departure with the child became known in the servant's quarters even before her father-in-law had found Catherine. When he did, she could tell something serious was afoot.

"I sent for that scoundrel Yuvraj," he said. "I told him I knew he'd raped Durisani Gertrude. He denied it of course, but when I threatened to charge him with rape unless he, his wife and his bastard child left the estate, he knew I meant business. So I told him to be gone by this time tomorrow and good riddance!" He paused. "I've done my bit, now you tell Gertrude. If she doesn't snap out of her misery soon, she'll

Though the unexpected turn of events had taken her breath away, it was not unwelcome news! She too was now convinced that Gertrude had been raped by Yuvraj and his departure with the child was good tidings! Yet she had the task of telling her! But how? If one merely mentioned the child there was always a scene! Now she had to tell her she knew she'd been raped and that Yuvraj was the father of her son. She dreaded telling her! All she could hope was that Gertrude would be pleased to hear Yuvraj had been dismissed and that he was taking the child with him!

Catherine went to find her. She was in her room. Expecting a tantrum, she told her as tactfully as she could, but to her astonishment Gertrude seemed strangely unmoved.

"Catherine," she said, "when I read that letter telling me Richard's ship had been sunk and that there were no survivors, there seemed no point in living! All I wanted to do was to die, to be with him in whatever world we find ourselves when we depart this life. All I could think of was how to kill myself. When I saw the leopard's yellow eyes, I thought it was the hand of Providence! Then I was thrown, and I remember nothing more, except seeing Richard, my beloved Richard with his beard and wearing the turban he wore for the fancy dress ball in the *Ranpura*. Catherine, it was truly wonderful! Richard and I were together again in what I took to be the next world. Oh! We were so happy! We made love. It was beautiful!" She paused as if still lost in her dream; then she sighed. "I've clung to that magic moment ever since. It makes me feel Richard is near."

Catherine reached for her hand. "Oh you poor dear," she mumbled.

Trudi smiled ruefully. "But it wasn't a magic moment, was it? Now I realise I was raped! While I was concussed Yuvraj took advantage of me. That's why I'll never accept his child as mine!"

"But Gertrude dear, why didn't you accuse him?"

"Well Catherine, I suppose I wanted to believe it was Richard who had made love to me. And when I found I was pregnant I wanted the baby to be Richard's! I know you'll think me stupid, and I really knew it couldn't be his, but it was comforting to live in my happy dream world. But that world came to end when I saw that dark skinned baby!"

Catherine squeezed her hand. "Well, Gertrude dear, Yuvraj and his son will be gone tomorrow."

Trudi nodded. "Good, I never want to see him or his child again."

"Well Gertrude, there's no reason now why you ever should."

"No, no reason at all. But Catherine dear, I've been very foolish, and I've given you so much trouble! I expect you'll be glad to see the back of me too!"

Chapter 23

It was evening, the end of his first day as a prisoner of war in Rangoon. The terrible stories the English told about the way the Japanese treated their prisoners of war had frightened him, but so far, he'd been treated reasonably well. Well, he'd had to carry ammunition boxes for miles over those jungle clad hills and they'd been back-breakingly heavy, but it could have been worse. He was just thankful to be alive, thankful he'd not been ripped open by that bayonet!

When he'd joined his father-in-law's old regiment, he'd never imagined anything could be as terrifying as that fight in the jungle. Then the war had seemed remote, and he'd been pleased to wear the uniform of the First Sikh Rifles! When his father-in-law had seen him in his smart regimental uniform, he'd said he was proud of him and had added "Sepoy Yuvraj Singh, now you look a man." But almost as soon as he'd put his smart uniform on he was packing it away and donning fatigues and learning how to march, to fire a rifle and use a bayonet. In April, only three months after he'd enlisted, his company had been sent to Burma, to North Arakan and within a fortnight, though depleted by malaria and dysentery, they'd been sent to hill 275 to defend the town of Buthidaung in the valley below.

Hill 275 was covered with jungle, a thick mass of vegetation which provided good cover for them, but also for the enemy! That scared them, but the Halvidar had assured them the Japs would be heard as they pushed through the undergrowth and he insisted they kept their ears cocked, remaining silent at all times, and passing all reports and orders by whisper. But the jungle was far from silent. There were always strange noises; the call of a bird, the grunt of an animal, the rustling of leaves or the shaking of a branch and no one could tell whether it was the Japs or an animal! They'd been on edge always, often alarmed and unnerved. From the very first day he'd hated the jungle, he'd never liked being hemmed in; he'd always lived on the plains, the wide flat plains of the Punjab or on the tea clad hills of Ceylon. There you could feel the breeze and see for miles.

But as time passed, they'd begun to doubt whether the Japs would penetrate the jungle and having laid a barbed wire barrier, they'd felt more secure. Then boredom had set in, and they'd begun to relax, assuring each other that the Japs would attack along the valley. But one night their assurance had been undermined by the unmistakable sounds of rifle and machine gun fire and the bark of a field gun. It came from the south, but no one could tell whether it was from the hills or the valley below. Anxiously they'd listened for the tell-tale rustling of the undergrowth, their eyes scanning the darkness for any movement. Then like the wailing of some evil banshee, the screaming, the shrieking, the howling had begun. They'd been warned the Japanese did this to frighten and confuse their enemy. Well, it had certainly terrified him. With his heart thumping, he'd stood to with his bayonet fixed and his rifle at the ready. Then he'd seen dim figures flitting from tree to tree, the nearest only three away. He'd taken cover behind a tree himself and as the crouching figure ran towards it, he'd stepped out bayonet at the ready. With his right elbow tucked against his hip he'd held his rifle steady, and the Jap had impaled himself on the bayonet. With frightened sweaty hands he'd pulled it out and leaving the Jap to die had moved to a tree next to *Jemandar** Madesh Singh. He pistol in hand, was firing at another Jap. But he missed and fell as the bayonet pierced him. In the fierce hand to hand fighting that followed, he'd fired his rifle point blank at another Jap, thus saving himself from the bayonet.

Then the fighting seemed to move on, and he was alone, one of the lucky ones still alive. But as he breathed a sigh of relief, a Jap had suddenly emerged with his bayonet at the ready. A cold spasm of fear had run through him, as cold as the steel of the bayonet that was about to be driven into his belly. Panicking, he'd thrown his rifle down and had jerked both hands above his head. The Jap stopped and leering at him prodded his chest with the point of his bayonet. He yelled. "You dog, you surrender, ka?" He'd nodded vigorously, "Yes, yes, ka, ka, I surrender!" Thrown to the ground, his hands quickly bound behind his back, he was kicked in the stomach. Then he was motioned to stand up and encouraged by the bayonet, had been marched off. Soon he'd been joined by another of his company, bound and terrified as he. Not allowed to talk, they'd sat together wondering what, would be their fate.

Then one at a time they'd been led off to be interrogated about the defences of Buthidaung, how many men were there and where they were positioned. He'd told them he couldn't answer such questions; he was only a Sepoy. But they hadn't believed him, and he'd been punched and kicked all the more. With his mouth bleeding and his eyes swollen, it seemed the beating would never cease. But then the officer had told his assailant to stop and pointing to his turban had said "You Sikh, ka?" When he'd hastily replied, "Yes, yes, ka, ka," the officer had said through the interpreter, "You join your fellow Indians who fight with us to kill the English, yes?" Without thinking he'd said "Yes, yes, ka, ka," again, and the questions and the beating had stopped. Then he'd been taken away.

The next morning with other prisoners, he'd been made to trek through the jungle and over the hills to the railway in the valley below to bring ammunition and supplies back to the front. For a whole week they'd done this, fed only on rice and watery gruel. The work was exhausting and whenever he or any of the other prisoners had slowed down the guards would shout "hurry, hurry" and beat him with their rifles. Finally, when the Japs had captured Buthidaung and supplies could be brought up the valley by road, he and his fellow prisoners, there were no English among them, had been marched back to the railway and sent to Rangoon.

Now sitting in the prison compound, he thought of Jasvinder. He remembered her fury when he'd told her the new Duri had sacked him. She'd told him he'd always been too familiar with Duri MacPherson, and she'd always known the Durisani had never liked him.

"So," she'd asked him, "what did you do to upset the new Duri?"

When he'd said he'd done nothing, that the new Duri had dismissed him because he was prejudiced and disliked all Sikhs, she hadn't believed a word. And when he'd denied doing anything to annoy him, she'd ridiculed him! But that was nothing like the scene she'd made, when he'd told her they had to take Durisani Gertrude's child Sandeep, with them.

"Why? Why should we?" she'd screamed. Then suddenly understanding, she'd scowled, "Ah! He's your child, isn't he? Your child by that unchaste woman Durisani Gertrude, she who vaunts her naked legs and her shapely breasts! So, she's rejected your child, has she? And now you expect me to take it!"

She'd said nothing would make her have the child and had threatened to leave him and take Dharas their daughter, with her. It had been a terrible row! But he'd prevailed; he'd known she'd never leave him for she could see, like him, that though he may no longer have any affection for her, at least he fed her! So, from then on, they'd lived together yet apart, he promising, never to be unfaithful again and she accepting Sandeep with bad grace and finally agreeing after much argument that he should be passed off as the twin brother of Dharas.

When they'd arrived at her father's house, he had been startled and had asked endless questions. "Why had he left that good job in Ceylon and why did they now have two children, when he understood God had blessed them with only one?"

He'd told his father-in-law that Duri MacPherson was deeply prejudiced against all Sikhs and had dismissed him unfairly. As for the children, he admitted they'd only expected the one, but he said that to their great surprise, Jasvinder had produced twins!

Father-in-Law had seemed unconvinced; Sandeep's blue eyes troubled him. "Never seen a Sikh with blue eyes before," he kept saying, but then he began to sympathise with him. "It's time we got rid of the arrogant English," he'd declared. "It's time India became independent." Then he'd put an arm around him. "Yuvraj, my son, I can't feed another four mouths on my Army pension. You must find work."

But work as a driver had been hard to find. There were plenty of simple labourer's jobs, but they weren't for him and so one day he'd joined his father-in-law's old regiment and after swearing an oath of loyalty to the King Emperor, had become a Sepoy in the 1ˢᵗ Sikh Rifles.

Now as he climbed onto his prison bunk and settled on the bare boards he wondered if he'd ever see Jasvinder again. Though she never roused him, he had to admit she'd been a good wife. Yes, he had treated her badly, but perhaps one day she'd forgive him. He sighed, the night was hot and sultry; it was difficult to sleep.

When morning came it was a relief and he and the other prisoners were marched off to the exercise yard. There were twenty of them, four others from his company and some from the Punjab and Rajput Regiments. All were Indians, there were no English. He studied the Halvidar as he began to speak. His regimental badges were strange, unlike any he'd seen before, but he seemed friendly enough, asking them about their families and what part of India they came from. He told them he'd been captured in Malaya, but when he said he'd served in the 17ᵗʰ Dogra Regiment, he like the others had been mystified. Why wasn't he wearing the Dogra regimental badges?

His musings were interrupted by the Halvidar asking, "Why did you fight for the English?" "Why," he continued, "have so many of your comrades given their lives for the English? Why," he demanded, "Why should the English rule over India? What right do they have to make our country an English colony?"

He'd strutted before them his eyes flashing angrily, and his hands punching the air to emphasise his questions. "Why," he persisted, "should the English be allowed to exploit the Indian people and steal their riches?" Then with a gesture of disgust he asked, "And why do we allow the English Sahibs and Memsahibs to live such pampered lives of luxury while poor Indians starve?"

These were questions Yuvraj had recently begun to ask too! And by the muttering he could hear, it seemed others had asked such questions as well! For a while the Halvidar let them ponder his questions, then, he spoke of the First War of Independence, "which the English," he said, "dare to call the Indian Mutiny." He told them how brutal the English had been once the mutiny had been suppressed. He reminded them that Muslims had had pork and Hindus beef stuffed down their throats before being shot.

"The English," he said, "took no prisoners. Those they captured were tortured; then killed. Yet now," he declared angrily, "the English accuse the Japanese of brutality to their prisoners! Have you been tortured or threatened with death?" The men shook their heads.

"No, they haven't tortured us. Why?" He paused. "Why? Because they are our Asian brothers!"

Suddenly he changed the subject. "Who has heard of Subhas Chandra Bose?" A few raised their hands.

"Mmm," he grunted. "Well, let me tell you about him. He's a Bengali, the President of the Congress Party. For a time, he followed Mahatma Gandhi's policy of non-violence, but Mahatma Gandhi has achieved nothing and so he became convinced that freedom can only be won by force. When the war in Europe broke out, the English arrested him, but he escaped to Germany. There he met the Japanese Ambassador who invited him to Japan where the Japanese Prime Minister General Tojo, suggested he went to Singapore where a great many Indians, captured in Malaya had joined the Indian National Army to fight the English alongside the Japanese.

In Singapore Subhas Chandra Bose addressed them and to enormous applause was proclaimed Head of the Free India Provisional Government and promptly declared war on the English. Then with General Tojo, he took the salute as ten thousand soldiers of the Indian National Army marched past. Ten thousand of them!" the Halvidar paused to let them digest the number. "Those troops," he went on, "wear the badges I proudly wear and now they are now helping our Japanese brothers to drive the English out of India. This," he proudly said, "is our Second War of Independence. This time we shall be victorious!"

He'd gone on to explain the organisation of the INA and how they were retrained to fight the Japanese way. Then exhorting them to join he told them he'd want their decision the following morning.

"Those who volunteer will be welcomed, those who do not, will remain prisoners. They," he'd added ominously, "will have to work for their food."

Chapter 24
. . . .

"**J**ustice House, please". The Tonga Wallah loaded her bags and she climbed in. She'd left Allahabad barely a year ago, happy at the thought of starting a new life free from the vindictive Lady Cynthia, but now as the tonga clip-clopped its way to their reunion, she was sure of a difficult reception. But she comforted herself, now they both knew the truth or most of the truth, for she was sure Lady Cynthia would never accept that Sir Humphrey had raped Ruby, her mother! Nor did she relish the thought of meeting her father again, for he like Yuvraj, had taken advantage of a woman not in control of herself! And how would she tell them about the child? During the whole journey she'd worried about it! Though she'd never written to tell them about her pregnancy, she knew Catherine had and they would surely ask about the boy for he was after all, her father's grandson. But what could she say? Her fantasy of carrying Richard's son had ended traumatically and she'd wanted nothing to do with the child, she'd rejected him.

When finally, she knew the child could never be Richard's, his death had been mercilessly ratified and a desire for vengeance had relentlessly grown. That desire to avenge him had manifested itself in a compelling desire to join the fight against the Japanese. Doing so she hoped might help quell the guilt she'd begun to feel about abandoning the child who though conceived in rape, was nevertheless a living being for whom she like all mothers had a God-given duty to nurture and protect. She hadn't nurtured him she'd rejected him and her sin had now begun to weigh heavily!

The crunching of wheels on gravel disrupted her thoughts. Nervously she braced herself for a difficult reception. The Khitmagar led her out into the garden, where Lady Cynthia was enjoying tea in the shade of the deodar tree.

She welcomed her coolly, the conversation being stilted and routine. Had she had a good journey? Had the sea crossing been calm? Had the train been on time? How was Catherine? How much damage had the Japanese bombers done in Colombo? Then after a long silence and with a steely look in her eye, Lady Cynthia had asked, "Where is this child of yours?"

"Lady Catherine, I no longer have it."

"You no longer have it! Has the child died?"

"No. As far as I know he is well."

"As far as you know? Gertrude, stop speaking in riddles! Is he well and where is he?"

"He is with his father and as far as I know, he is quite well."

"Oh! So, who is the father? Some young learnee tea planter, I suppose!"

"No Lady Cynthia, his father is a Sikh."

"A Sikh! You tell me the child's father is a Sikh? Have you an English woman, been having an affair with a Sikh? I find that truly repulsive!"

"Lady Cynthia, I most certainly have not had an affair with a Sikh; He raped me when I was concussed after being thrown by my pony."

"Oh! So, you're crying rape, are you? I suppose one might expect that of you! You really are your mother's daughter!"

Lady Cynthia's cynical refusal to believe her and the allusion she'd made to her mother had infuriated Trudi who without another word had left and gone angrily to her room. Lady Cynthia had been more offensive and spiteful than she'd feared. She sighed, she'd known it would be difficult, but Lady Catherine had excelled herself. Deciding she would have to make her stay as short as possible, she wondered how, after those insults and her own abrupt exit, she could possibly face dinner with her. Surely it could only lead to a repetition of Lady Cynthia's earlier intransigence! But how could she excuse her absence?

A tap on the door startled her. A servant appeared; she had a note in her hand. "It's from Lady Cynthia, memsahib. Shall I wait for an answer?" She smiled at the girl, "Yes, please."

She unfolded the note.

"My dear Gertrude," she read. I have clearly upset and offended you by my hasty and thoughtless comments. I have to admit I often react too quickly and without thinking at news that surprises and upsets me. It's one of the sins for which I have to ask our Father's forgiveness. And Gertrude, I ask you to forgive me too.

Cynthia

Such a rapid and fulsome apology had surprised her and finding her notepaper she'd penned a thankful acknowledgement. Now she felt able to attend dinner and meet her father.

When she arrived, it was evident that Sir Henry had been well briefed by Lady Cynthia and for that she was thankful, and the three of them dined in a subdued and formal mood, without reference to the child. When the meal was over and they had as usual drunk the King Emperor's health, to Trudi's relief, Lady Cynthia begged to be excused and retired pleading the need for a good night's sleep. She was about to do the same, when her father asked her to stay for a game of chess.

After the first opening moves, he'd twirled the brandy in his glass and having taken an exploratory sip asked her, "Are you sure I can't tempt you?" She thanked him but declined and watched him select a cigar, examine it with a practised eye and light it with a spill from the candle. He moved a knight.

"Gertrude my dear, I know how devastated you must have been by the loss of your Richard. Though we never had the pleasure of meeting him, we were both greatly distressed for you." He reached for her hand. "And now my dear you're stuck here in India until this wretched war is over and both Lady Cynthia and I think it's high time you put Richard's loss behind you and found yourself a good husband."

His suggestion had shocked her. She made no reply but moved a pawn to threaten his knight.

"Sadly," he continued, "Philip Brodie has recently become betrothed to Rebecca MacPherson." He caught her eye. "She's a friend of yours, isn't she? You used to ride together I remember."

"Oh! How splendid. Philip's a good man, father, I'm sure they'll be very happy."

"But there's Major Dennis White! He's a kind, decent upright fellow. I've always said he'd make a good husband for some lucky girl. You remember him?"

She most certainly did, hadn't she written in her diary that he had no spark of adventure in him, that if she ever let him bed her, he'd write a formal thank you letter the next day?

"Yes, Father, I do, but nothing would induce me to marry him, in fact I have no intention of marrying anyone!"

The conversation was not proceeding as her father had clearly hoped, nor was his game of chess, for Trudi had taken his knight.

"Oh dear!" he exclaimed, as he triumphantly moved his Bishop to take her pawn.

"So, what are your plans?"

"Well, Father, I want to do something in this war against the Japs. I want to do something for Richard's sake."

"That's very laudable Gertrude, but what have you in mind?"

"Father, I'm not sure."

"Well, Archibald the Chief of Secretariat tells me he's looking for a trustworthy English woman to help with confidential papers. I could have a word with him."

"No, Father that's not what I want. I want to be more involved with the war."

"What about nursing then? You've done some First Aid training."

"Yes, but I really don't want to be a nurse. I want to help the Army in some other way. Do they have women auxiliaries?"

He'd not been able to answer her, but he'd said Major White would know. "By chance we've asked him to dinner tomorrow," he added.

"Really?" It seemed her father had some matchmaking in mind!

When Major White arrived, it was quite evident to Trudi, that he'd been encouraged to believe she was ripe for the picking! It had amused her and mischievously she had done nothing to allay his expectations! And when she'd told him of her desire to help the war effort he'd seemed manifestly concerned.

"Father has suggested I might find work with confidential papers in the Provincial Secretariat, but I really want a more active role. I want to be closer to the action. Tell me, are there any jobs for women in the Army?"

He'd hesitated as if unwilling to reveal their existence. Then he shrugged his shoulders. "Well, there is the Women's Auxiliary Corps, the WACs as they're better known. It was formed a year ago to help the Army with clerical and domestic duties, but I don't think it's suitable for you my dear Miss Leafe. Why don't you accept your father's excellent advice and work in the Secretariat?"

"I want to be more involved in the war. But tell me, why do you think the Auxiliary Corps is unsuitable for me?"

"Well, it's mostly made up of Anglo-Indian women; the WAC is really not suitable for the English!"

His demeaning attitude towards the Anglo-Indians had irritated her but pressing him further she succeeded in extracting a reluctant promise to find out where and how she could enlist.

He'd been as good as his word and a few days later, she'd happily boarded a train for Calcutta and had been warmly welcomed into the WACs. "Well educated English ladies like you are badly needed to lead our willing native women," she'd been told and had been commissioned as a Probationary Second Lieutenant. A month later having completed her initial training, her Probationary status was removed, and she'd been appointed as an Assistant to the Staff Cipher Officer at Military Headquarters, Calcutta.

When she first met her new boss, she was startled for he a young Captain in the Signals, wore a black patch over one eye and had lost an arm in the fighting in Malaya. He welcomed her and told her she'd be taking over the job of a young subaltern who was desperate to see active service. She would be responsible for the safe custody of secret publications and code books ready for issue to units in the field. After a few days training she'd been installed in the post.

Although she was the most junior officer, she too attended the Staff Officers' periodic briefings on the war in Burma. The Army had retreated northwards before the all-conquering Japanese. Nothing seemed to stop them, neither mountains nor jungle nor river, and their ability to outflank and move behind their adversaries, had compelled the British to make one strategic withdrawal after another. Now the British retained only a toehold in Burma, a tiny area on its border with India and Assam. Imphal and the mountain village of Kohima were its last strong points, accessible only by a narrow mountain road from Dimapur a hundred miles away in India. For the first forty miles the road was "all weather", but thereafter it was no more than a track winding tortuously through steep hills, often disrupted by landfalls. As the only overland supply route it was excruciatingly slow and inflexible. Some urgent supplies could however be flown in by plane landing on a small airstrip at Imphal. But with Japanese troops nearby, landing and taking off was a hair-raising business. Often supplies were dropped by parachute, but inevitably some fell into enemy hands. But at Kohima no airstrip could be made, for Kohima sat on a ridge, where the Deputy Commissioner had his bungalow and where the tiny pre-war community had lived with its club house, gardens and tennis court. Now this pleasant ridge was covered with shell craters and its trees festooned with discarded parachutes. Not only was it difficult to supply the troops with ammunition and victuals, but it was all nigh impossible to provide secure communication between Imphal, Kohima and Military Headquarters at Calcutta. Laying telephone lines between the three was impracticable, so all messages had to be passed by radio and as these could be intercepted by the enemy, all radio traffic had to be sent in code. Yet it seemed the Japanese often had advance warning of British intentions, and this suggested that they were able to break the British codes.

To solve this problem headquarters had decided to use a Top Secret cipher system, the *One Time Pad**. This would be issued to Imphal and Kohima and the safe and urgent delivery of this new code became a matter of great urgency. Two officers were selected as couriers, one for Imphal and the other for Kohima and the new codes were to be delivered by air. With its airstrip, this was possible at Imphal, but Kohima had no airstrip. Shown a map of Kohima the pilot of an Auster Artillery Spotting plane was asked whether an Auster could land on the ridge containing the tennis court. And if it did, could it take off again? Having carefully examined the map and measuring the ridge, he declared it was far too short. "Even if it was a hundred or so feet longer," he said "It would be bloody tricky. But" he added, "It could fly low over the area and a parcel could be thrown out onto the tennis court. That wouldn't be difficult."

And so the plans were finalised. The officer with the codes for Imphal would fly in a Dakota and land on the airstrip. For Kohima the courier would fly in an Auster, which would descend over Kohima ridge and the package containing the codes would be thrown onto the tennis court. To distract Japanese fighters from the Imphal/Kohima area it was planned that a squadron of *Hurribombers** would attack railway installations at Mandalay at the same time

The night before the delivery, Trudi had prepared the codes ready for ⁻ issue and early the following morning the courier for the Imphal run duly arrived, signed for his package and departed. But there being no sign of the courier for Kohima, Trudi reported his absence. Her harassed boss appeared. "Stupid fool," he muttered angrily, "got himself run over by a Jeep! I'll have to go in his place!"

"You can't sir. How could you handle the package with only one arm? You could miss the tennis court and the codes might be lost. Besides you're not fit for Active Service. Let me go instead!"

At first, he'd refused, but she'd insisted, and finally realising that with only one hand it would indeed be difficult, he'd relented. And having been involved in the planning, she'd needed no briefing and so had been driven hastily to the airfield.

"Well Trudi, there it is." Her boss pointed to a tiny single engined aeroplane. Some men were standing nearby and as they drew up, one wearing flying overalls saluted. "Are you ready?" he asked. Her boss looked embarrassed. "It's not me. The fellow we'd planned to send has been injured in an accident with a Jeep. Second Lieutenant Leafe here is going in his place. She's been fully briefed."

The pilot looked surprised and eyed her up and down but made no comment. Then he opened the passenger's door. "That's your seat, 'fraid there's no parachute!"

As he helped her strap herself in and don her flying helmet, she saw her seat was alongside his. Thanking him, she studied the door through which she'd entered. It would have to be opened before she threw out the package. She found and felt its handle. She prayed it wouldn't jam! Then relieved, yet excited, she studied the cockpit. She'd never been in an aeroplane before; this would be her first flight! The pilot introduced himself as Jerry, "I'm an Artillery Officer. Usually, I direct the guns onto their target but," he said, "But I'm often used as a postman!" He seemed very busy. "I'm checking everything's OK before we take off." Then he grinned, revved the engine and the plane began bumping over the grass. She heard him talking on his microphone, then the engine raced, they picked up speed, the plane levelled out and suddenly they were airborne.

She looked around; everything on the ground was getting smaller while the view was getting bigger. Studying the ground below and the mountains ahead, she soon became aware that the stick between her legs was constantly moving. He saw her watching it, "D'you want to have a go?" he asked. Thrilled, she nodded and grasping the controls she nervously flew the plane. At first it required her full concentration and sometimes he would gently move the control column to correct her, but after a while she found it needed only a light touch and then the plane seemed to fly itself and she could glance quickly around and enjoy the view.

Then he was pointing ahead and shouting "That's Dimapur! I'll take her now." Reluctantly she relinquished control and studied the collection of buildings that was Dimapur. That was where they would refuel. He made a perfect landing, and leaving the plane, they were briefed over a hasty sandwich, on the situation at Kohima.

"On the night before last," the officer said, "the Japs launched a frontal attack on Detail Hill." He pointed to a map. "Here's the Ridge at Kohima, with the tennis court and the Commissioner's Bungalow and here is Detail Hill a mile and a half to the south-west. Our troops suffered heavy casualties, but so did the Japanese. The fighting is still continuing but there have been no reports of any fighting on the Ridge or near your tennis court, though recently there has been spasmodic shelling." Jerry thanked him. "We'll be OK," he told Trudi.

Then they were airborne again. For Trudi the first leg of the flight had been an exciting adventure, but now that she had a better idea of what lay ahead, she felt the first pangs of fear. But she put them behind her. She and her new friend Jerry were irretrievably committed and there was no going back now! Looking down she caught sight of the road to Kohima twisting and turning through the jungle with lorries struggling nose to tail. And somewhere up ahead in the mountains was Kohima. Her fears returned. She felt for Richard's ring, perhaps she would be with him today. They flew on in silence, then Jerry pointed. "Kohima," he yelled. He put the plane in a shallow dive, pulling out scarcely above the trees. "There's the Ridge," he shouted. "Get ready." She eased the door handle back and holding the package tightly in her other hand, she shouted "OK". He swung the plane to the right to line up with the tennis court, then flying even lower he shouted "Now, throw it now." She threw it and watching it tumble towards the court and then bounce and bounce. She felt the plane bank sharply. "Let's get out ...." Jerry's voice tailed off, drowned by the noise of the instrument panel shattering. She looked around. He was slumped over the control column, blood gushing from his throat. The plane was diving. She grabbed the control column and pulled it back. To her relief, the nose came up, but then a wing dropped, the nose went down again, and everything began to spin. Suddenly there was a deafening crash; the plane had hit the trees. She saw the wing crumple and the plane begin to slither down through the trees. Everything was upside down, only her straps kept her from falling. But she had to get clear and with a frantic thump she hit the clasp, the straps released her, and she fell. She remembered bouncing off something and landing awkwardly. Hastily she scrambled clear. She looked back. She could see him. He was motionless, held as she'd been, by his straps. Desperately she thought how she could rescue him, but with a sudden "whoosh" the plane was ablaze. Driven back by the heat, she watched helplessly as the flames consumed him and the wreckage.

Chapter 25

For an instant she was paralysed with fear. Then she heard gunfire, the rattle of machine guns and the erratic snap of rifles. Moving to hide behind a tree, she gasped as pain tore through her arm. She ran a hand over it, it was painful to touch. And there was blood on her forehead. She felt dizzy and sat on the ground. What could she do? Jerry was dead, his body burning in the wreckage and she alone, lost in the jungle. She was terrified, there could be Japs around!

"Please God help me," she muttered. Where was she? Somewhere near Kohima, she knew. Getting up, she looked around hoping to see some signs of the village, but she could only see trees, more trees and undergrowth everywhere. Then she saw him. He was darting from one tree to the next. She saw another. They broke cover and advanced towards her, their bayonets at the ready. Instinctively she raised her hands. They were wearing turbans! "Oh! Thank God you're Indians", she fought back her tears. "Thank God, thank God."

A turban grunted. "You English?"

"Yes, yes."

"English woman, you are right, we are Indians, but now we are members of the Indian National Army and you, Memsahib," he said the word vindictively, "are now a prisoner of war." He jabbed his bayonet towards her. "Go, follow him."

For what seemed an age she struggled through the undergrowth obediently following the soldier in front, then reaching a small clearing she saw trenches. All seemed empty except one; there she saw a wounded man. The sight of his bandaged head made her feel her own. It was sticky with blood. She felt faint. She sat down. More troops appeared. They too were Indians. She hoped they would be less brutal than the Japanese, but the scornful eyes that examined her did nothing to reassure her. And some of those eyes were full of lust. Frightened, she avoided them and tried to be calm. Then her escort told her to get up and to her relief he led her away. But that relief was short-lived for when she saw the man she was taken too, her fear returned. His hate-filled eyes bored into her.

"English woman," he snarled, "You are a prisoner of the Indian National Army fighting in our Second War of Independence. This time with the help of our Asian brothers, victory will be ours."

The smirk on his face worried her. He demanded her name, rank and number. Politely she told him. Then he asked about the plane, what sort was it? Why did it crash? What was it doing?" There seemed no point in lying, he could get the information from the wreckage easily enough, and not wanting to antagonise him, she answered his questions as truthfully as she could, though she made no mention of the codes.

"We dropped emergency medical supplies," she lied.

"Umph," he grunted. "We need some here, I have five wounded men. Are you a nurse?" He seemed a little less belligerent. She hesitated, thankful he'd accepted they were medical supplies, then thinking an ability to help his wounded men might make him less aggressive, she replied, "No. I'm not a nurse, I'm an admin officer, but I have done some first aid training." He grunted and ignoring her first aid skills, began asking her about the strength and disposition of British forces in Kohima. She told him she knew nothing of such matters, but insisting she must know, he kept on questioning her. Finally, he lost his temper.

"You are lying you filthy English whore," he shouted, his angry eyes pierced hers as he grabbed her shirt and ripped it open. As her hands flew to cover her breasts he saw her rings, her mother's and Richard's. With an oath he tore them from her fingers.

"Ah," he exclaimed as he pocketed them, "They will make a small reparation for what the English have stolen."

Then with an evil smile, he said, "I shan't need your services tonight, so go." And handing her back to her guard, he told him, "Tell the Halvidar the prisoner is a nurse. Get her working on the wounded."

The ferocity of his interrogation had shaken her, she'd been certain he'd rape her. He hadn't, but she was sure it would only be a matter of time! All she could hope for was that by nursing his wounded men he might see her in a better light. But would her limited training prove equal to the task? She was taken to the bunker where the wounded lay. There were five, but in the dismal light it was difficult to see them, let alone find how badly injured they were. Two she saw had bandaged heads and a third was groaning quietly; the other two were quiet and still. She had difficulty finding their pulses. One she concluded was probably dead and the other scarcely alive! She turned to the one who was groaning. A dressing had been applied to his chest, but it was saturated with blood. She asked his name. "Harbajan Singh," he mumbled. Carefully she eased the dressing away. The blood had congealed, but the wound looked angry and inflamed. She asked the guard if there was any clean water and where the dressings and medication were kept. She rinsed her muddy hands, swabbed his wound and managed despite her aching arm, to apply a clean dressing. That was all she could do, but he thanked her. Having tended to the other two, she was massaging her own arm, when a soldier arrived with rice and warm gruel. He told her he was now to be her guard and the Halvidar had said she was to stay with the wounded. She thanked him.

He wore a turban, yet another Sikh! Now she'd begun to hate turbans. Turbans and beards; they had brought her nothing but pain and misery! In the dim light she studied her turbaned guard. His face seemed familiar!

"Indira, Indira," she heard him whisper. Her heart missed a beat! Indira, Indira! That was what Yuvraj called her! She turned away; it must be a bad dream!

"Durisani, Durisani Gertrude," he was whispering. "Do you remember me? I am Yuvraj Singh, the father of your son."

"My God; it's him, it is him!" His eyes met hers.

"Durisani, I beg forgiveness. I was bewitched by your beauty, and I thought you wanted me. But now I know I raped you. Please forgive me so that when I die in this war, God will forgive me too."

Meeting him again, here in the jungle, he an enemy soldier and she a prisoner of war had left her stunned, flabbergasted. She couldn't believe it! And he was admitting he'd raped her; and not only that, he was asking forgiveness! She shook her head; surely this must be a dream! She looked at him again. It really was Yuvraj! Could she ever forgive him? She'd hated him ever since she'd known he was the father of the son she'd borne. Yet she had to admit, he hadn't forced himself upon her. In her confusion, she knew she'd given herself to him. But could she forgive him? She said nothing for while; then she whispered. "Tell me about our son."

"When I saw him last, he was six months old. He was very well, Durisani. Everyone admires his blue eyes."

"Yuvraj, I'm a Durisani no longer." She smiled involuntarily. "Perhaps you should call me Indira, that's what you've always called me isn't it?"

"Yes, Durisani, I've always called you Indira, but never face to face!"

"Well, we can't let them hear you calling me Durisani. I forbid it. Call me Indira for both our sakes! Now tell me what you have named our son."

"His name is Sandeep, Sandeep Ashok Singh; Sandeep is a good Sikh name, Indira."

"Sandeep," she repeated the name. She pictured the tawny child. Sandeep, it had a good Indian ring about it; it seemed a good name. She asked him where the child was.

"He is with my wife Jasvinder and our daughter Dharas. They are now in Lahore with her father Pratap Sardar Singh."

"Well, I'm sure Sandeep is better with Jasvinder than with me. She'll bring him up as a proper Sikh. So maybe, Yuvraj, in my selfishness I did the right thing." Saying that seemed to ease her troubled conscience.

"Perhaps, but I fear he will be unhappy as he grows older. Jasvinder hates him and her father knows he's not her child. I worry about him, Indira."

They heard some one coming. It was the Halvidar.

"We are moving out to take up our positions for a dawn attack on Detail Hill. The Jamandar says you, Yuvraj Singh, are to remain behind to guard our prisoner," he gave Trudi a contemptuous look. "Make sure she tends the wounded." He made a cursory inspection of the men and as he left, he glared at her, "Rajendra Singh needs attention." Obediently she went to Rajendra, but as she knew, he was already dead.

Returning to Yuvraj, she heard him whisper. "Indira you are in great danger here. The Jamandar really hates the English. He's a nasty man; he'll rape you I'm sure. Then he will pass you on to the Japanese. You must escape, it's too dangerous here. Let me help you. Let me make some small atonement for my sin."

The thought of freedom excited her, but what if their bid failed; what if they were recaptured? Thoughts of the vengeance they would exact if she was caught frightened her. But if she remained a prisoner the Jamandar would surely interrogate her again. Then he might beat her, even rape her! Yes, Yuvrah was right, as a prisoner she was in great danger. He'd said he'd help her; she couldn't refuse him! The risk was worth it and if she was caught well, she wouldn't surrender easily. Death would be better than capture.

"Yuvraj, you say you'll help me escape, but how?"

"Tomorrow Indira, the Japanese and Indian troops will launch an attack at Detail Hill, the most southerly strongpoint on the Kohima Ridge. That's where all the fighting will be. I propose we make for Garrison Hill about a mile to the North. The gradient is much steeper there, so it's a much more difficult target, and it's very unlikely there'll be any fighting there, at least not for a day or so. If we leave in two hours time, after our troops have left and go north, we will skirt the fighting and could be below Garrison Hill by daylight."

"You make it sound easy. Are you sure you can find the way?"

"Yes, I have a compass and I've been on two reconnaissance patrols to learn the lie of the land."

"But can we do this in the dark?"

"Yes. We need the cover of darkness, but there is a quarter moon. That will give us all the light we need."

So having agreed they would make their escape that night, Yuvraj went to find water and food. As he left, he said, "We'll need a white flag to show we're surrendering. Find something white."

A white flag was essential, she knew, but "Where," she asked herself, "will I find something white?" She searched carefully, but could find nothing even remotely white, everything was grey or khaki. Only one thing she knew would be white. She pulled down her trousers and removed her knickers. Though now more grey than white, they would have to do; there was nothing else. Carefully she tied them to a stick, then rolling it up she stuffed it down her trouser leg. She took a few steps and thankfully found that it didn't hinder her walking. Then she went to minister to the wounded. Only three were still alive. All she could give them was water; there were no more clean bandages. So, she did her best to adjust their old dressings and offer them words of comfort.

Yuvraj appeared. "I didn't hear you come," she said. "Shush," he hissed. "Indira, you must learn to move quietly like me. Have you made the flag?"

"Yes," she nodded. "I have it here, in my trousers."

"Good," he whispered. "Now eat some food before we go."

When they'd eaten the cold rice balls, he left. "Come out quietly and join me in a minute or two," he whispered.

They set off creeping quietly from tree to tree, he leading and she following one tree behind. When moving through the undergrowth they had to be as quiet as possible and progress was very slow, but thankfully at times the forest floor was clear and then it was easier and faster. Often Yuvraj would stop and listen carefully and when he was satisfied it was safe, they'd move on again. The trek seemed endless, her nerves at fever pitch. But finally, he stopped and pointed. There in the faint moonlight, through the trees she could see the dark shape of a hill. "Garrison Hill," he whispered. "We'll climb to the edge of the trees and wait there till dawn."

When they had reached their objective, the moon had faded and in the pink rays of the rising sun she could see the bunkers high on the hill. Then hiding behind a tree, she did as he had told her. Waving her white flag, she shouted as loudly as she could, "British Soldiers please don't shoot. I am an English woman. Please let me come to you."

She saw rifles pointing at her and shaking with fear, prayed they wouldn't shoot. They didn't, but there was no reply to her plea.

"Shout again," Yuvraj said. She did so, waving the flag energetically. Again, they didn't shoot, but again there was no reply. She shouted a third time, but still they remained silent.

Yuvraj shook his head. "They are suspicious. They can see there are two of us. We must crawl up the slope. You go first. Continue to shout and wave the white flag. I will be behind you."

The thought of being in the open without cover terrified her, but telling herself it was better to die, than be recaptured, she lay down, held the flag high and crawled out into the open.

"Go further. I am right behind you," he whispered. She did so.

"Shout again," he said. She did so. Now she could see faces behind the rifles, but again they didn't answer.

"Go on, Indira." She heard Yuvraj's insistent voice. "Stand up and shout. Let them see you really are a woman."

With her heart in her mouth, she stood up. An inner voice screamed "Any second now, they'll shoot." But they didn't shoot and in a trembling voice she shouted, "Thank you for not firing. I am an English woman. I am an officer in the WACs. Please let me and the brave soldier who has rescued me come to you."

For what seemed an eternity, there was no reply. Then an English voice replied, "Advance and be recognised."

Chapter 26

"Get up, get up, sir." Strong arms pulled him to his feet, and he came to. He shook his head to get his brain working. He saw flames, hungry flames devouring the bridge.

"Come on, sir," Andrew the young Sub, dragged him towards the bridge ladder. Now alert, he shouted "You go first." Following Andrew, he scrambled down. He looked back. The fire had taken hold and was spreading; surely, he thought, this must be the end of the *Strongbow*! Then as if in confirmation, a massive explosion ripped through the for'ard funnel. A blast of searing heat bowled him over. He bounced off something and found himself in the sea. Surfacing, he gasped for air and swam clear; it was dangerous to be too close. If she went down, she'd take him with her. He looked back. All he could see was a mass of flames spreading from the bridge to the after funnel. Where was Andrew? He searched for him and others but without success. He could see nothing but the burning wreckage of his ship, now almost stopped in her tracks. Who could escape from that inferno?

He turned, behind him towered the huge Japanese cruiser, now so close. They'd been about to launch the torpedoes when that salvo had struck! If only they'd had another minute, then those torpedoes would have been on their way, and surely, they couldn't have missed! He swam further away; the ship was beginning to break up, she was awash amidships.

He looked for the *Zaanfontein*, but couldn't see her. He hoped she'd manage to escape. Still there was no sign of Andrew. What had happened to him? He'd been right alongside him! Hadn't he been blown overboard too? And he could see no one else! Maybe there were others on the other side of the ship. He heard a muffled explosion, and her bows begin to lift clear of the water. He watched her hang there for a moment, then a great bubble of air broke the surface and she slid quickly into the depths. The *Strongbow*, his first command was no more!

How many had gone down with her? Surely, he couldn't be the only survivor! But would he survive? For the moment he was floating, but how long would it be before he too slid into the depths? The nearness of death scared him. He thought of his beloved Trudi and the plans they'd made to marry and the life they'd hoped to share. "Dear God, don't take me yet," he cried. "Let me see her again." Once more he looked for the others. The sea was still disturbed by the sinking; great bubbles of air were rising and whirlpools forming. No one could remain afloat in that! Then he saw a carley float. There were men on it. They seemed to be paddling his way. He waved an arm. Had they seen him? He waved again and shouted. Then they were near and firm hands were hauling him onboard.

"Are there any others?" he asked. Petty Officer Allen shook his head. "We've seen no one else, sir. We'd almost given up looking, then we saw you." Richard counted, there were just seven! "My God," he thought, "We were seventy-two!"

The enemy cruiser was coming nearer. A boat was being lowered. It hurried towards them and bumping alongside grabbed them and headed back. Wondering what lay ahead, he studied the cruiser. It was enormous, bristling with guns. Then they were climbing on board and being herded against a bulkhead. Then after some jabbering, Petty Officer Allen and the men were moved aft, while he was taken away and led up ladders to the bridge. There he was made to stand before the Captain, who said something he couldn't understand. A junior officer nearby translated, "Captain Sasaki welcomes you aboard the Imperial Japanese Ship *Maya* and wishes to say he was impressed by your brave attack." His comments surprised him. "Please thank Captain Sasaki for his kind words."

He heard the translator repeating his message; then Captain Sasaki spoke again. "He asks what is the name of your ship?" He told him. He heard more Japanese; then "Captain Sasaki says he sees you wear the insignia of a Lieutenant. What role did you have in the *Strongbow*?

"I was the Captain." Captain Sasaki looked surprised and held out his hand. They shook hands and he heard the translator say "Captain Sasaki says you did well." Then he was dismissed. His reception had been courteous, even friendly. It had astonished him. Might the terrible things he'd heard about the Japanese be untrue?

He was even more surprised when having been taken to a small cabin, he was given some overalls to wear while his clothes were taken away to be dried. Then there as a knock on the door. His guard opened it and the translator appeared. He introduced himself as the ship's Intelligence Officer. He seemed friendly and asked his name and rank. This he happily revealed; telling himself he would answer no further questions, but his interrogator asked for details about his ship, its armament and capability. When he refused to reply, he was pressed for an answer. When he refused a second time his interrogator's polite and agreeable manner quickly changed. Now angry and threatening, he banged the arm of his chair.

"You are a prisoner of His Imperial Majesty. You must show him respect and answer the questions I ask on his behalf." He repeated the questions. Again, Richard did not respond.

"Answer me," his interrogator screamed. Richard spoke, "The information you want is clearly shown in *Jane's Fighting Ships**. You must have a copy!" His anger subsiding, his interrogator smiled, "Yes, we do, the Imperial Japanese Navy holds Jane's Fighting Ships in the highest regard!"

The tension had eased. "Clever bastard," Richard thought, "He was going to check my answers against Jane's, to see if I was lying." His interrogator became friendly again and took another tack. "Tell me about your family. Where is your home?" Richard was happy to answer and did so. It seemed to please his interrogator, who smiled and then asked him about the new British naval base at Trincomalee, and what warships were based there. Another ugly scene followed when he said he didn't know. He was asked again and again until finally his answer was accepted. Then he was left alone. This was the first of many interrogations he endured. But though he was sworn at when he refused to answer he was never beaten in the *Maya*, nor in the freighter that took him to Japan. It seemed that like sailors the world over, the Japanese crew had a fellow feeling for survivors and in both ships he was fed and treated well enough. But that was to change when he and the others were put ashore at Kobe. Then there'd been thirty-three of them, a mixture of British, Australian, American and Dutch. Lined up, they had been made to march through the town where hostile crowds swore, shouted and spat at them. A few miles outside Kobe they'd had their first sight of the prison camp, a collection of shabby huts, enclosed by a high perimeter fence. At one end of the parade ground, which formed the central feature, stood the Camp Commandant's office, with the Rising Sun flying over it. The Camp Commandant a stocky, sallow man with a straggly black moustache and slit eyes beneath arched eyebrows sauntered forward, a Samurai sword hanging from his waist. He inspected them, swearing at some and slapping the face of others with his gloves. Then, through an interpreter, he spoke:

"You are prisoners of His Imperial Majesty and we, who are his representatives, must be obeyed without question. You are no longer arrogant Europeans, but cowardly soldiers who unlike our brave Japanese troops, have chosen to surrender. We loyal soldiers of the Emperor look upon you with contempt. From now on you will serve the Emperor in whatever way we choose."

His hatred and contempt was matched by the guards, who insisted the prisoners should look them in the eye when passing and then bow. Failure to do so earned a savage blow. Orders were given in Japanese and any prisoner, who hesitated not understanding what was required, was deemed slow to obey and beaten. So, for their own safety, the prisoners soon learnt a few Japanese expressions; one of the earliest being "kocchi koi". This, meaning "come here", had to be obeyed quickly. "Benjo" meant "lavatory" and "mizu", "water". "Mizu", unless followed by "kuasai", meaning please, would always be ignored, though even the addition of "kuasai" didn't necessarily result in water being given; it depended on the mood of the guard. "Tenko" meant "roll call", always taken early in the morning before the working parties were organised and prisoners marched off to Kobe to unload freighters in the port.

Daily rations were cruelly small, invariably consisting of watery soup with a tiny scrap of vegetable and a small rice ball. And prisoners had to work to earn their ration. No work meant half rations. So, officers, who were not allowed to leave the camp to work in the port and those who were too sick to work, were put on half rations. Had it not been for the Other Ranks, many would surely have died of malnutrition, for as the Other Ranks unloaded the freighters, they stole and ate as much food as possible and binding their shirt cuffs tightly round their wrists and their trouser legs round their ankles they poured rice, sugar and any other food they'd stolen down arms and legs and smuggled it into the camp. The sick and dying were given priority, but sooner or later everyone on half rations had a share of this extra food. Not only did this help ease the men's hunger, but the outwitting of the guards lifted the men's spirits and restored their pride.

Dreams helped too. To forget this hell, if only for a moment or two and dream of home and one's loved ones spurred their determination to survive. And everyone was desperate for news of the war. When new prisoners told them that at last the Allies had stopped retreating, news of any Japanese defeat was as important as food! Occasionally snippets of news would be heard by those working in the port or a newspaper would be found, and its headlines translated by one of the prisoners who had a rudimentary knowledge of the Japanese language. However, it was dangerous work, for if caught, the perpetrators would be savagely beaten. But the search for news could not be stopped. Some news items were clearly such fabrications of the truth that they made the prisoners laugh. These they concluded were published to maintain the morale of a war-weary population.

As time passed it began to become obvious that the Americans were getting ever closer to Japan itself and one morning a silver plane with four engines was seen flying high overhead. Though they pointed it out to one another, no one could recognise it. The guards saw them and, in a rage drove them back into the huts, striking the stragglers angrily with their rifles. But their fury only served to cheer the men. It must have been an American plane otherwise why were they were so angry? Soon the working parties in Kobe began to hear the air raid sirens more frequently and the silver planes flew overhead in ever increasing numbers. Returning from the port the men spoke of increasing bomb damage and began to worry that they too might be killed. Then to their great relief, the working parties were diverted to the countryside to help the farmers.

With the prospect of defeat becoming increasingly likely, the guards grew ever more violent, beating the prisoners whenever the mood took them and blaming them for the American bombs they said were killing Japanese women and children. But their violence did nothing to allay their gnawing fears that Japan's defeat was inevitable. What then, the guards asked each other? How would they survive? And what retribution would the Americans demand for the way they'd treated the prisoners? Some guards suddenly became more tolerant, but not the Camp Commandant. He reduced their rations. Already half-starved the prisoners wondered whether any would survive to be rescued when the war ended. Then they heard of the "Kill All" policy. Some said it was yet another ploy to frighten them. But then a malevolent guard told them as he beat a prisoner, that Camp Commandants had been ordered to prepare plans for the annihilation of all prisoners of war. None were to be left alive to tell how they had been treated by their Japanese guards. It seemed there was no hope!

July gave way to August and the prisoners though starving were still alive, but subject to bouts of unpredictable and increasing violence from their now desperate guards. Then one morning a brilliant flash lit the sky. A flash so brilliant, far brighter than the sun, so bright indeed that they dared not to look at it. Then a deafening, thundering noise had battered their ears. It had gone on and on! Those working in the fields had seen and heard it too. They too spoke of seeing a huge cloud rising high into the sky. No one could explain it and it became the subject of much whispered conversation. The guards seemed stunned, and one had been heard to say a city had been destroyed by one bomb! No one could believe that! Surely, he must have been misheard; he must have said the city had been destroyed in one air raid. But whatever the truth, the guards seemed frightened and confused.

Three days later another brilliant flash had lit up the southern sky. Again, they'd heard that thundering, rumbling noise. They remembered the other, that had been a single explosion too, yet the guard had said the city had been destroyed! What city was it? And was this another city to have been destroyed by that incredible weapon? The news intrigued and thrilled them.

What could this powerful weapon be? But their excitement angered the guards and for the next few days all prisoners were confined to their huts, only those who worked in the kitchen being allowed out.

But one morning, when the kitchen workers went to prepare the first meal of the day, they found the camp eerily silent. No guards could be found! It seemed they'd all stolen silently away. At first no one could believe it. Surely it was a trap, surely the Japs were about to implement their "Kill All" policy! A search was hastily organised, but no guards were found. They began to wonder what had happened. Could it be that the Japs had surrendered? That at last the war was over?

The Senior Officer among the prisoners, an American Major called for tenko and when all were assembled, parties were organised to search for food, medicine and clothing and a council of Officers and NCOs was formed to decide what should be done. Soon sacks of letters addressed to prisoners and their letters home were discovered. These were distributed immediately, but there was none for Richard! Perhaps, he thought, no one knew he'd survived the sinking. It was not an encouraging thought! Other findings included piles of Red Cross parcels containing biscuits, chocolate, other food items and cigarettes. The parcels were issued, one to be shared between three men and their contents greedily consumed. But apart from the Red Cross Parcels only a few bags of rice, some seaweed, decaying cabbage and a little dried fish was found, plus some flour, sugar and tea, enough to feed the prisoners on half rations, for no longer than a week! What would they do then? All they could hope for was that the war really had ended and that the Americans would arrive before the food ran out. But how would the Americans know where their camp was? Hurriedly, a search was made for any material that could be used to make a sign that could be seen from the air. Stones were hastily collected and laid out on the parade ground to form large letters, P O W. Then with the whitewash they'd found, they painted them white.

All next day the prisoners searched the sky for any signs of an aircraft. Some were seen in the distance, but none came near. But early the next morning a single-engined plane was sighted heading towards them. As it flew overhead, the men shouted excitedly and waved their arms frantically. They watched it turn, then dive and head towards them again. All eyes were glued on it; surely, they told each other it could only be American. When it skimmed over them, its engine roaring, someone shouted "It's a Helldiver." Then as it climbed and turned, it did a victory roll. Now everyone was certain it was American, for they had seen the star on its wings, and the victory roll must have meant they'd been seen. In high spirits they began to believe the war really was over and soon they'd be rescued. In the afternoon, sooner than they dared hope, more planes could be seen. They were Helldivers too, four of them. They watched them circle overhead; then one dived and dropped something. It bounced and finally came to a stop. Men ran to it. The box it once was, had broken scattering its contents far and wide. Tins of spam, fruit, sugar, biscuits and other items were hastily collected before the next plane dived.

When the planes had left and the food gathered, the men had a great feast, gorging themselves on meat and fruit, tastes they scarcely remembered. Next day more Helldivers came with more food and then one of the huge silver bombers flew overhead and more packages rained down from its belly. Some contained messages. All were the same, addressed to the Senior Officer. They read "Remain in camp. A US Officer will arrive in due course to lead you to Kobe, where a ship awaits you." A mood of euphoria settled over the men as they waited. With food aplenty the men could not stop eating, though their stomachs accustomed only to minute rations, rebelled, but nothing could stop them satisfying their ravenous hunger!

Two days later the promised American arrived and, helping each other as they went, they hobbled along the familiar road to Kobe. There waiting for them was the promised ship, an American cruiser. That was the first leg of the long journey home. At Yokohama all were subject to medical examinations and prepared for the next leg. The few "Limeys" were to be flown by flying boat to Hong Kong to join a troopship waiting to repatriate British POWs from the Prison Camp there.

Chapter 27

"The Methodist Mission, please."

"Very good, Memsahib", the Tonga Wallah whipped his horse into a gallop. Nicola had suggested Trudi should visit her if ever she was in Calcutta, so now she had a few days leave, she'd decided to see her. Her wounds had been treated and physically she was well, but the events at Kohima had left her mentally scarred. The flight with Jerry, exciting at first, had ended so dreadfully, he dead and she alone and terrified. The joy at seeing those Indian troops had quickly turned to fear. Fear turning to terror at that interrogation. Then, she'd remembered Nicola and that Psalm of hers, "In God I trust. I will not be afraid. What can mortal man do to me?" She remembered she'd said it again and again, but still she'd been terrified! Yet her prayer had been answered! Yuvraj had come! Now since her escape, she couldn't get him out of her mind, for while she'd been welcomed by the English troops, they had seen his Indian National Army badges and had arrested him as a traitor! She'd pleaded for him, telling the Major he'd helped her escape, but he wouldn't relent. And when she'd been evacuated to the safety of Calcutta, he'd been sent back to await trial for treason. It was so unjust; he'd risked his life rescuing her! He should have been given a medal for bravery!

The Tonga drew to a halt. She paid her fare and evading the throng of begging hands escaped into the Mission. An Indian woman approached with enquiring eyes. Trudi smiled, "May I see Sister Nicola, please? I hope she can spare me a little of her busy time."

The woman salaamed, "Mother Nicola finds time for everyone, Memsahib. She truly is our Mother. Please follow me." She led her into a courtyard from which through doorways she could see the sick and infirm. Then climbing a few stairs her guide gently opened a door and there was Nicola; Nicola wearing a grey habit, but looking as beautiful as ever, her hair blonde and flowing, just as she remembered.

Nicola turned and smiled; her blue eyes shining with delight. "Trudi dear, how good it is to see you; and you're in Army uniform! Come let us have some tea."

Over tea they reminisced, Trudi telling Nicola how happy and fulfilled she looked and Nicola, noticing the scar on Trudi's forehead voicing her concern. Trudi pooh-poohed her sympathy and remembering her guide saying, "Mother Nicola is truly our Mother," asked her why they called her Mother.

Nicola smiled. "Mother Mary died suddenly, and I was asked to take her place. I felt so inadequate, but they pressed me and believing it was God's will, I accepted. So, now I'm Mother Superior, but I'm afraid I have much to learn before I can fill Mother Mary's shoes." Then changing the subject, she asked Trudi about "that handsome Naval Officer, Richard."

Trudi told her he had asked her to be his wife and then in a trembling voice she continued "I agreed, but now he's dead, his ship sunk by the Japanese."

"Oh! my poor dear!" Nicola wrapped a protective arm around her, "do you want to tell me about him?"

Trudi did and unburdening herself spoke, about the happy time she and Richard had had in Colombo, about Yuvraj and the son she'd borne and rejected. Nicola listened quietly, commiserating over Richard's death and seeming overcome when she heard about Yuvraj. "Oh! my poor dear," she said as she held Trudi's hands, "But tell me, have you never seen your son again?"

"No, Nicola no, I have never wanted to. I never even wanted to know his name," she stopped for a moment, "until………," her voice trailed off.

"Until what Trudi?"

"Until I was captured."

"Trudi what do you mean captured?"

Trudi gave a great sigh. "I was taken prisoner in Burma. Let me explain." Nicola's eyes widened in astonishment as she listened attentively. Finally, Trudi concluded, "Yuvraj told me he'd named the child Sandeep and that he is with his wife Jasvinder in Lahore. He said his wife dotes on Dharas their daughter but hates Sandeep."

"Oh! Poor child," Nicola's concern was very evident. "He must be very unhappy with a stepmother who hates him. Do you never want to see your son again?" The question hurt. She too had a stepmother who hated her. How could she let Sandeep, her son suffer a similar fate?

"Nicola, I'm not so sure now. Now that I know Yuvraj to be a brave and honourable man. He rescued me and he didn't really rape me."

"Trudi, are you saying you were a willing partner?"

"No, but Yuvraj would have thought so!" She explained she was concussed and, in her confusion, had mistaken him for Richard.

"Do you remember our fancy dress ball in the *Ranpura?*"

"Yes, you wore a nurse's uniform, and I was a Tudor lady!"

"Do you remember what Richard wore?"

"Yes, he wore a turban and with his beard he really looked like a Sikh."

"Yes, Nicola he did, didn't he?"

"Trudi, why are you telling me this?"

"Well, Nicola as you might have guessed, Yuvraj is a Sikh with a beard and turban and in my concussed state, I thought he was Richard, and I encouraged him!"

She'd gone to Nicola to unburden herself in the hope that Nicola would understand and comfort her. But returning in the Tonga she'd begun to realise that Nicola's commiserations hadn't helped. Instead, she'd had made her aware how wicked, how selfish she'd been in rejecting her son, her son Sandeep now at the mercy of a stepmother who hated him. She had only thought of herself! Yet she of all people knew only too well how awful it was to be hated by the person you took to be your mother. She shook her head in despair. It would have been better if, like her mother, she had died in childbirth, or had been killed at Kohima. Yet she hadn't died in childbirth, nor had she been killed. By a miracle she'd been saved at Kohima and Yuvraj was that miracle. When they had finally reached safety at Garrison Hill, she'd been questioned briefly about her capture and how she'd escaped. But the next day her interrogation had begun; a grilling that had lasted three days. The Intelligence Corps Major had kept on asking the same questions but despite his persistence, she couldn't give him the detailed information he wanted about her INA captors. When the questions concerned Yuvraj, she had been able to answer them fully and honestly, always being careful to praise him for his bravery. "Without him," she kept on saying, "I would still be a prisoner and likely to have been killed or raped." While the Major had acknowledged her danger, he kept pointing out that "Sepoy Yuvraj Singh had enlisted in the First Sikh Rifles and had sworn an oath of loyalty to the King Emperor." Then he would say, "He has reneged on that oath and by wearing the uniform of the INA, he has clearly shown himself to be a deserter and a traitor."

His hard line had frightened her and when at last the interrogation was over, she'd asked him where Yuvraj was and what would happen to him.

"He's in detention, awaiting trial for desertion and treason. You will almost certainly be called as a witness."

"I shall be pleased. I shall tell the truth" She replied, "but what will happen to him if he's found guilty?"

Well, he's the first soldier of the so-called Indian National Army to have been captured, so the court may want to make an example of him. He may be sentenced to death, or he might get life imprisonment."

"But that would be grossly unfair. When he helped me escape, he knew the Japanese would kill him if he was caught, but in spite of that he led me safely back to the British. And now you say he will be executed? There's no justice in that!"

"Well," he said, clearly wishing to bring the questioning to an end, "it's up to the court."

His prophecy haunted her and as the months went by Yuvraj's likely fate dominated all her thinking. And while he was detained awaiting trial, she found to her horror that she had become somewhat of a heroine, with people congratulating her on her brave escape. But she always belittled her own efforts and made a point of praising the courage and skill of her hero Yuvraj.

But her supposed bravery was forgotten when news of the Allied landings on the beaches of Normandy reached them. All news bulletins were eagerly awaited, and everyone held their breath and prayed that the Allied landing would not be repulsed. In Burma too there was good news, though it was scarcely mentioned in the British Press. The Japanese had begun to withdraw from Kohima and the Army was advancing towards Mandalay. In July, when it seemed possible that the Japanese could, and would be beaten, Trudi was called to attend the Court Martial of Sepoy Yuvraj Singh. When he was brought in, she saw how smart he looked in his well pressed Indian National Army uniform and how calm and possessed he was when the charges of desertion and treason were read to him. Asked how he pleaded to the charge of desertion, he answered in a firm voice "Guilty." But when he was asked to answer the charge of treason, he replied "Not Guilty."

Then as a defence witness, she was asked to leave the court. Later when giving evidence, she emphasised how courageous Yuvraj had been in planning and helping her to escape. She wanted the Board to hear the truth and kept repeating "Without him, I would still be a prisoner and likely to have been killed or raped." But they seemed to take little notice of his bravery and having accepted his guilty plea to the first charge, found him guilty on the second, the charge of treason. He took the verdict without flinching, but as he was taken away, his eyes met hers. They seemed to wrap themselves around her as if for a final time. Did he really care for her? Was that why he'd risked his life for her? Was he to be the second man who loved her, to die? Sleep shunned her that night. Yuvraj's eyes haunted her as she pondered his fate.

She heard the sentence the next day. "Sepoy Yuvraj Singh you have admitted Desertion and have been found guilty of Treason," the President announced; "I therefore have no option but to sentence you to death." Yuvraj's eyes had been fixed immovably on hers. Now their message was clear; no longer could she hold back her tears. As he was taken away, he pursed his lips at her and involuntarily she raised her hand. A flicker of a smile crossed his face; then he was gone.

In a state of shock, she left the court. That he would be executed because of her was too cruel to bear. Surely, she consoled herself, he'll appeal. Two days later when she was able, she sought permission to visit him.

"We only allow relatives to visit the condemned," she was told. "But in any case, I'm afraid it's too late, he's already faced the firing squad."

In a daze and burdened with guilt she returned to her office but could do no work. Finally, when it was time, she went to the mess for tea and absentmindedly picking up a copy of The Times of India, a headline caught her eye.

INDIAN SEPOY EXECUTED

Yesterday at dawn Sepoy Yuvraj Singh was executed by Firing Squad at Military Headquarters, Calcutta. When Yuvraj Singh enlisted in the 1st Sikhs he had sworn an oath of loyalty to the King Emperor, but when captured by the enemy he brought shame on his regiment by turning traitor and joining the so-called Indian National Army to fight alongside the Japanese. The Court Martial found him guilty of Desertion and Treason and to dissuade other foolish Indian soldiers from doing likewise, rightly decided to make an example of him and ordered his execution. The Editor is pleased to learn that a Military spokesman asserts that only a tiny fraction of our brave Indian soldiers have joined the so-called Indian National Army when captured.

Her hands were shaking as she put the paper down, trembling with rage and indignation. It was only half the story. No mention had been made about him helping her to escape! No mention of his courage either, or his loyalty to her, an English woman! The truth had been vilely distorted! And those words 'only a tiny fraction of our brave Indian soldiers have joined the so-called Indian National Army' were a travesty of the truth! Surely, they must know of those ten thousand Indians who had marched past Tojo, in Singapore, proudly wearing the uniform of the Indian National Army? Clearly the censor had been at work. The authorities were obviously frightened more would desert!

Over the next few days, she found it difficult to concentrate on her work and seeing how distraught she was, her boss suggested she took a few days leave. Gratefully she accepted and packing a bag she took a Tonga to the Mission.

Nicola welcomed her. "Trudi, you seem very distressed. What has happened?" Trudi told her of the Court Martial, the verdict, his execution and of "that scurrilous report in the paper".

Nicola listened intently; then asked, "You say he pleaded guilty to desertion, but not guilty to treason?"

"Yes, Nicola. He was honest and freely admitted that he'd deserted, but when he was charged with treason, he claimed the King Emperor ruled illegally. "He is King Emperor by conquest," he said. "His forces defeated us in our First war of Independence, which he had the effrontery to call the Indian Mutiny and now he rules not by the will of the people, but as a conqueror! For that reason," he declared, "I cannot recognise him as my King Emperor and therefore it is not possible for me to be a traitor. I am not alone in this; for ten thousand of my countrymen are fighting alongside the Japanese to liberate our country."

Nicola sighed. "He was right of course; Trudi. Many like me have always questioned our right to rule India."

"Yes, I remember you airing such views in the *Ranpura*. I was quite shocked then, but now I'm beginning to agree and Yuvraj mustn't be allowed to die in vain; India must be given its independence!"

For the next few days, she stayed with Nicola enjoying the Mission's tranquillity and helping the Sisters treat the sick. Giving succour to those who lived on the street, the dregs of humanity, who had to beg for every mouthful, had given her time to come to terms with the death of the two men who had shown their love for her. When reluctantly she had to return to duty, she felt a little more resigned to their loss.

The mood in Headquarters was becoming more optimistic by the day, for now there could be no doubt that the Allies were winning the war in Europe. And as the Americans seized more and more islands in the Pacific, the expected invasion of Japan itself could only be a matter of time. And there was good news in Burma too. British and Indian troops were at the gates of Mandalay.

In January, when the Headquarters Staff were celebrating the capture of Akyab and its airfield, Trudi was called to the office of the Chief of Staff. Somewhat alarmed, she went to see him.

"Ah! Second Lieutenant Leafe. I have some good news for you. In recognition of your bravery in delivering classified material to Kohima and your subsequent capture and courageous escape, I am pleased to inform you that you have been "*Mentioned in Despatches*"*.

Surprised and angry, Trudi told him in a voice trembling with emotion, "I cannot possibly accept such an award. Not when Sepoy Yuvraj Singh, the man who bravely risked his life to bring me safely back to the British lines, has been executed for treason!"

The General looked surprised. "This award recognises your bravery, Miss Leafe!"

"For that I am honoured sir, but for the reason I've already given I cannot possibly accept it."

"Well, Miss Leafe, I'm afraid you have been mentioned, whether you like it or not!"

"That may be so sir, but knowing that Sepoy Yuvraj Singh was unjustly executed, I cannot wear the oak leaf."

Despite his efforts she would not change her mind and her refusal to wear it was finally accepted.

Christmas came and went and on 8th May 1945 victory in Europe was celebrated. Now the war against Japan had to be won and much bloody fighting against Japanese troops who preferred death to surrender, was forecast. But as the Allies assembled their forces for the invasion of Japan, reports were received that the Japanese city of Hiroshima had been devastated by what the Americans called an atomic bomb. An American bomber, named 'Enola Gay' had dropped a single bomb, equivalent in power to twenty thousand tons of TNT, on the city. Following the explosion an enormous mushroom cloud had risen high into the sky, beneath which only the skeletons of a few concrete buildings remained to mark what a few minutes earlier, had been a thriving city! The world was stunned, but the Japanese refused the offer of peace talks. Three days later a second atomic bomb was dropped on Nagasaki with similar awesome results and Japan finally agreed to surrender.

The ending of hostilities was celebrated on the 15th August and all efforts in Military Headquarters were then focused on the surrender of Japanese forces in Singapore, Malaya, Burma and Hong Kong, the capture of those to be tried for war crimes and the liberation of Allied Prisoners of War. Now with less need for ciphers and codes, Trudi became involved in the effort to find and rescue the POWs. It was a busy time and it seemed they were working harder than ever.

Then towards the end of August she found a strange letter in her mail. It had been addressed to Miss G Leafe, Oliphant Estate, Nuwara Eliya, then forwarded to Justice House, Hastings Road, Allahabad, where her father had redirected it. The original address had been written in a shaky hand which she found hard to recognise. Mystified and with her heart thumping, she tore it open.

Dearest, dearest, dearest Trudi, she read through tear filled eyes.

I am still alive. Tell me you are too. How I long to see you and hold you in my arms again.

I am now on a troopship bound for Southampton. We call at Singapore but sadly not at Colombo, so I won't have the chance of seeing you. But dearest now the war is over catch the next ship home and marry me. Our wedding has been delayed too long! We mustn't waste another day.

Chapter 28

She kissed Ruby Eliza and reluctantly gave her to Amah for her nightly bath. She'd been so good during her christening on *H.M.S. Chester*, the cruiser in which Richard served. He'd looked the proud father when the Captain had congratulated them as they cut her christening cake in the Wardroom. Her name, the Padre assured them, would be engraved on the ship's bell, which had served as the font. It had been a truly memorable day.

"Call me," she told Amah, "when she's in bed, so I can read Ruby Eliza a a bedtime story and give her a goodnight kiss."

She saw Sandeep and Richard playing snakes and ladders on the veranda. "You did well today, Sandeep dear." His blue eyes lit up as Richard added, "Yes, everyone said how well you behaved."

"Did you enjoy yourself?" she asked him. Sandeep laughed and said how big the ship was and how he'd liked going out in the boat.

Dear Sandeep, she reflected, how that terrible train journey had thrown them together! She'd found the son she'd rejected and now he called her Mummy. She sighed happily, so much had happened since that unexpected letter from Richard had come. For years she'd thought him dead, sunk with his ship somewhere in the Indian Ocean. Then that wonderful letter had arrived. She still had it now, the ink smudged with tears, tears of joy and disbelief. He'd wanted her to catch the next liner home so they could be married. She'd asked to be demobbed early and to her joy was released within a month. Then with her father's blessing she'd sailed as soon as she could find a ship and he was waiting on the jetty for her as the ship berthed at Tilbury. It had been such a blissful reunion he looking thinner, than she remembered, older and careworn too, but still handsome with that beard of his and those loving eyes. They were ecstatic to be reunited, hardly knowing whether to laugh or cry! On the train to Chagford, he'd been reticent about his time in captivity, but she had unburdened herself, telling him about Yuvraj and Sandeep. He'd listened attentively, holding her hand as she spoke, her face etched with worry. Finally, when there was no more to tell, she'd asked him to forgive her. Their eyes had met, and he'd embraced her.

"Dearest, what is there to forgive? You thought I'd died you were grieving, and you were concussed too!"

He sighed as he shook his head.

"I should never have worn that stupid Sikh rig. I felt a fool at the time, and I can understand how you came to mistake this fellow Yuvraj for me."

He stroked her hand tenderly, "And, dearest, he took advantage of you. He raped you!" He put a protective arm around her, "But now it's all in the past. It's our future that's important, and I want to spend it with you, with you as my beloved wife."

"Oh! darling," she pulled him towards her and kissed him. "And I want to be with you."

"Oh! Trudi dearest, how wonderful it is to be together again." A happy smile lit up his fa!ce; then he looked thoughtful. "But tell me, where is the child?"

She told him how she'd rejected him and that Yuvraj had taken him. "But now," she added "I have a great sense of guilt."

He'd given her an affectionate hug. "It's probably for the best. He's with his own people."

His sympathy and understanding had encouraged her. She felt she could tell him more! She told him about her time in the WACs and how she'd had to deliver those codes to Kohima. He listened with increasing admiration to the woman he was to marry. "You've had quite a war!" he remarked.

She smiled modestly, "Yes, for a woman I suppose I have. And I've been a prisoner of war too."

He looked shocked. "A prisoner of war? Oh! my dearest love, you a prisoner of the Japs?"

"Yes darling, we have that in common! But I was lucky; I was a prisoner for only two days. A brave Indian soldier helped me escape."

She told him about her capture and how she found Yuvraj, the father of her child. "I couldn't believe it was him, it was incredible, but it was Yuvraj! He'd been in the 1st Sikh Rifles, but when captured he defected to the Indian National Army."

"Oh! A traitor, eh?" Richard exclaimed, but seeing her face harden, he said no more and listened quietly as she told him how he'd helped her escape.

"He was brave! Tell me what happened to him?"

She told him about his trial and how despite his bravery in helping her escape, he'd been executed as a traitor. With tears in her eyes, she ended by saying, "I owed my safety, my life to Yuvraj and they killed him. How could they do such a thing? It made me feel ashamed to be English. I'll never forgive them for executing him. I can't bear the thought of him facing that firing squad. It always distresses me and now I feel guilty for rejecting his son."

In December 1945 they were married in St Michael's church in Chagford and had briefly set up home in Petersfield while Richard completed his Signals course at Leydene. Then in August he'd joined *HMS Chester*, a six-inch cruiser sailing to join the East Indies Fleet based in Trincomalee. Trudi had followed him a few months after the arrival of their daughter, Ruby Eliza and Richard had found a little bungalow for them, close to Naval Headquarters where she could see the *Chester* swinging at her buoy. And on most nights, when the *Chester* was in Trincomalee Richard could come ashore and join her and Ruby Eliza and life was blissful. But the *Chester* was often away and then she was lonely and her guilt about Sandeep would return. He lived, so Yuvraj had told her, with Jasvinder, who hated him. Now she'd come to feel for Sandeep, for she knew only too well how he must feel! Her worries for him persisted; she could do nothing to eradicate them. Then one morning feeling sad and miserable as she watched the *Chester* slip her moorings to sail for the Independence celebrations marking the end of the Raj, she'd had an irresistible urge to find the son she'd rejected. According to Yuvraj, he was in Lahore living with Jasvinder in her father's house in Hali Street. So, scribbling a hasty note to tell Richard what she was doing, and asking for his forgiveness, she packed a bag, gave Ruby Eliza a tearful kiss, told Amah to take good care of her and caught the train.

The sea crossing was calm and the overnight journey to Amritsar uneventful but finding the train to Lahore the next morning proved more difficult among the mass of excited people waving the new Indian and Pakistan Flags. She felt excited too, for at last she was doing something about Sandeep. She would be in Lahore soon, but as the train began to move, misgivings began to trouble her. Would she find him? She was confident she'd find Hali Street she'd seen it on a map; it was a turning off Poonch Street. But if she found Sandeep, what then? Would she just say "hello", talk to Jasvinder and her father about him, to make sure he was happy and well looked after, then go? But what if Sandeep wasn't happy? What if he was miserable? She began to wonder if she'd been not only impulsive, but stupid too! Would her journey achieve anything? Perhaps she should have let sleeping dogs lie! But despite her doubts and worries the urge to find Sandeep remained!

It was almost dark when the train pulled into Lahore. She found a rickshaw and asked for the nearest hotel. Exhausted after her long journey, she knew it was important she had a good night's sleep, for tomorrow she would have to have her wits about her.

"Good morning, Memsahib, welcome to Pakistan." The waiter set her breakfast before her. She smiled at him, "Thank you, may Independence bring you much joy and prosperity." All her thoughts had been concentrated on Sandeep; she'd forgotten it was the day India would be partitioned to form the new states of Pakistan and India! How could she have forgotten, she wondered as her rickshaw driver made his way with difficulty through the happy crowds waving their new national flags. But their happiness did nothing to ease her frustration at their slow progress. Then the rickshaw stopped. "Memsahib," the driver held out his hand. Here is Hali Street." Dismounting she gave him his fare and as she walked past the stalls and workshops, she saw boys playing marbles. They were Sikhs she knew, for they all had their hair set in untidy buns on the top of their heads. She asked them if they knew Sandeep Singh and where she might find him.

"Sandeep Singh? I am Sandeep Singh." A boy no more than five or six years old smiled inquisitively at her. He had blue eyes.

"You are Sandeep?"

"Yes, Memsahib."

She pointed to the marbles, now abandoned in the dust and wanting to gain his confidence asked, "Who's winning?"

"Me," he said proudly.

His smiling face and upright figure appealed. "Is that my son?" she asked herself. "What a lovely looking boy he is!"

He turned to play again. Expertly he flicked his marble. It bounced, hit another and sent it flying. Sandeep jumped for joy. "I've won, I've won," he cried.

She clapped her hands and he turned towards her, "What do you want, Memsahib?"

"I want to talk with your mother."

"Mother?" His eyes looked suddenly troubled. "I have no mother."

"Oh, Sandeep, I am sorry. Who do you live with then?"

"With Jasvinder and Dharas."

"Then could you take me to them please?"

He nodded and led her to a nearby house. He pointed to a woman, "That's her."

She saw a well groomed woman, of similar age to herself. A young girl was beside her, holding onto her *salwar**.

Seeing Jasvinder now a widow, brought memories of Yuvraj. Memories of his eyes fixed on hers as he was sentenced to death! How Jasvinder must hate me, she thought. Jasvinder looked at her with quizzical eyes. Nervously Trudi spoke.

"May I have a word with you? I knew your husband Yuvraj."

Her remark startled Jasvinder. "What do you mean, you knew Yuvraj?" She scowled, her angry eyes examining her. "Are you the English whore who seduced my husband and left me to bring up his wretched son Sandeep?"

"You say you knew Yuvraj, my son-in-law?" an elderly Sikh interjected. "Did you know he helped some English woman taken prisoner in Burma, to escape? He brought her safely back to the English lines, did you know that?" He gave her no time to answer.

"Why he should have done such a foolish thing I cannot understand! And how do you think the English thanked him? They tried him as a traitor and executed him!"

She lowered her head; then spoke quietly, "I was the English woman he rescued."

He looked at her aghast. "Why did you not tell them he'd rescued you? Why did you let them execute him?"

His questions were impossible to answer, but she told them how she'd pleaded for him, that her pleas had been ignored.

"I kept extolling his bravery and telling the court that without him, I would still be a prisoner and probably killed or raped, but they would not listen!"

She felt exhausted. The trauma of her escape, his trial and execution returned to haunt her again. And still they argued. Then finally they were silent. Had they accepted her answer? No, she knew they never would. She saw Jasvinder's father shake his head in disbelief and heard her telling him

"She's evil. She seduced Yuvraj and the English killed him because of her."

She had expected a difficult reception but not one as intimidating as this. Desperately she wondered how she could ask the questions she'd planned to ask about Sandeep.

"How is Sandeep?" she stuttered. But they didn't hear her. A rapid tapping on the door distracted them. Jasvinder opened it and an agitated Sikh rushed in waving his *kirpan**, his Sikh sword.

"Pratap Singh," he cried. "The Moslems have gone mad. They are running riot in the Hindu district, killing men, women and children. They keep shouting 'Pakistan for the Moslems, out with the Hindus and Sikhs'. They're butchering Hindus and burning their houses. Pratap, we'll be next!"

"Why are they doing this?" the old Sikh asked. "We've lived in peace together for years under the Raj. Why should they want to kill us now?" As they discussed the rioting of the Moslems, he'd pulled out his own kirpan and had begun polishing its blade. Then agreeing that the Moslems' madness was incomprehensible, he placed a hand on his friend's shoulder.

"We must prepare to defend ourselves in case they come!" He told him and with an urgent voice had added, "My dear friend, you must go; go to your own house now. We must lower our shutters and lock our doors and ask God for his protection. Surely this moment of madness will pass in the morning."

But it didn't. While Jasvinder, Trudi and the two children remained locked in the house frightened by the hubbub and the distant shouts of "Pakistan for the Moslems", Pratap Singh had kept guard on the roof. There he could see flames and smoke rising from the Hindu district and from the area where many other Sikhs lived. He spent all day keeping a lookout, but when darkness fell Pratap Singh came down.

"We must leave, there are many fires burning in the Hindu quarter and many in the Sikh area to the north," he announced. "Our turn will surely come, maybe tomorrow, so we must go, while we can. My cousin in Amritsar will surely give us shelter until it is safe to come back. We should be safe there Amritsar is in India. So now we must pack and early tomorrow before it's light, when it won't be so dangerous, we will go to the railway. In our prayers we must ask Guru Nanak to intercede for us and give us a safe journey. And Jasvinder, find your scissors and cut Sandeep's hair. Perhaps if he looks like a Moslem boy, they won't kill him."

So, their terrible journey began. The station was crowded with frightened Sikhs and Hindus struggling to board any train heading east, going to the safety of India and Amritsar. A train for Amritsar was in the station, but already it was full to bursting. People were on the roof and others on the boarding steps clinging onto whatever they could find. Even as it began to move, people were still trying to find a foothold on the train they hoped would carry them to safety. It was an age before the next one came. Like a tidal wave the crowd surged towards it. As it came to a halt, Trudi found herself opposite a door. Jasvinder, the children and Pratap, kirpan in hand were right behind her. Others followed, elbowing and pushing their way in. In a trice the compartment was full, people pressed hard against eachother and Trudi wedged against the window, with Sandeep squashed against her. She caught sight of a train coming to a halt on the other line. It must have come from India. Unlike hers it was strangely empty; there seemed to be only one or two passengers. She studied the nearest. He seemed asleep, his head lolling sideways. Then to her horror she saw his face. It was covered in blood and where his eyes had been she saw empty sockets! Through the next window she saw two other people. They were also still, and they too were covered with blood. Were they Moslems? Had they been fleeing from India? If they were, where were the others? And who could have committed such a brutal act? Were the Hindus and the Sikhs going mad too? She said nothing to the others but closed her eyes and repeated Nicola's psalm over and over again, "In God I trust. I will not be afraid. What can mortal man do to me?"

At last, the train began to move, and the tension began to ease. Sandeep was wedged between Jasvinder and her. "Sandeep dear," she whispered, "Would you like to look out of the window?" His little face lit up as he nodded. She squeezed him round and settled back as best she could, thanking God for their escape. The train was making good progress now and their spirits began to rise. They were on their way to safety in India. But then inexplicably the train began to slow down and soon it was hardly moving at all. Puzzled she saw that those who'd been clinging on had disappeared! Then the door was flung open with cries of "Pakistan for the Moslems" and hordes of frenzied men were climbing onboard and attacking the startled passengers with daggers and knives. Pratap was wielding his kirpan and an attacker fell, but other men with knives surrounded him and he fell too. Everywhere there were men shouting and stabbing. As Jasvinder and Dharas were attacked, she managed to cover Sandeep with her body. A screaming man, his eyes full of hate, raised his knife to kill her too, but then apparently startled that she was "white", mumbled "Memsahib", turned and disappeared. For an age she remained frozen with fear, her taut body stretched over Sandeep until at last the cries of the injured broke into her terror. There was blood everywhere! Dipping her hands in some she spread the blood liberally over Sandeep's face. "Lie still," she told him. "Pretend you've been killed; act as if you're dead." She found Dharas, crumpled under a body. She was already dead. Pratap was lifeless too, his head almost severed from his body. Jasvinder was moaning, blood flowing freely from a gash in her throat. Using her headscarf, Trudi bound the wound as best she could, but the blood still oozed. Then she began attending to the others, but many were already dead, and others were bleeding so badly she knew they couldn't survive. As she worked, she prayed the attackers wouldn't come back. When at last the train begin to move again, it seemed her prayer might be answered, that they would reach Amritsar and safety.

Then the savagery, the madness, the horror of it all overcame her and she began to sob uncontrollably. Through her tears she saw Sandeep, his face covered with blood. He looked terrified he was trembling. She pulled him on to her lap, hugged and kissed him. "Oh! Sandeep, Sandeep," she sobbed as she stroked his head. "Why, why have we two been saved? Sandeep, you must come and live with me now. You are mine and I'll never, never let you go." She wiped away his tears and hers and looked eagerly for Amritsar. Finally, to her joy she saw buildings approaching. It was the station. It was Amritsar. "Sandeep dear, surely we'll be safe now."

The station was crowded, people everywhere. The train hissed to a halt, someone opened the door and holding Sandeep tightly by the hand she climbed over the dead and managed to get out. At last, they were safe! She turned to look back. So many had hoped the train would carry them safely from the murder and mayhem in Lahore. But it hadn't! It had been cruelly ambushed and now like a scene from hell, it was full of dead and dying. The badly wounded were being stretchered off, while a few despite their injuries, struggled clear. Surely it was a miracle that she and Sandeep had been spared! All she wanted now was to escape from the station with its awful smell of death.

A policeman guided her to the Stationmaster's Office. There to her relief, she saw an Englishman. He introduced himself as the Superintendent of Police and began questioning her about the journey. She answered his questions as fully as she could and when she'd finished, he told her, "They've gone mad. They just want to kill each other. Yours is the second train from Lahore the Moslems have ambushed and now the Hindus and Sikhs are seeking revenge and attacking trains too."

He shook his head "God knows how it will end!" Then sending for his driver he told him to take her and the boy to a nearby hotel.

Three days later Trudi was told it was safe to resume her journey and finally she arrived home to be reunited with Ruby Eliza. Was it only nine days since she'd set off to find Sandeep? Then it had seemed a simple journey to Lahore, a journey to ease her conscience about the way she'd treated her son, a journey of penance. After that she'd hoped she would be able to forget Sandeep and his father and resume her blissful life with Richard and Ruby Eliza. But it had been a truly mortifying experience, one which had made her realise how wicked she'd been. And the hatred Jasvinder and her father had shown her had frightened her. Both were certain that Yuvraj had been executed because of her! That she couldn't convince them otherwise was indeed penance enough. Nothing she said or did had won the slightest forgiveness! And her fears that Jasvinder hated Sandeep were clearly true. Now watching Sandeep laughing and splashing in the bath, she gave thanks for the Guardian Angel who'd mercifully watched over them during that terrible slaughter.

"Father God," she'd asked time and time again, "Why were we saved? What have I ever done that you should save Sandeep and me?" It was a question she would ask for ever, though she doubted it would ever be answered!

She caught sight of the time. "Sandeep dear, we must hurry now," she said as she dried his trim little figure. "Richard will be with us soon. He's the man I love, and he'll be a good father to you." She hugged him. "And I'm your real mother. I lost you when you were born but now, Sandeep dear, I've found you and I'll never lose you again!" She held him at arm's length. "We'll have to do something about your ragged hair, but oh! you are such a handsome son! And you're my son."

She hugged him again. "Sandeep," her voice suddenly anxious, "Sandeep dear, can you learn to call me Mummy?" He looked serious, "I've never had a real mother, only Jasvinder and she hated me," then he smiled "But I love you, Mummy."

"And I love you, Sandeep dear."

She turned to brush away her tears, then she kissed him and in a busy voice declared, "You can't wear those dirty clothes of yours." Richard mustn't see the bloodstains! "I must find something clean for you." She wrapped the towel around him. "Come on, we'll see if anything of Richard's will do." Obediently he followed her and watched her pulling things out of the drawers. "Oh! dear," she cried holding up some shorts. "He's much, much bigger than you, but these will have to do." She found him a shirt too; it was an old rugby shirt. That was all she could find! As she helped him put them on, she wanted to laugh, but daren't, she knew it would upset him.

"Sandeep dear, what can we do?" Hurriedly she found a needle and thread and tacked the shirt above his knees. "You'll have to wear these for Richard and tomorrow we'll go shopping and buy you some proper clothes."

He lifted his arms and looking down saw his feet protruding from his baggy trousers. "You will buy me some proper clothes tomorrow?"

"Yes Sandeep, that's a promise."

"Trudi, Trudi, where are you, my love?" Richard ran into the bedroom. "I've been so worried about you." He pulled her to him and kissed her.

"I've been so worried!" Then he saw the boy. He was holding her hand and studying him intently.

"Richard dear," she whispered anxiously, "I've brought Sandeep home."

"Dearest, I just thought you might. He's your son and I'll be a father to Sandeep and to Ruby Eliza!"

He looked at the boy and laughed. "That shirt suits you, Sandeep. We need another Rugger man in the family!"

THE END